BELLE SCOTT;

OR,

LIBERTY OVERTHROWN!

A TALE FOR THE CRISIS.

By oppression's woes and pains!
By our sons in servile chains!
We will drain our dearest veins,
But they shall be free!

BURNS.

THIRD THOUSAND.

COLUMBUS:
D. ANDERSON.
CINCINNATI:
GEO. S. BLANCHARD.
1856.

E. MORGAN & SONS,
Stereotypers, Printers, and Publishers
NO. 111 MAIN STREET, CINCINNATI, O.

CONTENTS.

CHAPTER XXX.

CHAPTER XXXI.

CHAPTER XXXII.

CHAPTER XXXIII.

CHAPTER XXXIV.

CHAPTER XXXV.

CHAPTER XXXVI.

CHAPTER XXXVII.

CHAPTER XXXVIII.

CHAPTER XXXIX.

CHAPTER XL.

CHAPTER XLI.

CHAPTER XLII.

CHAPTER XLIII.

CHAPTER XLIV.

CHAPTER XLV.

CHAPTER XLVI.

CHAPTER XLVII.

CHAPTER XLVIII.

CHAPTER XLIX.

BELLE SCOTT.

CHAPTER I.

In the autumn of the year 1852, a young man about twenty-five years of age, was seated in front of a boarding-house, in an obscure street in New Orleans. The smoke from his cigar rose in curls above his head, while he seemed to be quietly enjoying the cool evening, and resting from the labors of the day. Edgar Reed was a journeyman printer, who for greater profit in his trade, had recently come from New York. A tall gentleman, about sixty years of age, who limped a little as he walked, took a seat by him.

"And so," said Mr. Carter to Mr. Reed, "you have not only made up your mind to go on your hunting excursion, but have got all ready to start!"

"Yes," said Mr. Reed, "I believe all is at last ready. We have laid in a full supply of powder, lead, and caps; we have good rifles and a tent; and provisions enough to last us a month."

"I dare say," said Captain Carter, "that you have powder and lead enough to kill all the deer you will find; and as much baggage as old travelers would start with on a journey round the world; that 's the way you young folks do; but it's no matter—when you get older you will be wiser."

"I think," said Mr. Reed, "we had better take too much than too little, for if we shall want anything in the place to which we are going, we cannot get it. You once had the kindness to give me some lessons on the art of hunting deer; please repeat them; you are an experienced hunter. I never shot at a deer in my life."

"It's all very simple," replied Captain Carter; "when the Mississippi rises so as to overflow the country, which it sometimes does in places, for many miles on both its sides, the deer, and other game are driven to the high points of land: they stay there in herds, and of course fall an easy prey to the hunter. The river is now up, and the place you are going to is the very best that I know of. You will find the bucks on the highest points of land; the does and fawns shelter and hide themselves behind logs and fallen trees. At other times you will find the deer in thickets; they always choose such as conceal them best. When you come across a deer, you must be cool. If your hand shakes at all, as you raise your rifle, put it down and don't attempt to fire, till you get as careless as if you were about to shoot at an apple on a tree. Better let the deer go, without a shot at it, than to shoot and miss. Don't get too close; you will kill oftener at seventy-five yards, than at fifty; because at fifty, you will be too confident and miss your aim. When you are ready, point your rifle down to the fore-foot of the deer and raise slowly till you get it ranged with the breast of the animal; then move it about an inch or two back; hold it firmly, fire, and the game will be yours."

"Thank you, captain, I'll follow your directions to the letter, and I have no doubt but that I will succeed."

"How long will you be gone? and who goes with you?"

"I intend to be absent two weeks. I cannot afford to lose more time, and could not go at all, unless with the confident hope that the profits I shall make from my game will be equal at least to my earnings if I staid here. Mr. Patterson goes with me. I am tired of hard work, and wish some rest and change of scene and occupation."

"As for your profits," said Captain Carter, "unless you are more successful than I have ever been, you will find the balance on the wrong side of the account. I have gone on a dozen such trips, and so it has always been with me. But go by all means, whether you make or lose money by it: your health will be improved, and in every other respect you will be the gainer; but it is eleven o'clock; good night."

"Good night, Captain Carter, we shall hear from you again."

CHAPTER II.

EDGAR REED.

Mr. Patterson called on Edgar the next day, and informed him that his mother had been taken dangerously ill; of course he could not leave her. With the exception of his rifle, he presented to him his share of the whole outfit, and Mr. Reed, having all things in readiness, determined to go alone. He soon found a steamboat, and was on board with all his equipage, and ascending the Mississippi.

Late in the evening of the following day, the boat reached the point at which he was to land. Rain was falling, and the night was dark. An officer of the boat had promised to make arrangements for him with the keeper of the wood-yard. His baggage and himself were soon put ashore. A brief conversation took place between the clerk of the boat, and Mr. Talbot, the owner of the wood-yard; and Edgar was committed to his care. He was conducted into a hut, in which were only two chairs, a rude bench, and table. His host was covered with a jacket, made of green flannel, that reached nearly to his knees; he had on his neck a kerchief with red and yellow bars; and a great number of keys and seals hung at the end of his heavy watch-chain. His movements, and air of self-reliance showed him to be one accustomed to command. Two surly-looking negro men came to the hut, on the floor of which, without bed or covering, lay four other negro men: a rifle stood in a corner of the room, and the stock of a revolver stood out of one of the large pockets of Talbot.

"Anything new in New Orleans, sir?" said he to Edgar, who for reply handed him a roll of newspapers. He began to read them by the light of his lantern. After some time, he gave directions to the two men who were awake to prepare a bed for Edgar, by arranging the tent, and other materials he had brought with him. In a few minutes Edgar was asleep, leaving Talbot still reading the newspapers.

After breakfast, the next day, Talbot directed four of the men, to get a boat and take Edgar and his baggage to the other side of the river, and about three miles below the wood-yard; to provide him with wood, and put up his tent.

The boat was soon at the place. The men had often been there with other hunters, and knew better than Edgar, what was wanted for his comfort. They put up his tent on the highest point of land, and near the river, placed in it shelves made with boards which they brought with them, and provided him with fire-wood ready for use.

They cut down a cedar tree, and piled up part of the tender branches in his tent, on which they placed his mattress; and covered the whole tent with the branches of the tree so thickly, that, except in front, no part of the canvas could be seen. They then made a pile of brushwood, on a point near the place where they had landed, and told him to set fire to it, as a signal, when he wanted them to come and take him off; or when, for any purpose, he desired their attention. Edgar gave them each a small sum of money, in addition to the compensation for their services that he had paid to Talbot; and they left him.

His first care, after their departure, was to place everything in order. His cooking utensils were arranged on one shelf; his rifle, bullet-moulds, and lead, on another; his books, pamphlets, and papers, on still another; and in a safe place, in a corner of his tent, he put his canister of gunpowder. These preparations kept him busy till nearly the middle of the afternoon: then, after cooking and eating his dinner, he dressed himself in his hunting gear, and started out, first to make an examination of his island. It was on the east side of the Mississippi river; at its highest point, the ground was not more than eight or ten feet above the surrounding waters. It was about three miles long, and half a mile wide, and irregular in shape: a small island that contained not more than an acre of land, was separated from the larger one, on which Edgar was, by a deep and narrow stream. With the exception of a few open spaces of small size, the larger island was covered with forest trees; sycamore, magnolia, cotton-wood, poplar, and cypress, upon which gray moss hung down nearly to the ground. Everywhere, were fallen trees, and half-decayed logs, and a thick undergrowth of shrubs. On the west and south sides, the Mississippi rolled its flood of turbid waters: on the other sides, the water extended as far as the eye could reach; and standing thickly in it, were large moss-covered trees, and bushes like those on the island.

It was night when he returned, wearied with the labor of the day. He prepared his supper, closed his tent, and slept soundly.

CHAPTER III.

THE HUNTER.

EARLY the next morning, our hunter was awakened by the chattering of hundreds of birds. The day so long wished for, from his early boyhood—so long the subject of his waking dreams—now beamed in the full brightness of early sunrise upon him.

After breakfast, he carefully dressed himself in his hunting clothing: his feet and limbs were covered to his knees with thick boots, to protect him from the bite of rattlesnakes; he had a blue cloth cap on his head, from the center of which, a tassel hung gracefully; and a closely-fitting jacket, protected him from the chilly air of morning. With his powder flask and bullet sack suspended from his neck, and his rifle on his arm, he was now ready.

He had not been from his tent an hour, before he saw through the bushes, a fine deer. He thought of all the instructions Captain Carter had given him, took slow and deliberate aim and fired. The deer bounded unhurt away; the forest echoed the sound of his rifle; and the island, so still before, seemed to be now alive with animals. In a few minutes afterward he saw another deer, and determined to be still more careful. He fired, and was keenly mortified to find that he was again unsuccessful. He then wandered through the tangled bushes, and over fallen trees and logs, to the furthest end of the island; here he rested himself, and then started on his return. He had got about half way to his tent, when he heard a slight rustling among the fallen leaves, and carefully looking in the direction from which the sound came, he saw part only, and but a small part of the body of a deer. The intervening branches nearly hid the animal from his view. The distance seemed too great for the reach of his rifle; but he was now half careless, and kneeling on one knee, he took deliberate aim and fired. The animal leaped high into the air—rushed with almost lightning speed for a mile, and fell. It ran in the direction of the tent, and when Edgar got to it, it was lying on its side, its eyes filled with tears, and panting for breath. He carried, or rather dragged it to his tent. His sadness was now all gone. He could shoot deer as well as other men, and needed only opportunity and practice to make him a successful hunter.

After he had taken good care of his game, he

started out again, full of hope—confident of success.

He had not gone far before he paused and looked around—then passed on a few steps and stopped again. He was almost sure that he heard some one calling to him, and after listening a short time, he heard distinctly the words "Master, master," and saw a negro man approaching with slow and feeble steps, and shaking as with an ague. His person was covered with tattered clothing, his feet with greatly worn skins of wild beasts bound around them with strips of bark. His eyes were sunk in his head, his hands and fingers long, thin and bony—his whole appearance showed disease and famine. Edgar was shocked at the wretched appearance of the man, and still more so, when he said, "Master, I am starving to death, please give me something to eat." He followed Edgar to his tent; food, water, and the remains of the coffee Edgar had prepared for his breakfast, were speedily given him. His eyes sparkled at the sight of the food, but after he had tasted it he became sick, and leaning back rested with his eyes closed against a post of the tent. Edgar prepared for him a cup of tea, and food better suited to his weak condition; but of this also he took but little, and then asked permission to lay himself down at the tent door before the fire. A few branches of the cedar tree were placed on the ground and covered with a blanket; a pillow was brought, the fire renewed, and the weak and weary man soon sank into a profound sleep; he continued in this state till nearly sunset, and then got up refreshed and craving for food. He was now able to eat much more than before; the muscles of his face relaxed, and he was certainly better and stronger than he was in the morning — still a wretched cough harassed him.

Our hunter selected from his wardrobe a full suit of his clothes, such as he could best spare, and directed the man to wash himself and put them on. A look, at first searching and distrustful into Edgar's face, and then, as if fully assured, another look full of gratitude and surprise, and a hearty "thank you, master, thank you, God bless you," was the response, and the reward for this kindness. As night came on the fire was increased, and Edgar and the stranger were seated by it.

"What is your name?"

"My name, master, is Aaron—Aaron Harper."

"Are you a slave?"

"No, master, I was born free; my mother and

father were both free; but I was kidnapped when I was a little boy and carried away and have been held as a slave ever since."

"Why are you here?"

"Master, I will tell you the truth. I ran away and was trying to get to Canada with my child. She is dead now, and I don't care whether I am free or not. I know I will die soon. I am worth nothing to any man. My poor, old, worn-out body would not bring a dollar on the auction block. I was near this place when the river rose, and I have been compelled to come here to get out of the way of the water; I could find but few roots to live on; and as for game—though there is plenty of it, I am too weak to get it. I heard a rifle-shot this morning and started to find the hunter; of course without knowing whether he would be a friend or a foe; and in this way I have met you." While he was speaking, his voice was low, composed, and respectful.

Although our hunter was kind and hospitable, yet it cannot be denied that this visit afforded him no pleasure. To leave New Orleans with high hopes of a brilliant hunting campaign—to be upon the ground, and then to have on his hands a sick negro to nurse, caused him no little vexation. But what could he do? The man was hungry—how could he refuse him food already prepared, and of which he had more than he needed! He was sick and wanted shelter—how could he refuse him a place to warm himself by his fire! There was a struggle in Edgar's mind between his pride and his humanity; but he was young, generous and hopeful; and humanity, of course, conquered all meaner feelings. It is difficult to blame him for these first impulses. He had his birth and education in a state in which there were but few people of color; and although he had seen a great many of them at New Orleans and other places, after he became of age, yet he knew but little about them.

After two days, the appearance of his guest had greatly improved. The deadly pallor had left his skin and it put on a more healthy look. He was more cheerful and active; and he performed many little offices about the tent by which he became useful. He cooked the food—kept up the fire—dressed the deer killed—aided greatly in carrying them to the tent, and always kept watch when the hunter was absent. Edgar conversed more frequently with him, and found day by day that his prejudices were wearing away, and that his guest, instead of being, as he at first supposed him, but little better than a beast, was a modest, sensible, intelligent, and grateful man.

It was now Sunday—our hunter laid aside his

hunting dress, and prepared himself to pass the day in his tent. After breakfast he opened a trunk and took out a number of books. He was surprised to find that Aaron took from his bosom an old book with its cover all black with constant use. Both sat down and read, but Aaron read slowly and with difficulty; Edgar found that he was reading a Bible, the print of which was too fine for his dimmed sight. He went to his trunk and from the bottom of it took out a larger Bible, sat down and said, "Let me read awhile to you."

"Thank you, master, thank you. It will be a great favor. My eyesight is so bad that I hardly know what I am reading. My book is an old one. I have taken as good care of it as I could, but it is soiled and worn."

"What shall I read?"

"Read, if you please, the 41st Psalm, master." Edgar turned and read: "Blessed is he that considereth the poor; the Lord will deliver him in time of trouble. The Lord will preserve him and keep him alive, and he shall be blessed upon the earth, and thou wilt not deliver him unto the will of his enemies. The Lord will strengthen him upon the bed of languishing: thou wilt make all his bed in his sickness."

As soon as he had read it, Aaron said, "Master, I am poor; I have worked hard all my days and have no land, nor house, nor food, nor clothing, only what you have given me. When I die, there is not a foot of ground that can be claimed as mine to lay my body in. I had no right, it was said, even to take care of my own child while she was alive. Another man claimed my own body and mind, as his property. Surely, if there is in the whole world a poor man, I am poor; and you have remembered me; you have taken care of me and given me clothes, and food, and shelter. Now the Bible is true, and God is true. He will bless you. I don't know how he will do it; but He will bless you. He will make your bed when you are sick; He will keep you from the power of your enemies." You will be blessed upon the earth. The Lord will deliver you in time of trouble, and preserve you and keep you alive. After this they were silent for a few minutes, and Edgar handed his Bible to Aaron and walked slowly into the forest.

CHAPTER IV.

JOHN SCOTT, ESQ.

A FEW miles from New Orleans was an old-fashioned house, two stories high, surrounded by forest trees. An avenue led from a gate, on the east side of the dwelling, to the door. Orange trees were scattered over the lawn, and rose-bushes, part of which were in bloom. The paint on the house had faded; and the roof was half-overgrown with moss. The avenue was covered with sea-shells, broken into fragments, but still white. A shower had fallen, and flowers, fruits, and the melody of birds filled the air with fragrance and music.

The front door opened into a hall, on each side of which were large rooms, with low ceilings, and small windows. In one room, packages, books and papers, lay on the chairs, tables, and carpet, which two black women and a mulatto boy, under the direction of a young lady, were placing in trunks.

The steps of a gentleman were heard upon the porch, rapidly walking toward the room. As he entered, he said, "What! Mary, not ready yet?

The boat leaves at eight o'clock to-morrow morning, and we must all be on board by half past seven or we shall be left for a week; no other boat fit to travel in will go up the river sooner."

"Oh, Papa, I am so tired; but we have now only to put these things in the trunks, and lock them up; in an hour all will be ready."

The gentleman was John Scott, Esq., the owner of the plantation. He was about sixty years of age. His features were regular; his eyes keen, bright and gray; his hands and feet small; his lips firmly compressed. He had marks of great activity of mind and body; courage and perseverance.

Mr. Scott had just left the room, when Mary said to the boy, "Run, Jim, and see who is coming? I hear a carriage in the avenue.

Jim returned and said, "Miss Mary, it 's Mr. Eyes, the same gentleman that was here yesterday, and that comes here so many times."

A flush passed over Mary's face. "Mr. Ives, Jim; not Mr. Eyes." The two colored women looked at each other and smiled.

"Run, Jim, said Mary, and take care of Mr. Ives' horse."

"Shall we quit packing now," said Sally, one of the women, looking at Mary?

"Why no, go on as fast as you can. What in

the world will you stop for now, with these things scattered all over the room? You really must have the trunks locked in an hour, or papa will be displeased."

"Well Missis," said Sally, "it's all one to us, and the sooner we get done the better."

Mr. Ives entered the room, and Mary exclaimed, "Why were you not here sooner? I have been looking for you all this afternoon."

"Oh, I have been so engaged in preparing for my journey. I have had all the business of my office to arrange before I leave, and the cases of my clients to look after; but I have got all ready now. Are you ready?"

"Nearly so; in another hour this hard work will be over. I am so glad that you can go with us. You have, of course, laid in a store of books?"

"Yes," said Mr. Ives, "I have more than we shall find time to read, even if we shall be two months from home, and at Richmond we can get moro."

"Do," said Mary, "exert yourself to the uttermost to cheer my father. My unclo was, as you know, the only relation that he had, out of his own household. Now that my uncle is dead, my father's sorrows have greatly increased. You must do all that you can to console him."

Mr. Ives said, "I will do so, as well for your

sake, as for his. It is strange that brothers should be foes for a quarter of a century; but when death comes, the feeling of brotherhood renews its power; and then the grief is more poignant than if they had lived in affection. These old Virginia family feuds have imbittered the lives of hundreds of excellent persons, who might otherwise have been as happy as mortals usually are."

"Well," said Mary, "I am now going for the first time out of my native state. I have lived so much at home, that I do not know how I shall feel and act in new scenes, and amidst strange associates. I half regret that papa insists upon my accompanying him, and I believe I would beg to be excused if he did not so much need my attention. You have been to Virginia, have you not?"

"I have never been further north than Lexington, but all the people south of the Potomac are so much alike in their manners, thoughts, and feelings, that we shall at all times be as much at home as if we were in New Orleans. Our trip will be short. There are no difficulties in the way of the speedy settlement of your uncle's estate, and when that shall be done we will return, and *then* my dear Mary."

Mary colored, but a smile would play upon her face, in spite of her efforts to look grave.

Although Henry Ives had never formally proposed to Mary, still they were affianced lovers. The eyes, the faces, the conduct of lovers reveal their hearts. Mr. Ives was a lawyer in good practice; he was about twenty-eight years of age. His brow was marked by hard study; his figure, slightly bent, was slender and graceful. At one time his friends thought he would become a minister; but although he had studied theology, he remained in the profession for which he had been educated.

CHAPTER V.

AARON'S NARRATIVE.

OUR hunter's interest in his guest, increased daily, as he became better acquainted with him. As they sat by the fire, in front of the tent, in the evening, after the labors of the day were over, he from time to time, obtained from Aaron, a history of his life, and made notes of such parts of it, as appeared to him worth remembering; correcting, as reporters do, some inaccuracies in the style of the speaker; while he endeavored, as closely as possible, to preserve the narrative, as he heard it. This was written in short hand, on loose pieces of paper, at intervals, and thrown into a trunk.

"My parents," said Aaron, "were both free. My father was steward on a ship that sailed from Alexandria to the West Indies. My mother, who had four children, of whom I was the eldest, in the absence of my father, maintained her family by daily labor. When I was seven or eight years old, a Quaker lady took me into her service, and taught me to read and write. She generally took me into a room up-stairs, when she gave me lessons. She told me not to let any person know that I was learning to read and write. As soon as I could read pretty well, and write a little, she took another colored boy in my place, as I believe, for the purpose of teaching him.

"When I was about nine years old, I was sent at dusk, by my mother, to a public pump; and while there, I saw a group of persons at a tavern, with the sign of a black bear, across the street; I went into the crowd; a slave-trader was just starting with a gang of slaves. One covered wagon, was nearly filled with women and children. I went near the rear of the wagon, a man picked me up, and threw me quickly in it; a man in the wagon seized me, put a handkerchief over my mouth, and tied me hand and foot. He told me, if I made any noise he would kill me; in another minute the wagon moved off. We traveled all night, and the greater part of the next day, which I remember was Sunday, before we stopped even to feed the horses. After a long journey, during which I was allowed to walk part of the time, with a man by my side as a guard, we came to what I now know to be, the eastern part of Alabama. Here I was sold, I do not know for how much, and delivered over to my master. He, too, was a trader, and after he had kept me a few months, he sold me to Mr. Thornton Jones, with whom I lived as house servant, until I was about twenty years of age. Mr. Jones was a Methodist class-leader; he discovered that I could read, and encouraged me to do so. He gave me two or three new Bibles, while I was with him; and often exhorted his slaves to be religious. It was his constant practice, on Sunday mornings, to gather us all together; read to us chapters in the Bible, and sing, and pray with us. He was generally kind, and gave his slaves as much food and clothing, as the best masters in the country gave to theirs. All seemed to be going on prosperously on his plantation, till one day, while we were hoeing cotton, two men came into the field, stopped all the hands, and said we were levied on by the sheriff, for a debt of Mr. Jones. We were allowed to stay on the plantation, for nearly a month, and then were taken to the court-house, and put in jail. Two days afterward, we were all sold at auction, by the sheriff. I was bid off at eight hundred dollars, by Harvey Willard; a gentleman of whom I had never heard before. He told me, he would be a good master to me, if I would be an obedient slave to him. This I promised him, and we set off together for his home, he on horseback, and I by his side on foot. But I was not long in his service. He was addicted to gaming, and one night took me to a tavern in a village, near his plantation, at which he met several other planters. He drank a great deal of liquor that night, and lost much money. About midnight he said, his cash was all gone; I was standing at his back, when he turned and said, 'I will stake this boy on this game.' The game went on, and I was handed over to a Mr. Adams, who won me. He took me in a few days, to a plantation near the middle of that state. I lived on it several years. My food was corn bread, with a little meat once a week. I was allowed two suits of cotton clothes, one straw hat, and one pair of shoes a year. His overseers were generally hard drivers, and made large crops. Mr. Adams was not often on the plantation on which I lived. His home was thirty or forty miles off. Soon after I went to his place, I married a woman older than myself, who had one child. She died in a few years, leaving me the father of one living child; my own child was a poor, weak, sickly thing. She was what people call broken-backed, and a more affectionate being never lived on earth: she would sit watching for me as I came home at night from the field; spring into my arms, and lean her little head upon my shoulder, and show by other tokens how deeply she loved me. After my wife died, no one but my daughter lived in my cabin, which was at some distance from the cabins of the other slaves. The only book I had was a Bible, and from that I taught her to read.

"When Lucy was about six years old, I was seized with dread that I should be sold, and separated from her. I tried to get rid of it, but it haunted me. I dreamed of it at night, and thought so much of it by day, that I became haggard and care-worn. I knew that if I was separated from her, she would die. No one loved or cared for her but myself. She was of no value to my master. The children called her bad names, because they said, she was ugly.

"This fear kept eating into my heart, till I could bear it no longer; I determined to run off. I knew the north star, and knew that somewhere in the world, there is a place to which, if I could get, I and my child too, would be free. I laid aside, each day, from my scanty meal a little food; and when the store seemed large enough, one dark night I took my sleeping child in my arms, and with all our clothing and food in a bundle on my back, quietly left our cabin, on a long, long journey, seeking for freedom."

(Here part of the narrative has been omitted.)

CHAPTER VI.

AARON'S NARRATIVE.

"At night we took a meal of corn bread. Again with Lucy in my arms, and my bundle on my back, I started on my journey. We kept on from night to night, till we came to the Ohio river. I had learned how to cross rivers. I made a float or raft of two logs of wood, of about equal length and size, placed in the water side by side, about four feet apart, then two more, but smaller, laid across the first; then two, which were nearly flat, placed across the corners, and close together; on these I put my bundle, and seating Lucy on it, held her with one hand, while with a stick in the other, I first pushed the raft into the river, and then rowed it as well as I could. I had never tried before to row a boat, or to cross a river, except by wading, or on horseback. My rowing was awkwardly done, and at first the raft only seemed to float down the river close by the shore from which we started. But by constant rowing, I saw that we were getting out into the stream. When we got into the middle of the river, the water ran so strongly, that my raft seemed unmanageable.

I worked hard at my oar, and after awhile, got out of the current, and was gaining the shore on the opposite side of the river. Just as I thought myself safe, Lucy started, and almost shrieked with fright; I turned to see what scared her, and saw, what seemed to be a furnace of fire, coming rapidly down upon us. It was a steamboat. I called out as loudly as I could, and rowed toward the shore with all my force. The boat swept past us without striking our raft, but another danger as great, seemed as if it would destroy us. The boat had made great waves, and the tossing of these seemed likely to break our raft in pieces. I pressed myself as firmly on it as possible, and the great waves drove us close to the shore. When we had nearly reached it, the logs came apart, and we both fell in the river, but we soon got out safe. My bag of food and clothes came also to the edge of the river; I caught it, and all wet as we were, we rejoiced that now we were out of the land of slavery.

"On the night before this, we met a colored man in the woods, who told us that we were but two miles from the State of Ohio, and that all persons in that state were free. I thought when we got there we would be free. As soon as we had climbed the river bank, we stood still. I said, 'We are free!'

"'Free, father! are we free now; free! will we be free all our lives?'

"My heart was full. The bright stars and the half moon were shining in the sky. All was still. I looked up and God seemed to be above us; I paused, and the hot blood rushed in gushing streams over my whole body; and then, lifting up my hands to heaven, I shouted, 'We are free! we are free!' I heard voices shouting in return, 'We are free!' The stars seemed to shout, 'We are free!' The clouds that floated in silver drifts above us, shouted, 'We are free!' Each golden wave of the Ohio, as it rolled along in its course, shouted 'We are free!' Every hill and every valley around us, shouted and shouted again, almost in thunder-tones, 'We are free!' All above and around us, seemed to be shouting to us, and to each other, 'We are free! we are free!' We kneeled down and kissed the ground and poured out our thanksgivings to God for freedom.

"I looked by the light of the moon and stars at my hard hands, and my heart leaped and beat in my breast when I thought, these hands are mine; these feet are mine; this head is my own head; this mouth, these eyes, this whole body—all my own. My whole self was a thousand times dearer to me now that they were mine. My child, too, was my own child; I pressed her to my bosom and was almost mad with joy.

"The morning soon came, and the daylight was sweeter than I had ever seen it before; the trees and the grass were greener; all nature had fresh beauty, such as I never thought of; I seemed to be in a land of dreams; Heaven itself seemed to be near me, and angels—good, holy angels to fill the air around, and to be rejoicing with us. I walked rapidly, for the earth seemed to bear me up; I felt no fatigue. My heart was full of joy. We traveled on three nights, walking as fast as we could; our provisions had got spoiled by the water, and we had been without anything to eat one day and night. Two weeks had now passed since we started. Sunday morning came; Lucy was very sick. It was raining hard, and cold: wet and hungry, with my child so ill that I feared she would die, I did not know what to do. If I trusted myself to any white person, I feared that we might be betrayed and sent again into slavery. If I did not find food, fire and shelter, my child might die. At last I determined to ask for food at the next house I should see. I came to a white frame house, built on a little hill, with a small roofed porch before the door. The out-buildings seemed to be new; there were a great many little trees and bushes in the yard. I stopped a long time before I could make up my mind to go there, but Lucy was hungry and cold, and it was raining upon us. I went to the porch; before I knocked at the door I heard some person reading; I waited—he was reading the Bible.

"Then shall the King say unto them on his right hand, Come, ye blessed of my Father, inherit the kingdom prepared for you from the foundation of the world: for I was a-hungered, and ye gave me meat: I was thirsty, and ye gave me drink: I was a stranger, and ye took me in: naked, and ye clothed me: I was sick, and ye visited me: I was in prison, and ye came unto me. Then shall the righteous answer him, saying, Lord, when saw we thee a-hungered, and fed thee? or thirsty, and gave thee drink? When saw we thee a stranger, and took thee in? or naked, and clothed thee? Or when saw we thee sick, or in prison, and came unto thee? And the King shall answer and say unto them, verily I say unto you, inasmuch as ye have done it unto one of the least of these my brethren, ye have done it unto me. Then shall he say also unto them on the left hand, depart from me, ye cursed, into everlasting fire, prepared for the devil and his angels: for I was a-hungered, and ye gave me no meat: I was thirsty, and ye gave me no drink: I was a stranger, and ye took me not in: naked, and ye clothed me not: sick, and in prison, and ye visited me not. Then shall they also answer him, saying, Lord, when saw we thee a-hungered, or athirst, or a stranger, or naked, or sick, or in prison, and did not minister unto thee? Then shall he answer them, saying, verily I say unto you, inasmuch as ye did it not to one of the least of these, ye did it not to me. And these shall go away into everlasting punishment: but the righteous into life eternal.

"After he had read, he prayed so loud that I could hear every word he said. He asked God to give him and his wife strength at all times, to do whatsoever he commanded them. He prayed for the poor and the needy, and for those who had none to help or comfort them, and for all those who were in distress in mind, body or estate. The tears came into my eyes, when I heard his prayer, for I felt sure that he would help us. As soon as he got up, I knocked gently at the door. It was opened. The man started when he saw us—stepped back and looked at me, as if he was scared. I told him, that my child was cold, sick and hungry, and begged him to let me warm her by his fire, and for a little bread and milk. Lucy looked hard at the warm fire, the first she had seen for a week. The man and his wife looked at each other, and then at us, and seemed troubled. Lucy too asked for a piece of bread; my whole heart was so intent on getting her warmed and fed, that I never thought of asking anything for myself, although I was hungry and weak, and nearly sick. The man asked me, if I was a runaway; I could not tell a lie with Lucy in my arms; I was silent. The man then went back to his Bible, and read out loud again, the same words that he had read before. His wife was standing by his side; both of them looked as if they did not know what to do. He said to her, that we were fugitives from slavery, and if they harbored us, he would be fined a thousand dollars, and have to pay one thousand for each of us to our owner, and to be imprisoned six months in jail, under the new law of Congress, if they were detected. That he had voted against his neighbor, Squire Phillips a few weeks before, when he was a candidate for the legislature, because he was a drunkard; and he feared Phillips would find him out and put the law in force against him. The man told his wife that for three days, he had felt as if some great trial was coming upon him, and while he was at prayer, that feeling came over him as a cloud of darkness. He said, they had set their hearts too much on the things of this world, and had always prospered.

"He walked in deep study, two or three times

across the room, and then stopped and looked his wife in the face, and said, 'Jane, what shall we do?' She made no reply. He then went back to the Bible still lying open on the stand, and read these words: 'Cornelius, thy prayers, and thine alms have come up as a memorial before God.' He stood still awhile and said, I see it plainly now; alms to the needy, are as acceptable sacrifices to God as prayers, and both together are remembered before him. Daniel prayed—prayed aloud, when he was commanded not to do so; and I will give these people alms, though commanded not to do so. He then told me to come in."

CHAPTER VII.

AARON'S NARRATIVE.

"VERY soon a hot breakfast was ready for us. Lucy was too sick to eat much, and I was too greatly concerned for her, to have any relish for even the good food before me. The lady gave her a cup of tea, and toast; undressed her, and put her in a soft bed. Oh! how my heart gushed with gratitude, as I saw my poor child so treated. She had never before slept on a feather bed, had never drank tea, and I had never been treated as a man till now. The lady bathed Lucy's face and hands, and nursed her as kindly as if she had been her own child. She told me that she was going to a meeting, about four miles off, and would not be back till lato in the afternoon. She told me to feel myself at home, to lie down on the same bed with Lucy. She darkened the windows, and bade me bolt the door. I told the man that I could read, and asked him to let me read over again in his Bible, the passages I had heard him read, while I was standing at his door. He hunted up the places, and brought the stand with the Bible on it, into the room where I was. Lucy soon fell asleep, and I sat at her side, and read the passages over and over again. I wondered how so good a man could doubt whether it was his duty to take care of my child; when he could do so with such words in God's book, right before his eyes. 'Whatsoever ye would, that others should do unto you, do ye even so unto them.' If his child was sick, and I could help him, would he not wish that I should do so? 'Whosoever offendeth one of these little ones, that believe in me, better were it for him that a millstone were hanged about his neck, and he cast into the sea.' I had always taught Lucy, from her early childhood, to believe, trust, and obey our Saviour—she did so from her heart. Could this man then have offended her, by letting her stay out in the cold rain, and refusing her food and warmth, when it was in his power to give her both?

"She was sick and in slavery, though not in prison; how could he refuse even for a moment to aid her! After a while the lady came home, and brought with her the preacher, she had been to hear. He was an old man, with white hair. At first he did not talk much, but after dinner they talked a great deal; my room was separated from theirs only by a plank partition; the door was part of the time ajar, and I could hear what they said.

"My friend's name was Peter Browne, and his wife's, Jane. The preacher seemed to be an old friend, and called them by their first names. He told them, to cultivate holiness of heart; to obey all God's commandments, and to seek, as for a pearl without price, perfect love and peace with God. He told them of the faith and trials of the early Christians; how they suffered all their worldly goods to be taken from them, and were cast into prison—that some of them were burned up in fire, rather than disobey any of God's commandments.

"Mr. Browne asked the preacher's opinion about the late act of Congress. The preacher told him, he thought it wrong, to talk on such subjects on the Sabbath day, and did not answer his question, till Mr. Browne said, 'What should I do if one of these fugitives should come to my house, and ask for food? What is my duty in such a case? It is impossible for any man to know at what minute it may occur to him.'

"Mr. Patterson said, 'It is our duty, to obey the laws of our country. The Scriptures expressly command that we shall be subject to the powers that be. And this commandment,' he said, 'was given, when the governments of the earth were much more oppressive than now.'

"Mr. Browne said, 'That was true, but the very

same apostles who wrote this, themselves refused to obey the command of their superiors, when they forbade them to preach the Gospel.'

"'Ah!' said Mr. Patterson, 'they chose to obey God, rather than man. This is our duty in all cases, where the commandments of men forbid duties which God enjoins.'

"Mr. Browne said, 'God does in all parts of the Bible command us to feed the hungry, to help the poor and needy; to be a friend to the fatherless, the widows and to all that are oppressed; and that the condition of slaves, was as helpless as that of widows and orphans, or strangers. Shall I, ought I to obey,' said he with great earnestness, 'any law of man, which either in words, or in substance, forbids me to feed the hungry, to clothe the naked, to help him who is ready to perish? Is it my duty to do so? If so, in what part of the Bible is such duty revealed? by what course of fair argument, am I to be convinced it is so?'

"'The Constitution, the organic law of our country, made by wise and patriotic men, requires the surrender of fugitive slaves. No human instrument ever has been, ever will be, perfect. The best men are controlled by circumstances, and must do as they can, in view of all the circumstances that surround them. Slavery existed in nearly all the states, when this Constitution was adopted; and the return of a fugitive from slavery, only places him in the condition in which he was born, and gives peace to the country. Without this clause, it may be, that our union never would have been formed. It does not make any man a slave; it only obliges us not to intermeddle with the slaves of our fellow citizens in other states. And as this is a constitutional provision, it is but right to make laws to carry it into full effect. It is a compromise of conflicting principles; and the laws that are made pursuant to it, should of course be obeyed by all good men.'

"'Yes,' said Mr. Browne, 'it is indeed a compromise; but what sort of compromise? The slaveholder robs his slave of all his earnings, of his wife, of his children, of his liberty, dearer than life; and we on our side have 'compromised' with him to protect and support him in this wrong-doing and sin. Is not he who keeps guard for the robber, to secure to him his prey, as guilty as the robber himself? Two men compromise away the rights of a third person, who is no party to their compact, and whose rights are either stricken down by their agreement, or kept down by it, and each agrees with an *oath*, to support the other in their joint iniquity: is *this* such an agreement as christian men may make or support? The return of the fugitive *does* place him in a worse state than he would be but for such return. He would be free if it were not for these laws making it *our* duty, as you say, to send him back. It is true, it obliges us not to intermeddle with our neighbor's slaves: but is it not our *duty* to intermeddle with them, when the fugitive knocks at our door and asks shelter and food, sympathy and protection? Is not this very agreement an open denial of God's authority? He commands us to do these things, and this is an agreement on our part, not to do them. Imperfection may exist of necessity, but not sin; God has not imposed a necessity for sinning on any people."

"Mr. Patterson said, 'But, brother Browne, remember, that many of our best men are bound by their oaths to support this Constitution; the whole of it, including, of course, all its parts.'

"'Yes,' replied Mr. Browne, 'but if a man takes an oath to burn my house, or murder my family, or to burn a city, or murder all the people he meets on the streets; does his oath give him any greater right to do so than he had before? If so, a man has only to take an oath that he will disobey every commandment of God, and every law of man, and then he will be guiltless, no matter what sins and outrages he may commit. If the thing itself is sinful, the oath to commit or to continue in it, is an additional sin. If two men rob you, and divide the spoil, and each binds himself by an oath to sustain the other in his wrong, does that give them any right to keep their ill-gotten gain? When a band of men at Jerusalem, agreed with an oath to kill St. Paul, they had no greater right to do so, than they had before. At least Paul thought so, for he accepted an escort, and escaped.

"'When Herod agreed with an oath, to give to the daughter of Herodias whatsoever she would ask, even to the half of his kingdom; had he any more right to behead John the Baptist at her request, than he had before? This too was a 'compromise,' between Herod and the dancing girl; the one demanded, and the other gave; but John the Baptist was not consulted in the compromise and was beheaded.'

"'Well,' said Mr. Patterson, 'the case is really a difficult one.'

"'I see now, no difficulty whatever in it,' replied Mr. Browne. 'It is my undoubted right to read the whole Bible, and to obey every commandment in it. God had the right to *command*, and as his accountable and moral creature, it is my duty to OBEY HIM. The one is the inevitable result of the other. It seems to me, that if it is not every man's duty to obey the whole Bible, it was not God's right to command every man to do so, and so the result would be impious at least. Now what God has made it every man's *duty* to do, He has given every man on earth the *right* to do. The duty came from God, and the right to discharge it, is also from God himself. Any law, therefore, which even tends to hinder any man from discharging any duty revealed in the Bible, impairs his religious freedom. Every man on this earth has the right to obey all the commandments of God, and this right has always been claimed in the United States. When, therefore, God commands me to shelter the outcast, to aid the poor and needy, to be a friend to the friendless, I can see no cloud upon my path of duty. I walk in it with the full sunlight of God blazing from the Bible upon me, and have no more doubt than I would have, if an angel from heaven were standing by my side, and guiding my every footstep.'

"'Brother Browne, that may be well enough; it seems all plain to you; but do you not fear that if you step aside into this new, and as yet, untrodden path, you may encounter difficulties of which you are not now aware? Is it not best to be on the safe side? Prudence is a virtue. You have a family to support, and have friends who are interested in your welfare; be cautious; no man was ever hurt by being prudent and cautious, while thousands have been ruined by rashness. Your good old father, who is now in heaven, never entertained such thoughts or followed any such courses as you seem now inclined to enter upon. Wait; be patient; pray; read your Bible; and meddle not with those who are given to strife.'

"'Why read my Bible, unless I do what it clearly teaches? Why shall I bow my knee to Christ and call him Lord, Lord, if I *do* not the things he commands? Why go to meetings, but for additional help and strength to discharge whatsoever duties God has revealed? It may be true that my father did not do as I intend; but each age has its own especial duties: the light that I have he may never have enjoyed. Prudence, may indeed be a virtue, but is it prudent to disobey God? Rashness has ruined thousands; but is it not rash even to madness, to disobey a clear command of God? There are dangers to my worldly interests in my path; but are there not also dangers to my eternal life, if I disobey a clear command from God?'

"'You are right, brother Browne, I see it, and what is more, I feel it too. You are right brother. We must at all hazards obey God; and if men, by their laws, command us to disobey him, it is our duty and therefore our right, to disregard all such laws, and we are cowards and worse, if we do not do so. The kingdom of God has ever been at war with the Prince of the powers of the air, and it would be strange indeed if we in our country should find no warfare. Asia and Europe have had their conflicts, which arose from their popular sins, and we may have ours; perhaps as fierce, as bitter, as bloody and unrelenting, as theirs. The human heart in all ages, has been the same. Civilization has only hidden its tiger passions, and these when aroused, are as fierce in their wrath as they were in the days of Nero, or on the plains of India. Slavery is the sin of America, as idolatry was that of ancient Rome; and the one may cost as many martyrdoms as did the other, before it shall be overthrown. The laws that sustain Slavery in this country, are as grossly wicked, as those that sustained the idolatry of the Roman empire; and it is as much our duty to disobey them, as it was the duty of the early Christians to refuse to worship idols. All sins dishonor God, and destroy man; and this sin of slave-holding, tramples down into the very dust, the children of the most High; classes them with the beasts of the field. God made man in his own image, and gave him dominion over the beasts of the forest and the field, and the fowls of the air, and the creeping things of the earth, and the fish of the sea. He only, of all creatures on earth, knows the use of fire; he only, laughs and weeps; and above all, he only, can be taught to worship and obey God; the beasts never can. God has surrounded him with his protecting care, by laws obligatory upon all men. He has commanded all men to love him, as they love themselves, and to do to him, as they would others should do unto them.'

"'You are right too, in another of your assertions. It is every man's right, to do everything that God by his revealed word, has clearly made it his duty to do. Now as God has in the Bible, revealed to man the whole circle of his duties; to God, to Christ, to the Church, to his father and mother, to his wife and children, to his friends and neighbors, to his country, and to all mankind; it follows inevitably, that he cannot be a slave; for no slave can discharge all these duties: his very position as a slave, makes it impossible for him to do so.'

"'The Bible assumes the existence of God; it also assumes the free agency of man. Both alike are true, and hence it is, that the Bible is the great liberator of the world; and those who teach it to others, and obey it themselves, are the best friends of human freedom. The missionary enterprise is therefore, above all others, that to which men must look, and on which, under God, they should rely, for the deliverance of the earth from tyranny and despotism.'

"Mrs. Browne now came in, and invited them out to supper. After supper the conversation commenced again on the same subject.

"Mr. Brown said: 'I have taken an oath to support the Constitution of the United States, and that instrument, you say, requires us to surrender fugitives from slavery. What am I to do? I wish to keep my oath. I have never willingly violated my plighted faith—and there is too another engagement upon me not less sacred. When I joined the Church, I covenanted with God, to obey all his commandments.

"'If the Constitution does indeed require us to surrender fugitive slaves, then the law which forbids us to harbor them, in its principle and spirit, requires us to withhold food and shelter from them, so that they may return as soon as possible to their masters; every act by which the slave is better able to go on his way to Canada, violates the spirit if not the very letter of that law. Here then there are conflicting laws; that of God commands me to feed the hungry — to shelter the outcast—and that of Congress forbids me to do so.

"'Prayers and alms are alike acceptable to God now, as they were in the days of Cornelius, whose alms and prayers were both remembered before HIM. A law of Congress that would forbid us to pray, would clearly violate our rights of conscience, and impair our religious liberty.

"'Does not the law that forbids us to show mercy to the poor, have the same effect? Is there no protection to religious liberty in this whole land?

"'Where is the difference between a law which commands us to renounce Christ in words, as a law of the Roman empire did, and one that commands us to disobey him?—between a law that forbids us to read the Bible, and one that forbids us to obey it, after we have it? I can see none. And if we are bound to do this by the Constitution, the religious freedom of the whole people of the United States, is as fully overthrown here to-day, as that liberty ever has been, or now is in any country on earth. I will not, for my part, obey any such law. 'As for me and my house, we will follow God, and keep his commandments.'

"My heart leaped with joy, when I heard him say this, for I feared for the very life of my child, if he should make up his mind not to do so. If he turned us out, who would take care of us? My child was sick; had a fever. I was hungry and could not work, lest I should be detected and taken back into slavery. I felt that we were now safe. The good man, Mr. Browne, had made up his mind to obey his God, as well as to pray to Him.

"Mr. Browne said: 'This man, has as good a right to give his children freedom, as to give them food.'

"I never heard anybody say so before; but I always thought so.

"Mr. Patterson said: 'The laws in the slave states support slavery.'

"'Yes, said Mr. Browne, 'in some of them they allow horse-racing, and gambling, and liquor selling, going to theaters, and selling bad books. It would be a strange thing if christian people did all these things, and then said, the laws allowed them to do so. The law compels no man to be a slaveholder. He can leave the state with his slaves, and set them free in the free states. Many have done so, and all who will not do so are without excuse.'

"'There must, I think,' said Mr. Patterson, 'be some mistake about my construction of the Constitution. Every man in the United States, has the undoubted right to believe in God, and to obey HIM. To read the whole Bible, and practice all that is taught in it. The people of the United States have always thought so. Surely there can be no error in this opinion, which has been held by the whole people, ever since this has been a government? I will look further into this matter. My opinions have probably been too hastily formed.'

"The next morning Mr. Patterson went away. We staid upward of a week at Mr. Browne's. Lucy was too ill to travel. When she got better, one evening we attempted to leave, and bidding Mrs. Browne farewell, with many thanks for her kindness, we set out. Mr. Browne went with us, but we had gone only a few steps from the house, when it was plain that Lucy could not go on. Mr. Browne told us to come back, and stay a few days longer.

"I ought to have mentioned that Mrs. Browne gave Lucy some clothes. They treated us with great kindness, which day by day increased."

CHAPTER VIII.

REV. MR. ST. JOHN.

NEAR the village of Burtonville, in the eastern part of Virginia, an old church had been standing for a century. The people who worshiped in it, had been for many months without a pastor.

On the first Sunday in November, in the year 1833, the Rev. Mr. St. John, by an invitation from the members of the church, was there to preach. He was without charge at the time, and had been highly spoken of as a suitable person for their pastor. A great many carriages stood near the church, with colored men as drivers and servants, lounging in groups about them.

Plethoric gentlemen, whose faces showed that their wine and their cheer was good; elderly ladies, whose glossy hair, neatly parted in front, set off the frills of their white caps with best effect; young ladies richly dressed; young gentlemen with neat canes, well-made coats, and jeweled pins; filled the pews. These people, from the village and the country around it, had come up to worship.

Mr. St. John was tall, gaunt, and lean. The skin upon his face and hands, had a sickly-yellow hue: nothing about him exhibited the great talents he was said to have, except his large black eyes; and they, when he was in repose, seemed to be slightly vailed with film; but when he became animated, they shone and glared with the light almost of insanity itself.

After the introductory service, he announced his text. "Servants, be obedient to them that are your masters according to the flesh, with fear and trembling, not with eye-service as men-pleasers, but as the servants of Christ."

All were surprised. The duties of servants! They were outside of the house with the horses! No person to whom the word could rigidly be applied, was within the walls of the building. The matter was new; all were aroused and attentive. We have no space to furnish our readers with the whole of this discourse. Extracts are all that our limits allow.

"It is the duty of servants to obey their masters. God himself has positively commanded them, in the text, to do so. To refuse, or to withhold that obedience, is to resist an ordinance of God.

"The relation of master and servant, is ordained and established by God in his infinite wisdom and goodness. It is of mutual benefit to the parties who enjoy that relation. It gives to the master, leisure for mental and moral culture; to the servants, the certainty of food, shelter, clothing, home, and relief from perplexing cares. True, the relation may be abused, and he was willing to admit, that in many instances it had been abused. But so, too, had the relation of husband and wife; parent and child; and all the relations of domestic life. Man is morally ruined by the fall, and the serpent's trail is in every household.

"The relation appeared first to have been established in the curse of Canaan: afterward it was not only permitted, but enjoined upon the Israelites to make servants of the heathen round about them. It has existed among all civilized nations, and in all ages since the flood.

"The most serious evils result to society from visionary schemes of philanthropy, that destroy it. Where it no longer exists, except as a mercenary relation, the master and servant have no common interest. They are heads of different households. The one has no certain home; the other, no established service; and hence the domestic arrangements of the master are frequently, and sadly disturbed for want of service, when it is most needed; and the poor servant, too often, is left to starve or beg. The sad condition of the free negroes and mulattoes in our own state, and indeed, wherever they are, is additional proof that the relation is blessed. They are destitute, afflicted, tormented by hunger, suffering with cold, in want and wretchedness, crowded together into seething and festering sinks of disease and vice. It is necessary only to see them as they are, to be convinced that those who have released them from their light service, have been deluded by erroneous views of duty. How much happier would they be, how infinitely happier for this life, and how much more hope for them for the life to come; if they could but have the care of Christian masters, and the gentle guidance and admonition of Christian mistresses."

He then, in touching language, showed the folly of those who, under the guise of philanthropy, have now actually organized themselves, with a determined purpose to break up this relation in the southern states. "They, or their ancestors, had, in their own states, taken from the couch of the sick and the dying, the care of servants born in the household, and at all times integral parts of the family; care, scarcely less tender and unremitting than a mother's love; and provided as its substitute, the watching of the hired nurse, who dozed and dreamed at the bedside of her dying mistress. And they now wish, against our will, to reduce our hearths and households to the same sad condition.

"It is the duty of all to resist these encroachments upon rights so valuable and so sacred. To resist, as Christians should, with the meekness of angels, but with the firmness of heroes and of martyrs. If the urgent demands now made upon us, were for a cloak or a coat, or to go with the exactors a mile, it would be our duty to yield; but when our hearthstones are no longer sacred; when the established institutions of the state and of domestic life, are ruthlessly invaded; then, it becomes us, by our self-respect, our love of wives, and children, and home, our love of the Bible and of holy things, to resist to the uttermost, the attacks so wickedly made, and so incessantly repeated.

"In a moment of weakness, and for want of due reflection, we have already yielded too much." He had shown that the relation of master and servant was a natural one; approved and sanctioned by the Father of mercies; "as that is right, we must take that as the stand-point, and viewed from this position, the trade, by which our servants were brought here, was also right; and that by means of which they follow their masters to new and distant states, is right. We have suffered the agents in these trades, to be denounced and defamed. We have," he regretted to say, "ourselves, too often given point to the sting of these reproaches, by refusing to admit into our society, well-educated, and well-behaved men, whose only offense is, to act as merchants, in transferring, when necessity requires it, servants from one state, already full of them, to another, where their services are of more value. We should humble ourselves, and repent of this gross injustice and deep wrong. We have sometimes done more—we have refused to these gentlemen the benefit of the sanctuary, and of alliance with the church. We do not so with merchants in other lawful traffic. This is but the result of prejudice and perverted sympathy. We have listened so often to the assailants of our institutions, that we ourselves have imperceptibly, become imbued in part, at least, with their unholy prejudices and unwise views, and suffer our conduct to be controlled by principles to which we are, in practice, opposed.

"Our repentance should be speedy and deep. We have wronged our best friends. They are of great service to the state, and to our institutions, and our gratitude and regard should be commensurate with the benefits they have conferred. What would become of the institution without these men? and what with all the benefits and blessings that result from that institution? They are," he said, "the very pillars of the commonwealth, which we by our insane prejudices, are pulling down. Let us reflect;" and again he urged, "let us repent in sackcloth and ashes."

CHAPTER IX.

BENNETT LEATHERS.

As Mr. St. John left the church, a gentleman stepped up to him and said: "Allow me, sir, to accompany you part of the way to your lodgings. I am so delighted with your sermon, that I wish to cultivate your acquaintance. My name, sir, is Bennett Leathers. You must have heard of General Wilmot; well, sir, he is my mother's own brother; and Colonel Woodman and Major Harvey, are my first cousins, so that you see, sir, I am of a good family. I live in Campbell county, where I have a plantation. I have listened to you to-day, and fully agree with you, in all the opinions you have advanced. Your arguments are conclusive; your logic is exact, and well applied. Indeed, sir, you have been of great service to the country. If you were to die to-morrow, sir, the country would owe you a debt of gratitude, which it never can repay. Slaves are better off than they would be, if they were free. Nobody but fanatics doubts that. Everybody who says to the contrary, sir, is a fanatic. The whole world calls them fanatics; all the newspapers publish them as fanatics; and they are fanatics, sir. There's my man, Joe; I have but one slave sir, and that is old Joe; the greatest thief and liar, sir, in the whole world, old Joe is—upon my honor he is, sir. Well now, I take care of old Joe. I give him food and clothing, and take care of him, and keep him when I can, from getting drunk. I don't work him hard, and keep no overseer, because you see, sir, I cannot afford to hire an overseer for three hundred dollars a year, and six barrels of flour, and two barrels of pork, and let him have a horse, saddle, and bridle, whenever he wants one, just to make old Joe work. So I am my own overseer; I sit on the fence all day, and make old Joe work in the tobacco patch, and in the cornfield. I get so tired, that it almost kills me, but I am getting used to it; and then the worst of it is, that last year, after all the crop was raised, and got all ready for the market, old Joe stole it all, little by little, till nothing at all was left for me; he traded it off to a mean white man, who keeps a grog-shop, for whisky and tobacco. I did not get a cent for the whole crop—not enough to pay the taxes on the land. Now would it not be a pity for me to turn old Joe loose on society, and leave him to shift for himself? He'd starve to death, sir, in two weeks. He would steal everything he could lay his hands on too; and would go to the penitentiary. I have tried to sell him over and over again, but when I take a trader to look at him, old Joe has got a fashion of throwing his elbows out of joint, and pretends it is the rheumatism, he calls it rheumatics, sir, and so no trader will buy him, because they say, sir, that he might do so, when they got him down South, and they could never sell him.

"I have come to this place for a few days, on a little private matter of my own; a little love affair, sir, under the rose. Miss Black is a beautiful lady; I met her last week at a party and fell half in love with her. Her father is a merchant, sir, but he is a wholesale tobacco merchant; and so you see, though you would hardly expect me to propose for a merchant's daughter, yet, as her father is rich, and she is his only child, her wealth may be equal to my family position, and so make an equal match, sir. I came here day before yesterday, and have called four times at her father's to see her, but she is too unwell to see me, and I am waiting at the hotel till she gets better. I am surprised too, at her sickness, for only four days ago, she was the very picture of health, sir, a blooming beauty, and as merry a young lady, as you ever saw, sir. I once before, paid attention to a merchant's daughter. She was from New York. I met her at the Springs.

She was a very learned lady. She believes a string of *isms* as long as her arm, and knows all the *ologies*. Her father is very rich. She will be worth two or three millions of dollars, when he dies. While she was at the Springs, she still kept up her studies. Every morning, she devoted one hour to chemistry, and every afternoon one hour to bigotry.

"Well, sir, I followed her to New York, put up at a hotel, and went to her father's house. I sent up my card, and presently a servant came down stairs, and told me 'she was not at home.' I went away, and called in the afternoon, and the servant came down and said, 'she was not at home.' Then I called the next day, and she was out then too, and so I kept calling for four days, but never could find her in. These city ladies, sir, go out a great deal. They have so much shopping to do, and so many friends to see, that it is really a hard thing to find them at home. So I went back to the hotel, and just made up my mind to keep on calling, till I could find her at home; and while I was standing in the parlor, a gentleman came up, and commenced conversation. He was very friendly, and we soon became acquainted: while we were talking, sir, another man came in, and they two talked apart for a little while. The other man went out, and soon came back somewhat in liquor. I was standing up, leaning my elbow on the mantlepiece, sir, when this other man jostled hard against me, and nearly pushed me down. They both apologized, and left the room a moment afterward; and when I felt in my pocket, a short time after they went away, my pocket-book was gone. I had barely money enough left to pay my bill, and bring me home, so that I had to leave, sir, immediately. I do not think the gentleman who talked to me in the parlor, had anything to do with it, because he was the only man that said a civil word to me while I was in New York. Everybody else was in too much haste to speak to me. He was a gentleman, sir. I am twenty-eight years of age, sir, and all my friends tell me that I ought to get married; and I will do so, provided I can suit myself, sir. I have two thousand acres of land up in Cabell county; but it is mountainous, and won't sell yet. It is full of mineral ore, and will be a great fortune by-and-by; so much, that with my plantation in Campbell county, and with my family connections, I think it right to marry a lady of fortune at least, if not of family. I know it is hardly right to marry out of my own family, sir. My grandfather married his first cousin, and my father married his first cousin, and as far back as I know or have heard of, my ancestors have all married in their own family. A good plan, sir, it keeps wealth in the family, and prevents those mèsalliances that sometimes come from marrying strangers. But I have but one cousin, who is unmarried, and she is so deaf that you have to speak to her through a tin horn, and then she can't understand more than half you say; and she is twice as old as I am too, so that you see, sir, I cannot follow the good old time-honored usages of my family. I keep a list of all the ladies who have received especial attentions from me, with the very date, when any particular event has happened that has brought the matter to a close. It numbers twenty-nine now, and if Miss Black shall follow the example of others, it will be thirty. Two years ago, I went out to Kentucky, sir, to see some relations, and there I met with a young lady, I should say woman, rather, for she was larger than I am; she is rich, too, the daughter of a gentleman who sells a great many mules and cattle every year; well, I went to see her, went once, and she sat and talked for two hours. I went again and something was the matter, so that she did not come into the room: I was in love with her, yes, sir, in love with her, and I went almost every day for two weeks. At last one day, just as I set my foot in the house, the door of a back room opened a little, a slight crack only, sir; I saw her face, but she did not say a word to me. I turned round for an instant, and a gun went off, the whole load struck me right on the neck; it knocked me down, sir; it was a shot-gun loaded with beans! I have not got over it yet; my neck, you will observe, sir, is a little stiff now. It hurts me very much just before a rain; I shall outgrow it, I have no doubt; the doctors and all my friends tell me so. I had always been told, sir, before I went to Kentucky, that I must not expect as much refinement there, as I had been accustomed to here in Virginia, and I had myself observed, that when a young man left Virginia, and went to Kentucky only for six months; when he came back his manners had not the softness they had before he left: but I did not expect to find such rude people in this whole world. I never set foot in that house again, sir—upon my honor, sir, I never will. I came back to Virginia, as soon as I could. I like your doctrine, sir. When I was a boy, I went to boarding-school, kept by old Dr. Stephens up in Amherst county. He starved us almost to death, sir; gave us nothing but mush and molasses for supper, and bread and herring for breakfast, till we got to stealing his geese, and that brought him to his senses, when he found out that we had roast goose in our rooms, almost every night. A great sin, that, sir, but I repented of it. Well, sir, while I was there, I became pious; I got to be so pious, that I would not walk as far as from here across the street on Sunday. Indeed I would not have done so on Sunday, to save your life. I think again of the happy days I enjoyed when I was pious. I 'll do all I can to practice what you have told us to-day. Indeed I will, sir; upon my honor I will, sir. I have counted the cost, and made up my mind, and I will do it. I will not be a doer only of the word, but a hearer also; no, that's not it; let me see how it is, sir. I am afraid I have forgot it already. Not a doer of the word—no, (oh, my neck hurts me so, that I cannot remember anything now, as I used to) not a hearer of the word—but a doer; that is it, sir, I believe. If you will go to Richmond, I will introduce you to the best society in the city. Richmond is a great place, sir. It gives law to the whole Union. Chief Justice Marshall gave law to the one party, and half a dozen of men there govern Virginia; and Virginia rules the Union by means of the other party. And so between them, they have governed this whole Union. Triumph of mind, of intellect, and intelligence, sir! let people make what form of government they please, whether it is a republic, or what not, gentlemen of birth, fortune and education, always will, in the long run, be the actual rulers. The people may vote, but the gentlemen will settle the principles they support, and then it makes no difference what men are elected to carry these principles into effect. Mr. Stephens told me so, sir; and he is the greatest lawyer, I believe, in the whole world."

Mr. St. John inquired, "whether they were near the place, to which he was going?" "Near it, sir?—why we have passed it almost a mile, but I am so delighted with your society, that I could but extend our walk as far as possible. Your ideas, my dear sir, respecting the slave-trade, exactly coincide with my own. Slavery is right. Everybody, whose opinion is worth having, knows that, by this time. All the churches that persons, like you and me, sir, care to go to, say it is right. Well then, that being so, of course it was right to bring the slaves here, and it is right to take them to the new states. The logic, sir, is as clear as sunshine. Do meet me in Richmond soon; I have a project in my head, that I want to consult my friends there about. I'll mention it to you now, sir; but in confidence, strict confidence, sir. It is this; we have been threatening to dissolve the Union so long, that our warnings have no good effect, as they once had. Now, sir, my plan is this; instead of telling the people of the free states, that we will dissolve the Union; let us threaten to burn the Capitol. That will surprise them; and it is so easily done too. If we attempt to dissolve the Union, the men that live up in the mountains, and on Mud creek, and Turtle creek, and in such places, may get scared; and vote against the measure, in our own State; but the other can be done without consulting them at all. Now, sir, here's the place you make your home at, while you are here. I will write to you in a few days, and I hope you will write me in reply. Good-by, sir. Oh, how delighted I am with your sermon! Rely upon it, the lessons you have taught, shall not be lost upon me. I will be a hearer of the word, and not a doer only. Good night, sir."

As Mr. St. John walked up the path that led to the house, he said: "That is a strange young gentleman indeed. He is no doubt very amiable."

As Mr. Leathers walked on his way, he rubbed his hands and said to himself: "The very thing—clear as sunshine. I wonder that I never saw it so distinctly before, as I now do. Sermons are good things; they place matters upon right principles, and enable us, who have less leisure to think about such things than ministers; to give a reason, and a good one too, for what we do and believe in. I always thought, that free negroes are a pest and a nuisance, and would be better off a great deal, if they all had masters, and I know it now. It will be better all round, for the blacks and whites, when all the negroes and mulattoes are slaves. They are not fit to be free. They can't take care of themselves. That thought of his, about negro drivers being made respectable, looks queer. Indeed it does; but he made the matter so plain, that no person can have any doubt now, about it. I'm glad of it, I am very glad of it."

CHAPTER X.

BENNETT LEATHERS.

The family of Bennett Leathers had all the ancient honor and respectability which he claimed. But he was poor. True, he had his plantation in Campbell county, and his immense tract of wild land in Cabell county, but these yielded him no present income. To supply his daily wants, he was compelled to borrow small sums of money from his friends, and these applications had become so frequent, that they were heartily tired of him.

Soon after he heard the sermon of Mr. St. John, he met that gentleman in Richmond. Their greeting was cordial. "I am so glad to see you," said Mr. Leathers, "because I want to consult you on a matter that may be of deep importance to me. I know that I can confide in you as a friend. Miss Black, sir, continued sick all the time I was at Burtonville, and I half believe she only pretended to be so, to keep from seeing me; because I have heard that the very day that I came away, she was out at a dinner-party. I wanted to unbosom myself to you, dear sir, and talked of my own affairs, sir, very freely, as you were a stranger, hoping that you would say something in reply, that would enable me to go further, and open my whole heart, but you did not—you were silent, sir. I have at all times, since that, regretted that I had not been more bold, sir, and asked your Christian advice."

"I shall be very happy to be of service to you, especially in the way of advice," replied Mr. St. John.

"Thank you, sir, thank you. It 's the very thing I want at this time. I get plenty of it from others, but I am almost sure their advice would not suit me. My matter is this, sir. You condemned as wrong, the prejudice that people entertain against gentlemen engaged in the slave-trade, and their families. They call 'em soul-drivers, sir; and reproach 'em with bad names. I felt the force of your reasoning, sir, and am convinced that you are right. I told you, too, that I would be a doer, or a hearer of the word, I don't remember which. Well, now, my dear sir, the case with me, is just this. I know a young lady, a widow, good-looking enough, and who has a cash capital of two hundred thousand dollars, at least people say so, and I believe she has twenty thousand at least. Her father was a member of Congress, but was afterward a clerk at Washington city, and rather poor. She married a negro-trader, sir, and he died a year or so after the marriage, leaving to his widow, who was much younger, his whole fortune. The family have lost their position—and I am almost sure that I can win her heart and hand, sir. You see, sir, how it is with me—here is a splendid fortune, and an accomplished lady; at least people say she is accomplished. Now how would it look for a Leathers—why sir, one of my ancestors was secretary to a governor in this colony, before the Revolutionary war; I don't know what the governor's name was, but when I see cousin Betty Leathers, she can tell me—she is the cousin who is so deaf;—the name of that old governor, and the pedigree of our family, are almost the only things she knows, sir; well how would it look for a Leathers to marry a negro trader's widow? That's the matter that troubles me; I could marry a tobacco merchant's daughter—I could do that, sir, if she was rich and pretty—but it appears to me as if it would be going one or two steps further down, to marry a negro trader's widow. But I see no reason in it, sir; the trade is lawful, and should be respectable."

"Ah, my dear sir, I see exactly, your difficulty. Do you love the lady?"

"I am not as yet, very well acquainted with her. I have kept away from that kind of people. When I meet a negro-trader in the street, I give him as wide a berth as possible, for fear that he may touch my clothes. But I am sure of one thing, sir; I am so fond of ladies' society, that I can love any woman who has a fortune, and will accept my heart. It's an easy thing to fall in love, sir; I have done so twice in one day and eight or ten times in one trip to the Springs; other gentlemen do so too. I believe ladies find it rather harder, and but few of them can be deeply, passionately in love sir, oftener than once or twice in six months. But courtship makes love—that's the sense of courtship."

"There is no wrong in your wishing a fortune," replied Mr. St. John; "you want fortune, and the lady and her friends want position. Each has what the other wants. Such contracts are fair, when the matter is well understood on both sides; and the parties, it seems to me, should be made happier by it. As for the disgrace that is supposed to attach to the lady, because she is the widow of a slave merchant, that is all the result of vulgar prejudice. The trade in slaves, is as well established as that in flour or tobacco; and slaves are staple commodities as well as wheat, and cotton and corn. Now why shall the dealer in sugar and cotton and wheat be respectable, and the merchant in slaves disgraced? It is an act of mere childish folly, and I do hope you will give the influence of your family position to break down this prejudice. I have fully made up my mind, to give my whole influence as a minister, to destroy it as soon as possible."

"Thank you, my dear sir," said Mr. Leathers, "that is exactly the advice I want. If I do win the lady, I shall if possible have you to unite us in marriage. Hold yourself in readiness, my dear sir, for my courtships are always short."

CHAPTER XI.

AARON'S NARRATIVE.

"My child was very sick; she had a cough and fever, and I believe, would have died but for the great care of Mrs. Browne. She afterward got well enough to travel, and I wanted to go on as soon as we could.

"In two days more Mrs. Browne said we could reach Canada, and then, even if my master himself should come there, he could not take us away; we would be as free there as he was.

"I wanted to be at work and get money, so that I could, by my labor, support myself and child. I meant to send Lucy to school, and thought it might be, that some day I could buy a bit of land, and build a cabin on it, and have a cow and poultry, and other things of *our own*. I wanted, above all things in the world, to see my child where she could draw one breath of air, and say, 'I am free!'

"One night Mr. Browne got his wagon ready; we bade Mrs. Browne good-by; our eyes filled with tears as we did so, and she wiped her eyes two or three times as she followed us to the door.

"We had gone about a mile, and were going down

a steep hill, at the bottom of which is a creek; before we got down the hill, four men came out from some bushes at the side of the road, and stopped us. One of them was Phillips, Mr. Browne's neighbor, who said:

"'Now, we've caught you at it. You always denied that you are an Abolitionist, and here you are caught in the very act of stealing niggers. You — a law-abiding man, as you always say — are mashing the whole Constitution of the United States to pieces under your dirty feet. You are throwing contempt on the laws of your country. You had me indicted and fined for selling whisky without license, and it's my turn now. Temperance men are not to be trusted; sooner or later Abolitionism will show itself in 'em. One leads right to the other.'

"Another man, Jim Bates, came to me and said: 'This is him, and this is the same humpback gal. I've seen 'em both a hundred times, and can swear to 'em on a stack of Bibles.'

"They took us to Down's tavern: as soon as we got there, the landlady came in, and looking at Lucy, said: 'I know that dress that child's got on; it is made out of one of Mrs. Browne's old ones that I've seen her wear over and over again.'

"I cannot tell how I felt. If a thunderbolt had struck Lucy to the ground, I could have borne it better, but for her to be taken back into slavery—for myself to be sold, as I was sure I would be, far away from her, was too hard for human nature to bear; I groaned aloud in the bitter sorrow of my heart. When I looked at Mr. Browne, I could find no help, because I knew that for my child and myself, all this had come upon him. I had begged him to let me into his house and warm my child by his fire, and give her bread, and for this he was a prisoner, and in the hands of his enemies.

"I watched him, for he was near me, and we were both in deep misery; I saw him lift up his eyes, and move his lips, and then he was calm, and looked on the people round him, with the same smile with which he had always looked on me.

"I asked him to buy Lucy. At first he told me he had no money; but when he looked at her, and studied over the matter a minute or two, he asked her price of Jim Bates.

"Bates said that he had no right to sell her; he was to arrest her and myself and take us back to our master: but that *he* would not sell her for two thousand dollars, if he could. 'I'd rather,' he said, 'take back one runaway nigger, even if she is but a humpbacked girl, than have any man's ten thousand dollars.'

The next morning we were put into a wagon, and started back. As they were taking us out of the State of Ohio, I still hoped that something would happen, so that we would be free. Every person that met us, I thought, would be a friend, and give us help; but they rode by as if our distress was no concern of theirs. We came to the Ohio river, and were ferried over it. Hope died in my heart. The whole world looked black, and the air seemed heavy. Before me was a life of bondage, without mercy for my child and for myself; the looks of a sullen master, the whip, separation from my child, and slavery for life. The world seemed as if no God was in it or above it. My heart swelled too full for tears. Death! I would gladly have died!

"We were taken to our master's house. He was glad to see us, but very angry that I had run off. He told me that this caper of mine had run him in debt five hundred dollars, and would break him up. I told him I was afraid I would be sold from my child, and that was my reason for doing as I had done. He put us together at first, in an upper room in his house, and tied my hands to a ring in the wall. After a few days I was taken to my quarters, with Lucy, and tied; and a white man left to keep guard over us. On the same day a man came and bought me. He gave a thousand dollars for me, put a manacle on my wrists, and told me to move off."

CHAPTER XII.

THE WEDDING.

THE guests had gathered at the house of Mrs. Tullis, to attend her wedding. All the family of the Leathers' who could attend, were there, including the first and second and other cousins, in degrees so distant, that no one except cousin Betty Leathers, could tell the exact relationship.

Cousin Betty, dressed in an old-fashioned, faded brown silk, represented the ladies of the family of the bridegroom. She had stiff brown hair, somewhat gray, large, watery blue eyes, and a large nose. She held in one hand a box filled with Scotch snuff, and in the other a tin horn.

The fat bride glittered in jewels. Her head rested upon her shoulders, without the apparent intervention of a neck, but under her chin was a gold chain, three strands of which distinctly enough marked the place where the neck is in other persons. Her fingers were adorned with rings, three or four of which were set with diamonds. The lady of course had invited her friends, and her three sisters older than herself,

Miss Euphemia Strong, Miss Clara Strong, and Miss Mary Strong were present.

Our friend Bennett had cast off forever the rusty suit, which he had worn so long that it seemed to be part of his identity. He was dressed as a member of so ancient a family should be on his wedding day, and on one of his fingers was a ring set with a large diamond.

The friends of the parties, had before been nearly strangers to each other; and when Miss Betty Leathers was introduced to Mr. Conway, a gentleman who had been partner of Mr. Tullis, the former husband of the bride, and who was engaged in the profitable business of slave-trader, the lady stood quite erect, much more so than any person present had seen her stand for ten years before, and slowly and coldly extended her hand to the gentleman. Mr. Conway, on his part, although he could not but observe the coldness of her manner, seemed to care but little about it. He shook his great bunch of watch seals, and adjusted a diamond pin. The Leathers', with the exception of Bennett, had no diamonds.

The coolness of cousin Betty, to the guests invited by the bride, seemed to be contagious. All the friends and relations of the bridegroom, by some apparent accident, collected in groups in one end of the room, while those of the bride, including her sisters, were some seated, others standing at the opposite end.

Miss Euphemia Strong, was entertained by Mr. Harrison, a gentleman who had a plantation in the interior of the state: for some cause, connected probably, with his own interest, he was often in the society of Mr. Conway and his partner. He had been engaged in buying slaves, to stock, as he said, his plantation in Arkansas; but although he had been stocking it for ten years, he was still buying more, it was so large!

Miss Euphemia asked the gentleman, if he had read a new novel of Cooper's.

"La! no, miss, I never reads novels; I got no time to read anything else but newspapers, and I read precious little of them. I read one novel once half through, when I was a boy, and that made my ha'r stand up on end, so that I have never touched another one, since that time."

"Oh dear me! how dreadful a-one it must have been, Mr. Harrison, what was it?"

"It was the 'Mysterious Rhodolpho,' or some such name, full of ghosts and horrors. I do think that such books ought not be printed."

"Our literature, Mr. Harrison, has been somewhat improved of late years. We have now, in America, writers who can successfully compete with those of whom Europe is proud."

"I don't know anything about that, Miss, and to tell you the honest truth, I don't care a button about it; I see no use in 'em all—what good do they do? They don't help a man to make money."

"But, sir, they cultivate the taste, and some of them have a happy effect upon the morals of the young."

"I never see any use in reading much, anyhow—them that don't read at all, get along just as well as them as does. I know several gentlemen, who can't read a word, and they make just as good livings, have as large plantations, and as many negroes and other stock, as if they could read. They raise just as good wheat and corn, and as much tobacco and cotton, as men does that reads more or less, every day of their lives."

"On this you are quite radical in your views on education. If they were carried out into practice, it seems to me, that the world would retrograde."

"I don't know what you mean by retrograde; it seems to me if its like going back a little. Well, I am in favor of that—going back, Miss, to the good old times of our forefathers—people had not so much trouble then as we have now. Then men bought and sold what they pleased, and how they pleased, and it was nobody's business but their own; now everybody is peeping and prying into everybody's matters, and everything that we do, is put in the newspapers. How do I know but the very same words that I am telling to you now, and you to me, will be in print before I die! Now, if so many people could not read, all this fuss would be put an end to."

"Good evening, cousin Betty. I have not seen you for a year," said Mr. Walters as he took a seat beside her.

"Yes, it is a new thing in our family," screamed cousin Betty, "for a Leathers to marry a negro trader's widow. But things are changed now—fashions change, and men change with them, you know. Mr. St. John tells me that it's all right, and the best people in the country approve of it. Who would have thought that a great-great-grandson of the secretary of Governor Berkley—a Leathers—would marry a negro trader's widow! I thought Bennett, cousin Bennett ought to have married in his own family, among his own people, as the patriarchs did; his father and grandfather and great-grandfather, each married a first cousin. It 's always been the rule among us, you know, cousin Thomas; but fashions change so, we can't keep the run of them."

"Yes," said Mr. Walters, "fashions have

changed somewhat since you and I came into society."

"I believe so. Yes, they say her father was a member of Congress, and afterward a clerk in one of the departments at Washington city. But I have inquired into the matter a little further, since I heard of their engagement. He was a congressman and a clerk, but before that he was only a schoolmaster.

"In my younger days it was not thought right for a gentleman of family, as ours is, to marry out of the circle of his own early associates. But now, if anybody has money—why anybody can marry a gentleman. I don't know but that it's all well enough—some people need position, and others need money, and when they unite, each gets what he and she wants, and both of them are suited."

While Miss Betty and Mr. Walters were still attempting to converse, Mr. Walters little daughter came, and leaning her head on his shoulder, said:

"Papa, I want you to do something for me."

"What is it, my child?"

"Oh but I want you to promise to do it, and then I'll tell you."

"Let me hear it first. I will do what I can to make you happy," he said, as he patted her cheek.

"Papa, I want you to get teeth for me, just like the bride's. I was in her room to-day, and she took all her teeth out, and put them in a tumbler of water and let them stay there a good while, and then rubbed them with a brush and a towel, and fixed 'em in her mouth again. Oh it was so nice."

"Mr. Walters smiled, and stroked her hair, and told her it would make her mouth bleed to put them in."

"What is it the child wants, screamed cousin Betty. I heard you say something about bleed or blood, Mr. Walters. They called it blood-money when I first came into society; and some people who sold their servants, never would buy food or furniture, or build houses with the money; they thought ill luck would follow it. Yes, they always called it blood-money, when I was a girl—a little girl, I mean, Mr. Walters. But Mr. St. John tells me that these opinions are now discarded as idle superstitions, and people prize such money as greatly as any other. What is it the child wants?"

"Oh, said Mr. Walters, she has a childish fancy about dentistry, that will be forgotten to-morrow."

"Yes, people forget very soon nowadays. It was not so when I was a little girl. Then we could remember the grandfathers of almost every person in the whole country. There 's the Follingsbys; I remember old Follingsby; he was an Englishman. He was a stocking-weaver, sir; and now the Follingsbys are among the first families in the land. They own the whole estate at Ryecroft, and live in the mansion built by Mrs. Ryecroft, while her husband was away at Congress. She run him in debt ten thousand dollars for it, and broke him up. And there 's the Pierces. I knew old Pierce. He was my father's distiller. His sons were merchants; and now his grandchildren are married with the best blood of the whole country, and have all forgotten that I know their ancestor was a distiller; and they live at the Oaklands. And the whole family of Barnetts, who once owned that fine estate, have moved off to Missouri. And then there 's the Mowbrys. I knew their grandfather very well. He was my father's overseer. Many 's the time he has carried me to school, when I was a little girl, and now his descendants are great planters, in Louisiana, and have a great many servants.

"Yes, the child is right, Mr. Walters, people do forget very soon nowadays. Times have changed, and some people have changed a good deal with them. I don't think cousin Bennett has changed much. But it does look queer, Mr. Walters, indeed it does, to see a Leathers, sir—a Leathers—marry a negro trader's widow! But Mr. St. John says that it is all right, and I suppose it must be so."

Miss Strong said in a low voice to Mr. Satterby, a negro-trader, seated by her: "My sister has been a widow eighteen months, and has discouraged the advances of half a dozen gentlemen, during her widowhood. She has now accepted Mr. Leathers, and it really seems as if some of his friends think the alliance quite a condescension on his part. I assure you, that Mr. Leathers was importunate in his courtship, so much so, that he sometimes called on my sister three or four times in one day. He was deeply in love, and you know, my dear sir, that Cupid's flames spread rapidly in the poor, weak, female heart. You gentlemen, have nothing to do but become deeply in love yourselves, and then in spite of all our efforts, you are irresistible. A life of single blessedness, I know, is a happy one, but in some way you manage to convince us, that a life of double blessedness is twice as happy."

Mr. Satterby said, "That no gentleman, could doubt that, in her presence."

"Oh, you wicked man! how you flatter," said she, tapping him gently with her fan. "If you will visit Washington city, I will take great pleasure in showing you, whoever and whatever is worth your attention in it. There are delightful walks around the Capitol, and it is so pleasant to wander in them with a friend,—one who can appreciate you, and whose sentiments are but the echoes of your own."

Mr. Satterby replied, "That it must be romantic indeed. If he could possibly spare the time from his business, he would avail himself of her invitation, and did not doubt that, in her society, his enjoyment would be greater than ever he had experienced before."

Miss Strong gave him a sweet look, tapped him again with her fan, and left the room.

CHAPTER XIII.

THE WHIPPING-POST.

About twilight on the evening of the day of the wedding of Bennett Leathers, another and more motley crowd was gathered before the door of the court-house, in the same city. A large square, open at all sides except the south, on that side near its eastern end, was a row of brick-houses. The lower rooms were occupied some as retail, others as wholesale liquor stores. The upper apartments seemed to be sailors' boarding-houses. In front of this row, shaded by a grove of locust and poplar trees, stood the red whipping-post, tall and massive, with the stocks in a kind of second story. It stood at right angles with the buildings, so that one end of it fronted the court-house door, and the other the liquor shops. The dense crowd pressed in mass toward the whipping-post. In the midst of it was a man dressed in a velvet round-about, with a red kerchief round his neck; in one hand he held a blue cowskin; with the other he grasped a tall, spare mulatto woman.

On each side of the pillar of the whipping-post,

which was next to the court-house, were iron clasps large enough to inclose the wrists of a person, with fastenings to keep them in their place. The feet were secured by placing them in holes in the platform, large enough to admit the ankles of the sufferer, and then the boards were, by wedges, driven back to their place. In this machine Minte, the mulatto woman, was placed. The man then unbuttoned her dress, and exposed about as much of her back between the shoulder-blades, as could be covered with his hands. While he was doing this, a crowd of boys had climbed upon the upper apartment of the whipping-post, and others had seated themselves on the branches of the surrounding trees. When all was ready, the man said, in a loud voice: "Stand back, men, and keep silence, while the law takes its course." The hum of voices ceased, and all were silent in an instant. He then said to the crowd:

"This here nigger wench, has murdered her master's child, and she won't confess and tell where she has hid the body. The bird that ken sing and won't sing, must be made to sing, and I 'm the man to make her do it.

"Now," said he, addressing the woman, "I don't want to whip you—indeed it hurts my feelings always whenever I have to whip anybody, white or black; but I am a sworn officer and must do my duty to my country. Come now, own it up, and I'll take you right back to jail without hitting you even once."

"Indeed, master Blue, afore God, I never harmed that child in all the days of my life. If I was a-going to the judgment this very minute, I would tell you what I have always told you, and everybody else—that I am just as innocent of harm to that child as an angel in heaven. Oh, remember that I am human nature as well as you; don't whip me—for God's sake, don't whip me. I never was whipped in my life."

Stand back, men, shouted Mr. Blue, and then stepping back he brought down his cowhide with skill between the shoulders of Minte. A loud, piercing shriek—a quivering of every muscle in her frame—a look of intense agony upon her countenance, followed the blow. There was a pause for an instant, and then four other blows, each harder than the preceding, quickly followed. Minte's head dropped upon her shoulder—she was silent as if dead. Blue paused. "Now," said he, "you've had five; you've got to take nine-and-thirty to-day, and as much more another time—and this is only the beginning." Minte in a low voice said:

"Mr. Blue, Oh God! Mr. Blue, I no more did

it than your mother did. I am not a liar. Oh! for God's sake let me go or kill me right out—don't torture me to death."

Blue stepped back again, and five other blows rapidly fell upon the quivering form of his now silent victim; blood followed each blow, and the torn flesh hung in shreds upon her back. He paused, and opened her dress, so as to expose still more of her person. "Now," said he, "I have given it to you in doses of five at a time. I'll give you one dose of nine, and another of ten; but it does hurt my feelings, you may depend on it; and I'll stop the very moment you confess."

"Oh, Mr. Blue! what can I say? Oh God! Oh Christ! what can I do? I no more killed that child, than I killed yours; I loved it most as well as my own. Oh, men, have mercy on me! Oh, God, have mercy on me!"

"Have mercy on yourself, and own up; you might as well do it first, as last. I tell you that you will have to be whipped on three several days, till you confess. The committee has ordered it, and it must be done, and can't be helped; you've only had ten, and on sound flesh too—think of nine-and-thirty to-day, and nine-and-thirty more on the top of that when it gets just about half well; when it will be tender as your eye; so tender, that you will scream, when the doctor only touches it with his little finger. Come, don't be a fool, own the thing at once, and save your feelings."

Minte returned no answer; her head hung down heavily upon her shoulder. The look of agony had left her countenance; her muscles were all still. Blue threw some water in her face; she started, and then he again stepped back, and applied the cowskin with fury. A boy seated overhead called out, "She confesses! she confesses! stop, Mr. Blue." Mr. Blue stopped. "Do you confess now that you killed the child?" A low "Yes," followed his question, and Minte was released and carried by two men back to jail.

"She ought to be hung at once," said a by-stander. "If a negro nurse should kill my child, as she did that of her mistress, I would never put the court to the trouble of trying her."

"Yes," replied the person addressed; "we are too lenient entirely, too much so, sir. No man's family is safe now-days. Only last week, another case of the same kind occurred in Mississippi; and they will constantly occur till more stringent laws shall be adopted, to put a stop to such wickedness."

"I want no more law," said the first speaker: "let every man avenge his own wrongs, and these things will soon be stopped."

CHAPTER XIV.

MINTE'S TRIAL.

At nine o'clock on Monday morning, three weeks afterward, the same court-house yard was filled with people. Politicians canvassing for votes at the approaching election; peddlers exposing their goods and trinkets for sale; old women stood behind stalls covered with apples, cakes and candies; men were passing through the crowd, with maps and books for exhibition and sale. It was Quarterly Court. The first case to be tried by the magistrates, was that of the negro woman Minte, charged with murdering a child she had to nurse.

To this charge Minte plead not guilty; upon being asked by the court, she stated that she had no counsel, and had no means to pay counsel for her defense. The long and elevated seat usually occupied by the Judge of the circuit court, was filled with magistrates. Four only seemed to be actively engaged in the trial. The others occasionally stood up; or one at a time left the bench, and after a brief visit to the tavern, returned. Most of them were gray-haired country gentlemen. Two of them were lawyers who had retired early from the profession, and were now living on their estates as planters. The magistrates consulted for a few minutes and called up John Hansard, Esq., a young gentleman who had recently been admitted to practice, and asked if he was willing to undertake her defense? The gentleman assented, and they then asked Minte, whether she was willing to be defended by him? A sullen look and a gruff "Yes" from Minte, was the reply; and the trial began.

Mr. Hansard claimed for his client a jury; not, he said, that he doubted at all either the fairness or the capacity of the honorable court: to do so would be evidence only of folly and presumption; but he thought, and even insisted, that no trial could be had by law, where the charge involved the life of the accused, without the intervention of a jury.

The district attorney was never more surprised in his life, than by the assertion of such a claim. In all his long practice in that court, this was the first time that it had ever been made where a negro or mulatto stood for trial. If the accused have a jury at all, it must be a jury of her *peers*. The only peers of the accused were persons of her own color; all others were in fact, and by law, her superiors.

The court overruled the motion for a jury. Witnesses were called, and it appeared from their statements, that the prisoner at the bar had a child of her own, and was employed by Mr. Scott to nurse his child. That Mr. Scott lived in the country, and had come down to the city to remain but a few weeks, principally for the purpose of obtaining the advice of experienced physicians for his wife, who was in bad health. She was, however, able to visit her friends. That about the middle of the afternoon, of the day on which it was charged that the murder had been committed, Mrs. Scott, in a moment of irritation at some petty misconduct of Minte's child, had called it a brat, and shaken it by the shoulder as Minte was entering the room; that Minte flew into a paroxysm of rage, and abused Mrs. Scott to her face, and when ordered out of the room, muttered something which Mrs. Scott could not distinctly hear, but which she thought was a threat of evil toward herself or some member of her family. She saw but little of Minte during the day, and when she did so, she was silent and sullen. She was invited to take tea with a friend on that evening, and went early with her husband, leaving the child in the care of Minte. She returned about eleven that night, and retired, supposing that, as usual, Minte had the child in her care; and knew no better till she came down to breakfast about eight o'clock the next day, when she learned from Minte that the child was missing. Diligent search was immediately made for it in all parts of the city—the river, ponds and wells were examined, advertisements were inserted in the newspapers, offering large rewards for the discovery of the child, but all without success. All hope of finding her body was now over, and all effort to do so abandoned.

The district attorney now called up Mr. Blue, but his evidence was objected to, on the ground that the confessions had been obtained by torture from the prisoner. Blue stated with accuracy what he had done, and by whose orders he had done it. One of the magistrates, Colonel Thornton, declared, that for his part he was not only opposed to hearing evidence obtained by such means; but if his colleagues concurred, would go further, and take proper means to secure the punishment of Blue and his aiders and abettors for the outrages they had inflicted upon the prisoner. He was pained to hear that the practice of torturing colored persons accused of crimes, was not of unfrequent occurrence. There was no law that authorized it; it was directly in violation of law as well as of common sense and humanity. Confessions of guilt, made under circumstances when the party making them could not deliberate, were of no value. They proved only the pain of the accused, not their guilt.

The other magistrates decided that Blue should be sworn as a witness, and tell all that he knew; they would hear his statements; of course they would not be taken into consideration, when they deliberated upon the guilt or innocence of the accused. They would sift it after they heard it all.

Blue then said: "If it please your honors, this here wench was brought to jail, the next day after she murdered the child, early in the forenoon. I axed her about it, and she said she had nothing to do with killing of the child, and did not know who did kill it. She pretended she liked the child mighty well, and always used it just as well as she used her own. She said she was a free woman, and could have left her place with Mr. Scott, who was stopping at the Washington Hotel, just as easy as not if she had chose to do so. I axed her almost every day for two weeks, and she got so sullen at last, that she wouldn't talk to me any more about it. The Vigilance Committee" (here Col. Wilbur stopped him and told him to say nothing more about that committee. It was an association not warranted by law; formed, as he believed, for illegal purposes). Blue apologized, the other magistrates however told him to tell the whole story, and Blue proceeded. "Well, I took her to the whipping-post, and after I had drawn a few drops of her claret, she did confess that she murdered the child. All that night afterward she never spoke one word, and the next day she would not eat or drink, and laid on the floor of the cell curled up in one corner, making once in a while a great fuss and groaning. When she began to talk again, which she did in two days afterward, she denied worse than ever that she had killed the child, and still kept on doing so from that day to this."

A few persons appeared as witnesses for the prisoner. They knew nothing of the circumstances attending the child's death, but had known Minte two or three years, and she always was an honest, industrious woman—hasty in her temper, and when angry, turbulent in her language, but it was soon over and then she was as kind and obedient as ever.

The case was argued at great length by the respective lawyers. The arguments were listened to with attention, and then the magistrates drew their chairs together and consulted about half an hour: seven were now on the bench. Two thought the evidence insufficient. The other five, believed the prisoner guilty. Minte heard this opinion without any change of countenance. She was then asked what she had to say, why sentence of death should not be pronounced against her.

At first she made no reply, but when the question was again asked, and the matter explained to her, she rose and said: "Gentlemen, I didn't kill that child at all. I'm just as innocent of it, as anybody can be. After I gave the two children their suppers, I took them up-stairs and laid them on my bed without undressing them, and I sat by them till they both got to sleep. Then I went out, and was not gone more than five minutes, and when I came back this child was gone. I was scared at first, and did not know what to think about it, but I thought that as Mrs. Scott was going out that evening, and I had my own child to take care of, that she had sent for her child as she often had done, and got another servant to take it with her. I went to sleep soon afterward and never knew, till next day, that the child was gone clean away. Then they took me up and put me in jail, and that's all I know 'bout it. You can hang me if you please, 'taint no worse than has been done to me; but God knows I am an innocent woman."

"Didn't you confess," said a magistrate from the country seated at the end of the bench: "didn't you confess to Mr. Blue, that you killed the child?"

"No! I did not do any such thing."

"Why, Mr. Blue swears you did, and I have

heard (outside of the court-house to be sure), that at least half a dozen persons heard you confess it."

"If I did so, I don't 'member it; I 'member very well, that I denied it over and over again; I was in so much pain, that I can't rightly say just what I might have said at the time. I am innocent, and God knows it."

She seated herself and then an old man, a magistrate, stood up and pronounced sentence of death upon her, and told her when she was to be hung. Before he sat down he told her, that as the court were divided in opinion, they would all recommend her to the mercy of the governor, and he had hardly a doubt but that the governor would commute her punishment, to sale as a slave for life to some person who would take her out of the commonwealth.

CHAPTER XV.

AARON'S NARRATIVE.

"My heart seemed breaking. My brain was on fire. My whole body seemed stiff as if it had been frozen into stone. I could not see or hear. One thought only filled my mind and tore my heart—my child: she would die—die of grief, alone and uncared for—or if she lived, her life would be one long lingering agony worse than death. Her deformity, her worthlessness to her master, made me sure that he would not care for her welfare. I thought, too, of her great love for me—every little act of kindness in her whole life came up at once before my mind—I saw her sometimes sitting under a tree as far in my path as she dared to come to meet me in the evening, and springing into my arms, and laughing and crying by turns as she did so. I heard her tell me over again how lonely she had been all day without me, and how long the day seemed between the sunrise and the sunset—and I thought over again the happy Sundays that we had passed together in our dark cabin, where we talked and sung and read the

Bible all day long. Who now would care for her when she was sick? Who would bear with her fretfulness when she was tortured with pain, as she had often been? She would be placed in the care of some woman with children of her own, and her feebleness and affliction would make her a prey to all who chose to abuse her.

"I was sold—sold as a beast, and chained with other men; and they were taking me to a market where they could sell me again for more money. I had been sold before. I had been whipped and abused and half starved, and slandered and denied almost every right that men love; but none of these things seemed hard, compared with the greatest of all sorrows, that of being separated, as I thought forever, from the only being on earth who loved me. If I could have followed her to the grave, I would have been less sad; for I would then know that good angels had her in their care, and that she was happy forever. But now, what ruin might not be done to her very soul. All the lessons I had taught her would soon be forgotten amid the bad teaching and example of the other slaves. She would forget her Bible and her God; she would forget even me, and live as those live with whom she would be compelled to associate.

I looked for a moment along the line of the coffle, as it stretched out like a great serpent before me, winding with the turnings of the road, and moving, now up, now down, as it passed over the uneven ground, and wondered if, in that whole gang of slaves, there was any one who, like me, was separated forever from an only child! I thought I saw in the sorrowful faces of many of my fellows, marks of sadness and suffering, deep almost as the grief of my own heart. I groaned aloud, and other groans re-echoed my own. I sighed, and far along the line, sighs seemed to answer mine.

"I was fastened to the leading chain by a single manacle on my right hand. We had gone but a few miles when night came on. I now, for the first time, could shed tears, I raised my chained hand to my face; the tears ran fast over it: another thrill of agony came across me, and as I dropped my hand to my side, I gave a sudden jerk, and the ball of my thumb, wet as it was, slipped through the ring of the chain. I cannot tell my feelings. I had now the power to free myself again. I carefully held the ring, and the darkness concealed its position. Very soon the two men who were riding behind us, passed one on each side, up to the middle of the coffle, and at the brow of a hill I carefully threw the manacle over the leading chain, and with one leap I was at the road-side, another brought me into a thicket. I ran as fast as I could till I had got out of sight, then suddenly turned and went back to the road. I did so to get clear of the dogs that the drivers kept in a wagon, to hunt such of the coffle as might escape. I soon heard them baying in the woods, but after awhile they seemed unable to find my track. I ran on, looking behind me almost every minute. I then laid my ear down on the ground, and heard horses coming on. I found by the roadside, two logs lying close together, and laid down between them. Presently two men on horseback rode past me. One of them said:

"'It 's Jim's fault—he's as tender-hearted as a chicken. He did not screw the manacle tight enough. I always do so at first, and then loosen it afterward, when the hand begins to swell. Once I made a mistake, and the man's hand swelled till it withered; but that's better, you know, than to let a nigger get away. But the running off of this fellow won't make much difference, for we 'll catch him before daylight, and then, you know, Sam's rule. He always takes the runaway to the head of the gang, and there in sight of all the rest, gives him a cool hundred on his bare back, and that strikes a terror into the others, and makes them afraid to run. Discipline among niggers is a great thing, Mr. Fitsimmons; it keeps all quiet and in order, and without it it's no use to try to live.'

"Mr. Fitsimmons said he knew it was so, and very soon they passed out of my hearing.

"I got up as soon as they were out of sight, and went after them. When I got near my old master's house, there was a turn in the road, and something told me there was danger there. I got over into the field, and went around among some bushes. I saw one white horse, and could hear the other stamping his feet on the ground. I then ran to my quarters; the door was not barred; I opened it carefully, and found Lucy lying undressed across her bed. I went to the floor, and raised up a plank, under which I had put my jack-knife, some lucifer matches, and my Bible. I got these, took Lucy in my arms, and ran to the woods. I ran till I came to a stream of water, and waded down it a mile; then I went on my journey. As soon as I felt myself far enough out in the woods to be safe, we laughed, we cried, we leaped, we shouted for joy! I had not a cent of money in the world; no hat nor shoes, nor house nor home—nothing, nothing but my child and my Bible, and with these I was so happy that I could hardly live. Lucy, too, pressed her little cheek to mine, and tears of joy fell fast from her eyes."

CHAPTER XVI.

AARON'S NARRATIVE.

"I WALKED as fast as I could until daylight, and then found a shelter and hiding-place, near a stream of water. Here we staid all day without anything to eat. At night we again started, but I was so weak from hunger and distress of mind, that I could not travel fast. All that night we walked slowly, Lucy complaining that she was very hungry: when daylight came, I do not believe that we had gone five miles. We were both suffering so much from hunger, that I thought it best to go on in hope of finding something to eat. We were in a large wood with a great deal of underbrush, and no paths appeared to have been made in it. About an hour after sunrise, while I was looking around, I saw something lying by the side of an old tree that had fallen down. I told Lucy to sit down and be perfectly still. She did so, and I went round the tree very quietly until I got opposite the place where the object lay, then looked carefully over and saw a young fawn asleep. With a spring I made it my prisoner. Its cries brought Lucy to me. It was a beautiful creature, and she was delighted with it: when I told her that I intended to kill it for food she begged me even with tears to spare its life; when I was about to plunge my knife into its throat, she caught my hand and cried out in agony. I carried it in my arms until we came to a place well sheltered and near a stream, and then sent Lucy down for some water. Before she got back the fawn was killed. She stood looking at its dying struggles, and crying over it until its life was gone. I then dressed it, made a fire and roasted as much of it as we needed. As Lucy was without shoes, after a hearty breakfast I passed the day in making her, from the skin of the fawn, a pair of moccasins that came above her ankles. At noon and at night we again feasted on the venison, and then started on our journey, carrying the remainder of it with us.

"I felt very dull, my head ached, my limbs were full of pain, and now that the excitement under which I had been, had passed off, I could scarcely walk. Lucy walked by my side. We were following the course of a stream of water, and about midnight I became unable to travel further. We found a place where three or four trees were overgrown by a large grape vine that twined all around them down to the ground. I made a bed of leaves under this shelter as well as I could. Here I laid down. I told Lucy how to make a fire and prepare her food. My mind soon wandered; sometimes I imagined myself dying and leaving my child alone in the midst of this great wood, perhaps several miles from any human being; and if she returned to where she would meet with human help, the very helpers would themselves as their first act, reduce her to slavery for the residue of her life. Then I was startled by visions of wild beasts tearing her, and again by seeing her wasted to a skeleton and dying of starvation. In the midst of these distressing thoughts I lost my consciousness. I do not know how long I was in that state. The first thing I remember was, that I awoke as from a deep sleep, and found Lucy bending over me and pouring water on my forehead from a large muscle shell. She was wasted to a skeleton. She told me that she had eaten up all the remains of the fawn, and had been a long time without food, and was almost starved to death. I tried to rise but was unable to do so. Poor little Lucy sat by my side; her face was thin and thoughtful; but even in the agony that was upon it, I could see fullness of joy at my returning consciousness. She said she was so glad I could talk to her, that she had been talking to me day and night, but that sometimes I said nothing in reply, and at other times she could not understand me; that she had sat at my side all day during the days, and lain by me all night; that rabbits and birds came near us and looked at us, and then went away; that except the singing of the birds, she had heard no other sounds than her own voice and the groans of her father for many days.

"My senses were completely restored. I was sure that the disease had left me; but still I feared that before I became strong enough to walk, my child would starve to death. It was about daybreak when I came to myself, and while I was wondering what to do for food for Lucy, I heard a large frog croaking in the stream below me. I told her to take a stick and creep carefully behind it, and hit it on its back: she did so and soon brought it to me. I never before felt so thankful for food. It was soon prepared by the aid of a fire, and Lucy ate it with eagerness. I could eat but little of it. Before night I became able to walk a little by the help of a stick and the hand of Lucy. I had not walked a mile before I came across a horse that had died but a short time before. At first I did not see what benefit it could be to us, as its flesh was unfit for food; but on thinking a moment I saw that I had stumbled on a prize. With my knife I cut off the long hair from its main and tail, and then we found a hiding-place. With this we made a great many lines; and from some bones, by the aid of my knife, I made fish-hooks. They were very rough ones, but answered the purpose for which they were made. We found a pole and some craw-fish for bait, and very soon Lucy, seated under a large sycamore tree, began fishing in the stream. I sat by her and shortly, with my help, she caught a small fish, and then another and another, 'till we had plenty of food. We staid here several days until I became strong enough to walk with ease, and Lucy had recovered from the effects of famine. We then one evening started on our journey.

"Two nights after that, we came to a country with oak and other trees growing on it, in clumps of some half dozen together, and then with wide open spaces—some large and some small. The ground was all grown over with long grass and flowers. It appeared as if the foot of man had never passed over it. I got on the highest rise of ground, and looked carefully all around me, but saw no sign of human habitation. I laid my ear to the ground, and could not hear the barking of any dogs. We went into what I supposed to be the middle of this country, and I there found on a little knoll, the ruins of an old house that had been burnt; near it was a spring, now filled with mud and leaves. In the remains of a garden, in front of the house, was a large thicket of young fig-trees, the old ones appeared to have been destroyed, and these had come up thickly in their place. There was, too, in the rear of what had been the house, a large grove of oaks, and some peach, apple, and cherry trees. There was a cellar filled up with pieces of burnt timber and stones. I cleared out a corner of this place, and arranged the boards in such a manner as to shelter us from the sun; and we determined, if we could safely do so, to make it our home for several days, until our health and strength should be fully restored. Very soon after we had prepared our hiding-place, Lucy came to me with her face beaming with joy: she said she had found something, and asked me to guess what it was! I made many efforts to do so, but failed in them all—when she told me it was a bucket. This was indeed a prize. Down in the stream below the spring, deeply buried in the mud, was a wooden bucket; it was soon raised and cleaned, and the handle, which was loose, put in its place. This led us to look for other articles of value, and we found an old tin-cup, a case-knife, a fork with the handle off, and the prongs of an old pitchfork. What treasures, and how useful these things were to us!

"Large herds of cattle were grazing over this natural meadow. Most of them were too wild to let us approach them; but one cow had her udder full of milk, and she was quiet and tame. Oh! how Lucy feasted on the first bucket of milk that I got from the cow, and how rich we were, now that we had plenty of food, and the means of getting more. I made snares for rabbits, and caught a great many; cut down a small bush, and made a bow, and with my horse-hair lines, a string for it. I made arrows from the broken boards around me, and soon was able to supply ourselves with woodcock, partridges, and snipe. We did not merely feast, we fattened.

"I do not know how long we staid here; I suppose it was more than a week. Do not think that I wasted my time. I could not have traveled in my weak state. I was not strong enough to carry Lucy, and she was not able to walk much; so that I still think I acted for the best, in staying there until I became strong enough to travel.

"Generally, in the daytime, we stayed in our place in the old cellar, except that early in the morning I went out to kill birds and rabbits, and to milk the cow. The cow seemed also, to look upon our place as her home, and upon us as her friends; for regularly night and morning she came up to be milked. Our place, too, was on ground that rose so high above the country around us, that I could see a great way in every direction, if a man, especially on horseback, should approach us. Our time during the day was employed in preparing our food, and after that in reading the Bible. I here had, for the first time, an opportunity to read it day after day to my dear child: she sat by me and listened, and asked questions as I read, and I do hope that she was greatly benefited by what she heard. She was less fretful, her countenance became calmer, and her conduct more quiet. Much as she had always loved me, she now seemed to love me with more tenderness and force. Her eyes often filled with tears as I read to her.

"Once I read: 'If meat make my brother to offend, I will eat no meat while the world standeth,' and explained to her that it meant that the eating of meat was entirely lawful, but that if by doing a lawful act, it caused others who were of weak minds, to lose their love for Christianity, that then it would be wrong even to eat meat. She looked me in the face, and said:

"'Father, was it not wrong for master to *sell* you; he sold your flesh, was not *that* as bad as to eat meat? It offended me, it offended you, and it may be that it will offend others. Then how can he be a good man and do so?'"

CHAPTER XVII.

AARON'S NARRATIVE.

"IT may seem strange, but it is true, that I never before had become thoroughly acquainted with my own child. I had nursed her when she was a baby, but I had to work so hard, that at night I was too tired to talk much with her. Now I had, what I had very long wished for, full time to sit all day by her side, to talk with her, to read my Bible to her, and to enjoy fully her society. I never passed so happy a time in my life. The days flew by us swiftly; our various employments seemed not to leave us leisure enough for all of them. Lucy's love for me grew daily, as mine did for her. I had before that, supposed that I loved her so strongly, that I could love her no more; but my power of loving seemed to be increased. She often asked me if we were now free. We talked over our plans of living when we should get to Canada, a place which, to Lucy, seemed next to heaven. I was to go out in the fields and work—and she was to keep house, milk the cow and feed the chickens. Such plans of happiness came up before us, that we almost forgot for the time, our present distress in looking forward to the bright future.

"While we staid at the ruins of the old house the weather was clear and mild, but a change seemed to be coming on, and I thought we had better leave it as the cellar might fill with water. One evening about sunset, we milked our cow; Lucy patted her on the head, and bade her good-by. We took with us our bucket, cup, and pitch-fork, to which I had put a handle, and started, not without sorrow, from our home: although I was nearly recovered, yet I found it would be too great a burden to carry Lucy. She had to walk nearly all the way. This she did cheerfully, as her feet were well protected by her moccasins. We got along slowly, but well. The weather was cloudy, so that I could not see the North star, and from this point I must have made a mistake in my starting, which took me too far to the west, and ended in my getting here.

"We were now traveling through a country which was pretty well inhabited, so that I had to be very careful, for fear of being seen. One evening, just after we had started from our hiding-place, we were greatly scared at the sound of something rushing toward us through the bushes. Our hearts beat wildly; detection and a life of hopeless slavery seemed to be just before us; but when it came in sight—Oh! how glad we were to see only a wolf—not a man. It looked at us, and then ran away.

"We went on night after night, for I do not know how long—often suffering from hunger, sometimes, though rarely, from thirst, weary and sad, until early one morning we were startled by the distant cry of a pack of hounds: on listening, I had reason to fear they were on our trail. I snatched Lucy in my arms, and fled with terror, running even in broad daylight close to the fields. At last I came to a path, on which I saw the freshly-made tracks of several men; it led in the same direction I was traveling, and I followed it, heedless almost of all danger, except from the pursuing hounds, until I came to another that turned off from it, and seemed to lead out into the woods. I pursued that until our traces were lost. Soon afterward I came to a swamp, overgrown with large trees, and covered with the trunks of those which had fallen. In it was a little space of dry ground, surrounded on all sides by almost stagnant water; there, under a large tree, I made our stopping-place. I discovered that a pair of bald eagles had their nest, and young ones, in the top of a pine tree; one of the eagles, by accident, let a young rabbit, not yet dead, fall from the nest; we were hungry and I grasped the prize The eagle swept over and near us, with ruffled feathers, and screamed and flew away to her nest. They were free! they could fly and soar, and rear and feed their young, while I was compelled to hide from the face of my fellow-men. Several alligators lay on the logs by the edge of the water, basking themselves in the warm sunshine. We caught some fish, and staid here several days. I could, almost every morning, hear the hounds at a distance. I supposed from this, that other runaways were in the neighborhood, and that they were in search of them. At last one night, I heard a low whistle, which was repeated in a few minutes; then a pause followed, and it was answered in another direction. This was the first sound I had heard from human lips, except Lucy's and my own, for many weeks: but as I did not know whence it came, I hid myself, and put out my fire. The smoke of it had been seen, for two persons were evidently coming cautiously toward us. I laid Lucy down on the ground, and myself close by her side, and listened; my limbs trembled, and I feared that the beating of Lucy's little heart, would itself betray us. After awhile, the two persons seemed to be coming nearer to each other, and then I heard them speaking in a low tone. From their speech, I supposed them to be colored people, but I was not sure whether it might not be white persons speaking like them, to deceive me. It was a bright starlight night, and I saw one of them get up on a large log, and look carefully around him. He was a very short, heavy-set man, without hat or shoes; his clothes all in tatters, except a huge skin that covered his shoulders. Very soon the other approached him, who appeared to be a mulatto boy about seventeen or eighteen years of age. They talked together a short time, and the boy then came cautiously toward us, and in a low, but clear voice, said: 'Will.' I made no answer. He called again, and added, 'We are safe now, why don't you answer?' He came still nearer, and finding that I could not remain concealed, I stood up and asked him who he was? he replied, 'Lewis,' and seemed to be greatly frightened, when he found that he did not know me.

"The other man now came up; their tale was soon told. A party of five, had left Mississippi and were running away. They had been out a month, and during the rains had lost their course. They had suffered so much from hunger that one of them went crazy, and his howlings and other indiscretions had betrayed them. A pack of hounds had been put upon their trail, and the hunters had come upon them; at the first shot one had been killed, and another so badly wounded, that he died a few days afterward. They fled until they came to a large swamp, and took shelter on dry ground, near to what they supposed to be the middle of it. Their wounded companion died in great agony, and they had buried him. Their place was so surrounded by water, and so far in the swamp, that the dogs could not trail them; nor could the hunters get there on horseback. They determined to stay till the pursuit should cease, and then to go on. At night they went out in search of food; and in one of these excursions they saw my fire, and supposed that one of their companions who had separated from them when they were closely pursued, had kindled it.

"We left the place where I was, in the edge of the swamp, and started to go to theirs. They led the way, and after a very long, weary walk over fallen logs, sometimes sinking deep in the mire, at other times wading through stagnant water, we came to their hiding-place. They had built a little hut and filled it with leaves. They had a wild hog, an opossum, and an alligator all just killed, and we soon had an abundant meal.

"New and friendly faces and voices, gave Lucy great joy; she listened eagerly to every word they said, and looked by the light of the fire, steadily in the face of each speaker, as if she were enchanted. They seemed pleased with her, too. They had not seen the face of a child for several weeks, and Lucy was soon a great favorite with them."

CHAPTER XVIII.

MINTE.

In June in the year 1834, a traveler in the western part of Virginia, was slowly descending a steep hill. At a turn in the road he stopped almost involuntarily to gaze upon the beautiful landscape before him. At the bottom of the hill ran a deep, wide creek, the banks of which were shaded on both sides by great sycamore trees and wild rose-bushes and other shrubs and flowers in full bloom; which were mirrored in the slowly-moving green water below them. A flock of parroquets were wheeling in the air, and showing at each turn their brilliant plumage of green and gold.

On the western side of the creek was a fertile valley half a mile in width, which extended north and south as far as the eye could reach. Behind the valley rose a long line of hills, covered to their tops with trees, and beyond this range of hills towered majestically to the clouds, the Alleghany mountains, all green with the fresh verdure of spring. As the south wind blew gently over the forest, the waving trees showed unbroken terraces of moving living green, that rose pile on pile, and height upon height, until the vision was closed by the clouds that rested on the tops of the mountains. Wreaths of white mist were rising at different points of the landscape, which gently curled and waved, as like spirits they rose and melted in the air.

All along the valley were farm houses, and orchards and meadows of deep green, and fields of clover in full bloom. Large fields of ripe wheat waved like lakes of melted gold, as the wind blew gently over them; and there were great fields of corn, green as emerald, just shooting into tassel with red and yellow silk. The first pencilings of the morning sun rising over the North mountain, shed their mellow luster over the scene, and rose in long waves of golden light upon the dark green forests on the sides of the hills and mountains.

A road rough with loose stones and huge rocks, lay on the west bank of the creek, and followed its windings.

At a turn in this road which brought those who passed along it into view of the traveler, he saw first a buggy driven by a young man neatly dressed, and behind that a row of seven or eight wagons, each drawn by two horses, and filled with negro and mulatto women and children. Behind these wagons followed a coffle of eighty slaves. They were in chains. The iron ring around the right wrist of one, was attached by a chain to a like ring on the left wrist of another, and in the middle of these chains, were rings that attached the whole party to a leading chain that extended along the whole line.

They moved slowly along the uneven, winding road, and at a distance looked like some great monster undulating and twining with the inequalities of the ground over which it passed.

Upon riding nearer, the traveler saw an old man of sixty years, chained to a bright mulatto boy of sixteen. The old man's face was thoughtful, and full of care; the boy walked bravely on, but in spite of his efforts to restrain them, tears would start to his eyes and steal down his cheeks. Some of the men were talking composedly, and all were serious; the men were variously dressed, some of them in the coarse clothing of field laborers, others in well fitting garments of good quality.

Behind the coffle were five one horse carriages, each driven by a well dressed white man, with a colored woman seated at his side.

In the last of these carriages sat a woman so nearly white, that, but for her position, it would have been difficult to discover the traces of intermixture with the African race. Her soft black hair hung uncared for, shading her large lustrous black eyes; her features were as finely and delicately cut as a statue by the hands of an accomplished artist. She moved not, spoke not, looked not either to the right or left, and seemed to be wholly unconscious of objects around her; on her face sat, not sorrow nor traces of mental suffering, nor grief, nor anguish, nor misery—but despair.

If you have stood by the gallows when the doomed man took his last look at the scene before him, and at the sunshine: if you have stood by the side of the gay young man, when his warm blood was gushing from a wound inflicted by the assassin in the street, and he had just been informed that he had but a minute to live; if you have been at the deathbed of the hardened sinner, whose eye is now too dim to see the brazen serpent that Moses placed on a pole for the healing of Israel, and heard him whisper with his last breath, "It is too late—I am lost;" if you have seen the widow, standing by the grave of her only son, as the first clods fell upon his coffin; if you have seen the young mother frantic, as her babe has just fallen, quickly as the flower of the meadow before the scythe of the mower—then you may imagine the despair that spread its raven wings over the face of that poor woman.

The procession halted. A man dressed in gray clothing, burly and big, mounted on a fat and clumsy horse, rode up, and inquired for the owners or agent of the owners of the coffle of 'servants.' He was told that the owners were a few miles in the rear, but that the agent was the young man who rode in front. He pricked his steel into the fat side of his horse, trotted to the young man, and stated that he wished to buy a negro woman. He was told that the woman in the rear was for sale, and would be sold at a low price; but after a close inspection he refused to purchase her. Another woman was then shown to him. He examined her carefully, and the purchase was made.

"But," said the agent, "she has a little child, a girl about four years old; you must buy that, too."

The woman, who had been sullen and silent, now became furious; she declared that her child was free, and that the agent had no right to sell it. Two of the white men had, by this time, joined the group, and she appealed to them as witnesses that the child was free. After some delay they admitted her statement, and the child was handed over to the purchaser of Minte, her mother. The price was paid, and the company were starting, when a white boy ran up and said, addressing himself to the agent.

"Mr. Tibbs wants you to come right quick to him; something's the matter with the gal he has to take care of."

The agent went quickly to the rear, and there, seated upright in the buggy, by the side of Tibbs, sat Patsy, the woman already described. A single drop of blood rested just below one of the corners of her mouth; her face was sad, even in death, for she was dead: her heart had broken.

Poor Patsy! In her position as housemaid, in a family in Washington city, she had observed the deportment of cultivated persons, and her own manners were as quiet and refined as the best culture could make them. The same dreams of love and happiness passed through her girlish imagination, and warmed her heart, that cheer and soften the hearts of all her sex. And then she married—married the lover of her youth and of her choice—and loved him more intensely than she loved her own life. He was a free man, a mechanic, industrious and sober, and they both hoped that, by his industry, she would soon become free. Children clustered around their humble hearth, and the footsteps of their little feet as they followed her, made music to her heart.

They threw their arms around her neck, and she half forgot in their caresses that she was a slave. Her little boy, with his rich clusters of hair shading his bronzed forehead, was dearer to her, because he bore the manly image of his father. Her little prattling girl, wiped with her soft hands, the tears from her face, and soothed her with kind and comforting words when she wept from the fear of separation. The smiles of her infant were dear, as such smiles always are, to the mother's heart. And then came gloomy forebodings of her sale to the traders—not the most abject submission that a slave can offer, trembling as she does so, to a cold and heartless mistress, could remove from the brow of that mistress, the frown that gathered there when Patsy approached. And then her husband meekly offered to purchase her; but the whole purchase-money was demanded in one payment, and in cash; and he had no power to make it. He offered to labor for years on years, till he should become an old man; but that offer was rejected. Then followed nervous apprehensions of sale; so that Patsy started and trembled at the sound of every approaching footstep. And then came the hour so long delayed, so greatly dreaded, when the trader and his gang sprang upon her in her little home, and tore her from the arms of her children; the last look—the last embrace of her little Harry, and her girl, and her babe. Can you wonder that she died broken-hearted, far away from all she loved—with no kind hand to soothe the anguish of her dying hour, and that a drop of blood rested upon her face!

CHAPTER XIX.

THE DROP OF BLOOD.

THE traveler went on his journey, but that drop of blood on the pale face of that poor slave, as she sat cold in death, made a deep impression upon him. Perhaps the optic nerve was diseased. In after years, he saw it in places where its presence was least looked for. He saw it on bales of cotton, and hogsheads of sugar; on newspapers—even religious papers were spotted with it; on the pages of the novelist and the poet; on books of science and of ethics; on records of courts he saw it spread, until they were, in places, covered with crimson. He saw it on the ballot and in the right hand of the voter, till the palm of that right hand was red with blood.

He saw it beneath the blaze of gas-lights, where long rows of silver and cut-glass ornamented the table, and beautiful women and brave and learned men sat joyously at the feast; and there, in a moment of revery, that drop of blood oozed out upon each plate, and spotted each glass, until his soul sickened at the sight.

A beautiful young bride, decked in white robes, with orange-flowers upon her head and surrounded by groups of laughing girls, was arranging her hair before she went down to her marriage, cast a glance at the diamond ring which the bridegroom had just placed upon her finger, and turned white as Italian marble, and shuddered in every limb. The traveler at her side saw in that diamond the drop of blood, fresh and crimson. Was the vision of the bride made unnaturally acute by her excitement, and did she see it too? In a moment it was gone—the diamond shone in its bright splendor; the bride became composed, and in a few moments was—wife.

A young minister charmed by the fervor of his eloquence and his piety all who heard him—the traveler sat in his pew and saw that drop of blood spread itself over his manuscript, as it lay upon the Bible; till it covered every page.

He saw Christians meet together, to commemorate the love of *Him* who died for them; and that drop of blood floated like oil upon the wine, and spotted all the bread, as those Christians pressed them to their lips and prayed to be forgiven.

But he did not see it on the works of nature. The deep blue sky was stainless, as when it bent over Eden before the sin of man. The white lily bloomed radiant and glistening in its unsullied purity. The rose, seated in moss and dripping with dew, was immaculate in her queenly beauty, and the plumage of the dove, was all unstained.

He opened the Book of God—and its every page and line were "pure as the spirit that made it." There was no spot there—Oh no! all that his eye rested upon in it, was free from every stain and trace of blood.

He consulted the learned Doctor Stebbins, who told him that the optic nerve was diseased, and that the diagnosis indicated amaurosis, and made a long prescription—which did the traveler no good.

He consulted his beloved pastor, the venerable Doctor of Divinity—the Rev. Thomas Slowsee, who told him that his imagination was diseased, and tenderly and affectionately talked in mild and gentle tones and terms of fanaticism, and the danger of losing one's influence, and of organic law, and of the difference between religious and political questions, and the folly of meddling with strife that belongeth not to the meddler; but as the good man talked, he looked surprised; for he too saw the same spots of blood almost everywhere—even upon holy things—and he too shared in the fanaticism that at first he had thoughtlessly condemned; for the disease proved to be contagious—and had, like other contagions, its own peculiar laws. Those who would, could see the spots as the traveler saw them; those who would not, were blinded.

CHAPTER XX.

LITTLE BEN.

"WE walked nearly all night, part of the time we had to wade through water quite deep, until we came to the place where my new friends had their hiding-place. About twenty acres of ground without trees on it, rose above the level of the swamp; on it were two gentle swells of land.

"The hut of the party that I went with, was on one of them; and on the other was the hut of Little Ben. It was in the shape of a haycock, and made of the bark of trees that reached from the ground up to a peak at the top. A small hole, large enough to be entered by a man stooping as low as he could, was the only door. There was no window, nor any holes for light. Little Ben had caught a young wolf by the right fore-foot in a steel trap, which had broken the leg at the first joint, so that the foot was twisted inwardly, and did not reach the ground. He had made the animal as tame as a dog; and it was his constant companion. Little Ben generally dressed himself in skins; but on great days, he wore an old suit of regimentals which he had brought with him, and carefully kept. At the top of his hut was a long pole, on which was a flag made of cotton cloth, with the stars and stripes marked on it with charcoal and pokeberry juice. He had round his neck an iron collar, with two prongs that passed by his ears and went up several inches higher than his head. This collar had been so well case-hardened, that it could not be filed off. He was a short, heavy-set man, with a large head and muscular arms, and seemed to be very strong. His eyes were red and sunk deeply in his head, and over them were large, heavy eyebrows. He was between fifty and sixty years old, but his hair was jet-black and bushy.

"The next night after I got there, my new friends told me that Little Ben was in one of his ways, and would sing his 'Star-spangled Banner' song: that he always did so when the moon was full.

"Near his hut was the trunk of a large sycamore tree that had fallen down; on which Ben had made a place to stand when he sung.

"About ten o'clock he went out with his wolf, who seemed to understand what he was about, got on the fallen tree and began to sing. At the end of each verse he uttered a low, sad howl, in which the wolf joined, and then after a moment went on to the next verse, and the two howled together until the song was ended. Then he and the wolf howled for several minutes, got down from the tree, and the two went to his hut. I cannot tell exactly what he sung, but no one ever could sleep while Little Ben and his wolf were singing and howling his 'Star-spangled Banner' song. It seemed to be something like this:

Here 's Little Ben—all alone in the wide world—
He 's got no wife, now ;
He got no children now ;
Never had any house,
Never had any land,
Never had himself—
Master own me all.
The Star-spangled Banner, Oh! long may it wave
O'er the land of the free, and the home of the brave.

And then followed a series of howls.

Had a wife once,
She love him dearly ;
Lived great while together ;
On ole master's place ;
She sold now—'way up Red river—
Took her 'way from Little Ben—
Never see her more,
Never hear from her again.
The Star-spangled Banner, Oh! say, does it wave
O'er the land of the free, and the home of the brave?

Then he sold Rachel,
For a thousand dollars,
While I was out at work;
Lef' her in the morning,
Came home for dinner,
Rachel gone forever!
The Star-spangled Banner, Oh! say, does it wave
O'er the land of the free, and the home of the brave?

Then he sell Sally,
Down to New Orleans;
Sell her to a Frenchman—
I seen her once there;
She ride in her carriage,
Dressed up in silk and satin;—
Good to her ole father,
And she try to buy him,
But master wouldn't sell me!
Oh! say, does that Star-spangled Banner still wave
O'er the land of the free, and the home of the brave?

Then Tom he ran 'way,
Off in the swamp ground;
And the hounds they caught him,
And tear him till he dead!
Oh! say, does that Star-spangled Banner yet wave
O'er the land of the free, and this home of the brave?

Then Missis took Milly;
She whipped her and whipped her,
And wash her back with red-pepper,
To keep the flies off it—
And she whipped her again;
While her back was all sore—
And Milly she died,

And dey put her in de ground
And say she hab fever!
Oh! say, does the Star-spangled Banner still wave
O'er the land of the free, and the home of the brave?

Massa ride fine horse—
Missis ride in de carriage;
Nice heaven here for 'em—
Big heaven in de next world!
That Star-spangled Banner, Oh! when will it wave
O'er the land of the free, and the home of the brave?

"Sometimes, when the moon was full, he dressed himself in his old suit of regimentals, and sung and howled, accompanied by his wolf, all night. At sunrise they went into the hut and slept all day.

"He was harmless, silent and gloomy; yet with all his gloom, he was kind to all who were on his island, for he had made the place his own, and treated all who came there as his guests.

"He had corn and vegetables planted on the island, and caught birds and game for food. In some places there were ponds of water in the swamp, in which he caught fish. He always gave his guests food when he had it; and when his stock of meat and fish was exhausted he got more.

"We stayed here three days, one of which was Sunday. I was sitting on a log reading the Bible to my child, when Little Ben saw me from his hut and came to us. He sat down and listened a long time, and I read on because it seemed to please him. I read the passage about John the Baptist. He stopped me and said, 'Read that again.' I did so. He put his hands to his head and bent it down, almost to his knees, and sat in silence. I stopped reading as soon as I saw he was not listening. After four or five minutes he raised his head and said, 'I see it now.'

"'See what?'

"'I see it now; it's just this; the good Lord loved John Baptist. He was a good man; that king a bad man. But the Lord let him cut off John Baptist's head. What he let him for? just this: it didn't make any matter whether he live great while or little while in this world; so he let him cut off his head, and kill him in jail. The king live great while—forgot all 'bout John de Baptist—think he do no harm; a great man and live in a great house, and then he die too. All over with him then—all his king gone clean away. Only like another man then, and he have to answer for all he done to John de Baptist. Suppose he couldn't do it, what then?

"'I see another thing here, too: the good Lord lets a bad man kill a good man. May-be he lets a bad man make a good man slave, and keep him slave, and put a collar on his neck. I see it now.

He just lets people be, to see what they will do in this world; lets 'em kill one another, and make slave of one another, and whip one another. He looks on. Don't say one word, till it's all done; and then '—he paused.

"'And then what?'

"'I don't know what then; but it 'pears to me, that them that's killed and abused and made slave of, ain't so bad off then as them that did all these things. It 'pears so to me. I don't know much—Little Ben got no l'arnin', but it 'pears to me, that after awhile—may-be a good while—that the man who put this collar on my ole neck, will find it heavier than I do, and wear it a great while longer than I will.'

"Next day we took leave of our friends. Little Ben and his wolf went with us. He knew the paths, and offered to be our guide.

"He took my child in his arms and said he would carry her. Our way led along narrow and crooked paths, across logs; sometimes we waded for half an hour through mud and water: the large trees were all hung with moss, and the whole woods were dark almost as night.

"Little Ben went before me with my child in his arms, and acted as pilot. We heard no sounds but the croaking of large frogs, and the hootings of owls. We walked all day as fast as we could, but did not reach the edge of the swamp before night. Sometimes we passed through great cane-brakes, so thick that none but a person who knew the road could have found his way.

"When we got nearly to the edge of the swamp, he stopped on a dry piece of ground, and told us to rest here until night, and then to travel as fast as we could; for he said the men-hunters were always about the swamp with their dogs.

"'Look here,' said he, while he led me a short distance. I looked, and saw the skeleton of a man. On the bones of one of the legs was an iron ring. 'This has been here,' he said, 'for two years. You'll see a good many of them before you get clean away from this place. They kills as many as they catches. There, two more dead men close by here, and all round this swamp people has been killed. Did you ever hear of Watkins?'

"'No.'

"'Well, may-be, you'll see him. He's the one that kills our people, and catches all he can. He shoots 'em, and cuts 'em with his knife, and sets his dogs on 'em. He's always at it.'

"After awhile he said, 'Read some more out of your good book. May-be it's the last chance I'll have, in this world, to hear another word of it. I can't read.'

"I read to him until it was too dark to read any longer.

"'I think,' he said, 'if I could hear you read that book every day, this hotness would go away out of my poor old head. It seems to cool it. It sounds good to me. How odd it is that one man can read every word of it, when he chooses, and another man can't! It seems to me that people have to take care of each other in this world. I have shown you the way out of this swamp; ought not somebody show me the way through that big swamp, that all us people have to wade in all our lives.'

"After we had rested and taken some food, I was about to bid him good-by; but he said he would go on further with us.

"He again took my child in his arms.

"'Let me carry her,' said I.

"'Oh no! it does me good to carry the little gal. It 'minds me of the time when I carried my own little children. It makes my heart soft. It makes me cry, but all the time it makes me feel good too. Can't carry my own children any more; never see any of 'em again. All gone from me.'

"'Let me see,' said I, 'if I can't get that collar off your neck.'

"'No, it can't be done; I must die wid it on

me. Tried hundred times to get it off, but it won't come off. Got file but can't file it at all.'

"I still had my pitchfork, and other articles that I had found at the burnt house. We came to an open place in the woods, and the moon and stars made light enough for me to see.

"By my direction he laid down by the side of a log, and rested his head against it. I gathered up a great deal of moss and put around his collar inside, so as to keep it from hurting him. While I worked, the wolf stood by, looking keenly at every motion that I made. I then applied my pitchfork to his collar. The wolf growled furiously. Little Ben called him and held him by his lame foot, while I, with my foot on one side of the collar and the pitchfork, worked at it for an hour. It seemed as if I could not break it. At last, with one sudden wrench it cracked; Little Ben leaped up; he looked amazed and stupefied. The wolf looked in his face and whined.

"'I hear it crack,' he said.

"'It did crack. It's almost off.'

"'What dis collar come off me! I've had it on dis ole neck ten years; I live wid it on, sleep wid it on, and eat wid it on—part of my own self almost.'

"He laid down again, and with another effort the collar was broken. I opened it and took it from his neck. Little Ben took it in his hands, held it up, and by the light of the stars carefully examined it; then rubbed his neck, and threw the collar on the ground. The wolf seized it in his teeth and shook it as if it had been a wild animal.

"While I was taking the collar off: 'Listen,' said Ben, 'don't you hear dogs bark?' I stopped a moment and heard them.

"'It's a sign,' said Ben. 'I have had three collars filed off before, and always the dogs barked as they were taking them off. They never barked at all while men were putting the collars on me.'

"'What makes 'em do so?'

"'It's a sign,' he said. He then took Lucy in his arms.

"'Had you not better go back?' said I.

"'No; I want to stay with this child as long as I can—'minds me so much of my poor little children. Makes me think of ole times. Seems as if I never can leave you.'

"'Well then, come on with us.'

"'No; can't leave my own place. Lived thar ten years.'

"'Why can't you leave it, Ben?'

"'Don't know—bound to stay there till I die. Don't want to go to Canada. I like to live in de swamp—best place for me; see no white man dar. Dey freard of me; can't get nigh me; and wolf here howl when anything come nigh—so I know when any hounds about. Don't want to go anywhere where white man see me. White man put another collar on me. Black man take collar off. White man can't do it by himself.'

"We had traveled nearly all night as well as all day, and I could hardly walk; I told Ben so.

"'Come on a little further, and may be you will be out of white man's way.' We did so and found a hiding-place. Little Ben and his wolf left us, and we staid there till night."

CHAPTER XXI.

AARON'S NARRATIVE.

"At daylight the next morning, I heard some one walking carefully through the leaves. We laid down so as to hide ourselves. The man seemed to be coming toward us. Our hearts beat quickly; Lucy trembled, and I feared would scream; but we were still. The man came within ten feet of us, and stopped, looked around him but not at us. His side was to us. He was about thirty-five years old, and had no coat or vest on. His sleeves were rolled up above his elbows. He had a black beard which hung down on his breast, and long, black, curly hair. In a red belt around his waist there was a pair of large revolvers, and on the other side a bowie-knife with a silver handle. He held in his hand a short rifle. He was a man of powerful frame, and walked like a cat.

"In a few minutes he went away without having seen us. I knew it was Watkins from what little Ben had told us of him.

"We were so scared that we trembled nearly all day. If he had seen us we would have either been killed or taken back into slavery.

"It rained for several days after that, and we wandered through the dark nights, over fallen trees, and through the woods without a path, and through water, and deep swamps.

"My child got sick. We were both almost dead with hunger. One dark day we ventured to travel; Lucy walked, for I was too weak to carry her. She was before me and ran back greatly scared. 'Look here, father;' I looked and saw the skeletons of two persons. The bones were covered with green mould. A large rifle-bullet was in the front of one of the skulls.

"The next day we saw another set of human bones, but there were no marks of violence upon them. He had probably starved to death; I thought so, because we were nearly famished.

"We wandered on and on through the cold drenching rain, and over creeks so full that we could hardly get over them. No game could be seen. All was silent and dark and desolate. The gray moss dripped with water, no stars or moon appeared at night. Sometimes we heard the stealthy, cat-like tread of the panther, but that did not scare us. It did not want to enslave us. Again and again in our weary wanderings, we passed by the bones of men and women who, like us, had longed for freedom, and found death. Would we too find only death?"

CHAPTER XXII.

PATSY'S GRAVE.

On a rocky knoll by the road-side, where a narrow lane came down to it, two men were digging a shallow grave. Their work was soon done, and a long box made of rough boards, in which was the body of Patsy, was lowered into the grave. No other persons were there. The broken earth was carelessly thrown in, and the burial was over. They placed no stone to mark her resting-place, and made no mound of earth above it. The crescent moon was riding in majesty surrounded by hosts of brilliant stars, and white clouds were slowly floating like snow-wreaths over the clear blue sky. A balmy south wind murmured as it passed, bearing on its wings the fragrance of a thousand flowers, and when the men left the place all was as still, and calm, and sweet as was Eden before our first parents sinned.

A half-witted negro boy returning home from a mill, was riding slowly along the road soon after the men went away. He told his fellow slaves, that before he came to the place, he saw, standing by the grave, amid a cluster of sumachs, and sassafras, and persimmon trees, two white and glittering shadows, bright as the sun, and heard music so sweet and sad, that he cried like a little child; and that he saw them slowly going up into the air, but now their songs were full of joy; and that another form was with them, like a bright cloud when the sun is shining on it; and he looked at them till they went up far in the sky and faded like white mist out of his sight, and he could hear their music no more.

And down to this day, some of the slaves in that neighborhood say, that on a certain time in June, they hear at midnight, above that grave, delicious music, at first sad as the wailing of a broken-hearted mother for her child; and that as it rises higher and higher in the air, it becomes more joyous, till at last it is a rapture of sweet songs, and their hearts grow soft and warm as they hear it, and they feel happy as if they were in heaven.

The rocky knoll is still there, but the fence has been removed, so that it stands in a corner of the field, and persimmon, and sassafras trees, and sumach bushes cover it; and over the neglected and almost forgotten grave of Patsy, a wild rose grows and sheds its fragrance all around it, and guards the sleeping dust that lies below.

CHAPTER XXIII.

AARON'S NARRATIVE.

"ONE morning at the risk of being seen, we continued our journey. Very soon after daylight, I killed a partridge, that I saw sitting on a fence, with my bow. I found an open piece of ground covered with grass, at the foot of a large oak, nearly hid by hazel bushes. Here I made a fire, and roasted the bird. Lucy was eating it with great relish, her face bright with joy; I was sitting a few feet from her, watching and enjoying her pleasure, as much as if I had been satisfying my own hunger. Suddenly I saw Lucy's eyes open wide, and one loud scream burst from her. At the same instant, five large hounds sprang upon both of us; one hound, with ash-colored hair and large black spots, seized her by the throat and shook her as if he would have torn her head from her body; another caught her feet, and was tearing them to pieces. I sprang upon the dogs, and with one wrench with my hands, tore them away; other dogs were upon me, but I took no notice of them. In an instant, I killed the two that had seized my child, and I believe, had crippled all the others. They ran howling from me. I turned to follow them, and saw on horseback, a man dressed in black, with a white cravat on his neck. He seemed greatly scared, turned his horse and fled as soon as I saw him.

"Lucy seemed to be quite dead; no blood flowed from her wounds. I took her in my arms, and ran as fast as I could. After a few minutes, I saw that she still breathed. I soon found a stream of water, and washed her wounds, and bathed her face, till she opened her eyes and looked at me, but did not know me.

"After a while, I hunted the best hiding-place I could find by the side of the run, and nursed her until her senses came back, so that she knew me. She still trembled at every noise, and put her little arms around me, and looked up in my face so kindly, but could not speak. All that day and the night afterward, she did not recover her voice, and could scarcely hold up her head. Her neck was very sore, her legs and feet badly torn, and her body in pain, wherever I touched her. I cannot tell my feelings; if I could have died for her, I would have done so: whenever she writhed in pain, my heart seemed as if it would burst. I thought over nearly all my past life. It had been passed in slavery. My only child, all that I had on earth; all that I loved, or cared for almost in this world, had been hunted by dogs, nearly killed; and for what? She was innocent, and I alone was to be blamed, for attempting to run away from slavery. Now she was sick and wounded, and I could not help her; had not even food to give her; no friend to aid me; no shelter for her head, from the cold night winds, no clothing to protect her! How bitter was my fate! how sad the fate of my child.

"I knew it would be still worse, if we should be discovered; for then our capture would be certain. Early in the next night, weak with excitement, sorrow, and hunger, sick myself at my very heart, I took my poor, dear suffering child in my arms, and again started, to find if I could, a safe hiding-place. Lucy could now speak; she was nervous and frightened, but her face was calm, and as she rested her little head upon my bosom, she from time to time, consoled me with her kind words. At almost every step she suffered pain. I found a place that seemed to be secure, sheltered by trees, and near where we now are; and there, under a large, leaning magnolia, I made her a bed of leaves, caught a bird for her, and some fish for myself; but I saw each day, more and more clearly, that she could not live.

"One morning I had prayed with Lucy according to my custom, and was reading at her request, when looking earnestly in my face, she asked me:

"'Father, why should one man be born to be all his life a slave, and another man to be his master?' I could not answer, but took her in my arms; a smile brightened her wasted features, and she said:

"'Father, do you remember the sunset that we watched, one evening, when we were at the old burnt house? I see that sunset again. I see the red and golden clouds spread over the whole sky, and they turn and roll into each other; and two of them stand widely apart as if they were the pillars of the great gate of heaven. And far down between them I see brighter and still brighter glories; and away beyond them still there is a brightness, but it is not that of the setting sun. And I see in the great space around it thousands of figures, all clothed as if their garments were torn from the covering of the sun. And I see a garden, father, and in it a river clear as the light, and its waters go softly among trees green and beautiful and covered with fruit. And the figures are slowly, slowly coming to us. They will not take us back into slavery, father! they will not hurt us, they are near to us now! They have wreaths made of stars upon their heads, and their hands are stretched out and beckoning me to come to them, father: they are all around us; one of them is close to me—is bending over me, father.'

"I pressed her to my bosom, and looked in her face. She was DEAD!"

CHAPTER XXIV.

REV. MR. ST. JOHN.

THE reader will remember, that when the man who bought Minte rode up, and inquired for the owners of the coffle of slaves, he was informed that they were a few miles behind the gang.

On the top of a high ridge of the western slope of the North mountains stood a tavern, a white frame house, two stories high with a porch along the whole front, and four locust trees before the door. On the sign, in large golden letters, were the words, "Mountain Home."

In the parlor sat three men, one of them, Mr. Williams, a man of slender person, regular features and well dressed; another, Mr. Bullard, a stout, burly man with a red face and bushy, gray hair that stood up like bristles; and the third, a long, lean, pale-faced man whose limbs seemed to be unjointed, dressed in a full suit of black. This, oh reader! is our old aquaintance, Mr. St. John. Two years have passed over him since we last saw him, but he is still in the full vigor of active life.

"I tell you," said Williams, "it will not do; the thing is unheard of. I respect your motives, my dear sir, and have a high regard for your feelings; but, with the utmost deference," waving his hand toward Mr. St. John, "it cannot, and I think, ought not be done."

"Why not," said Mr. St. John. "I can see no earthly reason for your objections, except only the novelty of the enterprise, and I do see a great many in favor of my proposition. You know that now, among the best families who hold slaves, they are in the practice, some of them daily, and others I am sorry to say, only once a week, of assembling their slaves together and reading the Bible and praying with them. Who is there with so hard a heart as not to feel deep respect for these tokens of piety? And yet sir," and he raised his voice, "I do not doubt that the first slaveholder, who introduced this practice, excited remark and surprise. You know too, that our best ministers are slaveholders; yet I cannot but think that when a minister of the Gospel first bought a slave, he was persecuted for this exhibition of christian principle. It is, sir, I do assure you, only the novelty of the thing that surprises you."

"I admit," said Mr. Williams, "that your arguments are strictly logical. It is right to hold slaves; they are our property. It is useless to hold them unless we have the right to sell them, since they would be of no value to any one without the exercise of that right at pleasure. If it is right in one man to sell, it is right in another man to buy. The buyer and seller stand on an equal platform. It is right for the owner to take them from one state into another, just as he takes, at his pleasure, his other property. If he has the right to take them from one state into another, he has the right to secure them so that they can be so taken."

"Yes," interrupted Mr. Bullard, "that 's clear—I see it myself now. It 's no use to have niggers unless you can sell 'em—and it 's no use at all for us to buy 'em without we can take 'em down South again and sell 'em; and we can't do that without we chain 'em—I mean the men—for if we don't chain 'em, it would take all our profits to hire guards to keep 'em; and then where would be the use in the trade? and if the trade breaks up, why then, in course, the whole system tumbles down. I see it. But still, Mr. St. John, I don't believe one word in your new scheme. It 's all waste of time. I see no use for us to stop on Sunday, to keep the Sabbath day, as you call it, holy. It 's not a bit of use for you to hold prayers night and morning over the niggers;

'cause they 've got no souls, as we have: you never seed a nigger, in all your life, that had a soul, any more than a hoss has!"

Mr. St. John looked surprised.

"The negroes no souls, sir! why I never heard of such a heresy before. Do you really think, Mr. Bullard, they are but beasts?"

"Certainly," said Mr. Bullard, "I think so. Indeed I know it. Everybody else, that I know of, thinks so too; you think so."

"Indeed, Mr. Bullard, you do me the utmost injustice. No man has ever heard me express any such opinion. I am very sure that I never, even for a moment, entertained it. I have always thought that the negroes came from the same common stock that we do. But your argument, Mr. Bullard, is not extensive enough, for some of our people are nearly white; now as to those, they ought to be allowed the rest of the Sabbath."

"Indeed they ought not any such thing. They are all niggers, I tell you, white or black, and no man, woman or child who has one single drop of nigger blood in him or her, has any soul more than a brute, and everybody else thinks so too; you do, excuse me, sir."

"Indeed I do not think so, Mr. Bullard," said Mr. St. John looking him fully in the face, "I never thought so."

"Yes, indeed you do, and so do all the rest of us. Mind, I don't accuse you of lying. I never say that to a gentleman, if I can help it, for I know the consequences; but you do think so, and so do all the rest of mankind."

"Please explain yourself, my dear sir; please explain yourself, Mr. Bullard."

"Well I'll tell you, and it's just this. If niggers has got souls, some of 'em will go to heaven, and they'll tell all the angels such a mess of stuff on the white people, and us especially, that when we die, and go up there, there will be such a muss made, that we'll be glad to get out of the scrape."

"Mr. Bullard," said Mr. St. John, "you shock me. Do you expect to go to heaven?"

"Why certainly I do. Did you ever, in all your life, see a man that did not expect to go there when he died? Expect to go to heaven indeed!—certainly I do. But I can't go to a heaven full of niggers, without they are kept chained. I never feel myself safe among niggers without they are well handcuffed."

"But, Mr. Bullard, this does not prove your assertion, that I believe negroes have no souls."

"Well then, I'll explain myself. You see, ef they are humans, as we are, then they ought to be treated like humans. Nobody does that. I've been in the free states, and there too the white people go just as far as the law allows 'em to treat 'em like brutes. They don't sell 'em — good reason for that—they can't;—they don't hold 'em as slaves, 'cause the law 's ag'in it;—but they treats the whole of 'em as near to brutes as they dare to for the law, and some of 'em goes a great deal further than the law allows. Now there must be some reason for this kind of conduct everywhere, and the true and honest thing is, just because every man 's own sense tells him that somehow niggers is not human, like we are. Stand on that ground and you are safe; but the very minit you take that thar other ground, that they are humans, then, begging your pardon, the devil 's to pay with the whole kit of us."

"Well, but (said Mr. St. John,) I do not see that your argument is good; there are, and always will be, classes in society; and here we have a class of masters and a class of slaves."

"Very well, sir, here is, as you call it, a class of slaves—a class that you call men; but they ain't men, 'cause if they are men, then they ought to have men's rights; and they have not one bit of human rights."

"Well, sir, the Bible plainly teaches that men may be held as slaves. St. Paul sent back a fugitive slave to his master."

"How's that?" said Mr. Bullard: "I've read the whole Testament twice through, and there is no such thing as a nigger in it, from beginning to end."

"Certainly," said Mr. St. John: "there were no Africans in Judea; they never left their own country, until they were forcibly brought away; and that commenced not more than three hundred years ago. The slaves alluded to in the Bible, were not negroes."

"Who were they then?" said Mr. Bullard.

"Why, they were people of the same complexion with their masters; poor people who had been reduced to servitude."

"Oho! sir, that's it, is it? When you and other gentlemen talk about slavery being in the Bible, you mean white slavery, do you? Well, that may suit you, but it don't suit me at all, sir; not a bit of it. I want you to prove from the Bible, that niggers is rightly slaves; and you turn round and prove that poor white people ought to be slaves: well, that don't suit *me*. This business that we are in, is rather risky, and next year we may all be as poor as Job's turkey; so then we ought all be slaves, ought we? No you oughtn't. You've got a profession, and Mr. Williams, he might get be clerk for somebody; but as for me, according to what you say, I ought to be a slave.

That don't suit me. So then when I hear of you and other preachers, saying that slavery's all right, and that the Bible says so; you only mean that poor people ought to be slaves to the rich. Well that's comfortable—its quite refreshing; but for my part, I ain't willing to pay for preaching like that. Let those pay for it as likes it. Do you pray for it too, Mr. St. John? Preaching and praying ought to go together; a man ought not to preach one way, and pray another way. Don't you know that half the poor people in this country are grandchildren of rich men; and I suppose it is always so. Now it must be nice in these rich men, to pay a man for preaching in such a way as to make their grandchildren slaves, as far as preaching can do it. They must be smart people—sensible people them, sir."

"But my dear sir," said Mr. St. John, "they know that there is no danger of their children being made slaves; we only prove the *principle* by the Bible, and then apply it to the negro race."

"Well, I see that plain enough: you prove that niggers ought to be slaves, 'cause you say poor white people ought to be so; and niggers is no better than poor white people. That's real nice; you ought to go down to North Carolina, and be a candidate for congress; you would run *fast* if you didn't get elected, as soon as the people found out exactly what you meant—indeed you would, sir.

"Now sir, all this won't do. The only real solid ground we can stand on, is, that niggers are almost humans, but jest miss it a little; that they come pretty nigh having souls, but not quite.

"If you go one step above that, we're all gone, sir; we are all in for it, up to our eyes, sir."

"My dear sir," said Mr. St. John, "I really have been unable to convey my exact meaning. It is probably my fault, that I have not yet so fully explained myself as to be well understood. The relation of the slave to his master, is a beneficent one. It gives to the poor negro food and clothing, and shelter and protection. He is so ignorant and has so little capacity, that this is greatly desirable for him. To the master it gives steady service and faithful, though humble friends. You see, then, that in the relation, as God intended it, there is great good to both parties."

"Yes, sir, I see it clearly enough, and understand you much better than you think I do. The real thing is, that I understand you better than you understand yourself. A common thing, sir, for all. Some men may open their eyes and stare when you tell 'em so, but it is so, sir.

"Now this is what you mean. You say it's

right for you to preach that slavery is upheld by the Bible. Well, sir, there I don 't dispute you at all; so far as niggers is concerned, I agree to that. Well then if it 's right for you to preach so, it 's right for every other preacher in the United States to preach so too. 'Cause 'ef the thing 's in the Bible they all should preach it; just as it is thar, without caring a copper who it helps or who it hurts.

"Yes," said Mr. St. John, "I see that you do, so far, more fully understand me than many men who make greater pretensions to readiness of apprehension."

"Oh! as for readiness of apprehension, as you call it, which means I suppose, sir, quick-witted, we common people have just as much good mother wit, as you learned men have," said Mr. Bullard, "and sometimes, begging your pardon, sir, but by no means a-meanin' you, I think we have a good deal more—but that 's neither here nor there. Well then let me go on.

"Then you say that the Bible justifies white people being slaves, if they 're poor and can't take care of themselves!"

"Oh no! sir," said Mr. St. John; "I really have said no such thing."

"Begging your pardon, sir, you have not said so in words, but what you did say, means that, people as can't take care of themselves, ought to have somebody to take care of 'em; people as is bad off, ought to have somebody to find 'em a home, and food, and clothes, and protection. Now I know a good many white people in these here states, in North Carolina, where I come from, and in Virginny and Georgy, and all these states south of Potomac, who make a mighty bad out takin' care of themselves, and are sometimes bad off for corn-bread and clothes, and all sich things. Now if you and all the preachers will go about the country, and preach up that black people ought to be slaves, because they are so ignorant, and poor—by-and-by you will be getting to making white folks slaves, not all at once, but by little and little, edging in here and there, beginnin' with paupers, and men who have been whipped for stealing sheep and chickens, and so creeping along by degrees, till at last, rich men will not only own all the land, but all the people white and black that live on it. I tell you again, sir, that don't suit me. You prove too much for me, and not a bit in the right place. I want you to prove out of the Bible that niggers ought to be slaves,—I want it for a good reason too. It will help me in my trade, sir. Many a good bargain have I lost, because when I was getting it nearly closed, the man would stop and say, 'Well I don't like to sell human flesh and blood, the Bible 's again it,' or may-be his wife would come out and say so to him and I would have to go away. Now if you will find me plain good places in the Bible where it says it 's right to hold niggers, and sell 'em, and all that, I 'll give you the price of the best nigger in our gang, as soon as we sell 'em at New Orleans; I will make lots of money by it too, 'cause I can carry a little Bible in my pocket when I go out to buy, and with the leaves turned down and the places marked with a pencil, and then when I come across one of these here squeamish, half Christian, half devil cowards, I 'll just pull out the book and read it to him, and make money by it. But if it only means you may sell white people, it would get me into bad scrapes, for they would try to whip me. People see into millstones quicker than you think for."

"But," said Mr. St. John, "let us return to the point from which we started. You said that I believe negroes have no souls: this I denied; but you reiterated the statement: that was not fair, Mr. Bullard, you did me injustice."

"I meant no offense, sir; not a bit of it, and I am sincere. I say again that you yourself don't believe that a nigger has a soul no mor'n a hoss."

"Why, Mr. Bullard, I am really surprised that

you should say so, after I have told you exactly the contrary."

"Ah!" said Mr. Bullard, "I told you that I understand you better than you know yourself, and I do, too. Mean no offense, sir—not a bit of it. You *say* they are *men*, but you *treat* 'em like beasts: conduct speaks louder than words. Whenever I see a man preaching and praying to niggers, I git mad right on the spot. Ef they're brutes, what's the fellow preaching and praying to brutes for; ef they're men"—here Mr. Bullard paused.

"Well, what follows if they *are* men," said Mr. St. John.

"Well," said Mr. Bullard, "ef they're men they ought to be treated like MEN—that 's all that follows."

"I agree with you," said Mr. St. John, "they should be treated as men;—for that very reason I wish to stop to-morrow, that being the Sabbath, and give them rest and religious instruction."

"Well," said Mr. Bullard, "if they are men; they ought to be treated as men—and not like cattle; that 's my doctrine. If a man is a man, he *is* a MAN, sir."

"Don't become excited, Mr. Bullard."

Oh! I 'm not a bit mad at you, sir; I like you; I respect you: I don 't like your doctrine—my doctrine is, that white people ought to be free and niggers ought be slaves; and I believe, if a vote could be got to-day, more than half the people in these United States would agree with me in that p'int. But still I like you, because, sir, you talk and act right out what you are. Now I know plenty of preachers, and deacons, and elders, and class-leaders who would be very much scandalized at being where and what you are to-day. No offense, sir; in principle they are exactly with you, but they are too big cowards to be open about it, sir. I 've had secret partners in my business, who let me have money to buy niggers with and shared the profits of the trade, who wouldn't for the world have had their names mentioned concerning it. Big men in churches, great Christians, talk just as you do—act just as you do—only behind the curtain. I don't like that. Let a man be a man, or a mouse, sir. The thing 's right or it 's wrong. Ef it 's right, be a man and act it out; ef it 's wrong, why don't they keep out of our trade? And these very same fellows all the time say, slavery is right for niggers, and hold 'em as slaves."

"I do most decidedly condemn such people," said Mr. St John, "and it is for that very reason that I am here openly maintaining my principles. I practice as I preach, as every minister should.

"God is no respecter of persons; He is the father of all the people in that quarter of the globe called Africa, as well as he is of all the people in Asia, Europe, and America. It is only on the ground that the institution of slavery is merciful and according to his will, that it can for a moment be sustained. If it is not so, it should be immediately abandoned. God is eternal, and it follows from his eternity that there can be no to-morrow with him. All things are *now* to him. All men must repent of sin *now*. If slave-holding is a sin, it, like all other sins must be instantly forsaken. If it can be continued till to-morrow, according to the will of God, it can be continued to eternity according to his will.

"All very fine preaching," said Mr. Bullard—"very fine indeed, sir; but I tell *you*—I *tell* you, sir, that nine-tenths of the white people in this whole country, don't believe, and never have believed, a word of it, so far as niggers is in it. I don't dispute but what it 's right enough for white people—nor does anybody else that I know of; but, sir, when you come to put this here fine talking on niggers' heads, the cap don't fit 'em, sir. That 's my belief, and so I sell 'em and buy 'em and make all the cash I ken out of the trade; just because it 's all right, and as decent a business as selling sheep, or horses or any other trading in live stock. I 'll stick to it too ; the people 's on my side and they are right.

"But it 's no use talkin' to you about this ; we can't see alike, and what 's the use of disputes among gentlemen."

Mr. Bullard went away.

"I tell you, my dear sir," said Mr. St. John to Williams, "that the slaveholder who first introduced family worship among his slaves, was a benefactor to his country. It has added to the respectability of the institution, and placed it on its right foundation. He ought to have a monument erected to his memory."

"Of brass?" said Mr. Williams.

"I care not whether it is of brass or marble," replied Mr. St. John, "he ought to have a monument erected to preserve his name to all posterity. And all that I wish to do now is, to tread humbly and at a distance in his footsteps, and have family worship and the due observance of the Sabbath, and all the decencies and duties of Christianity carried into the slave-trade. Rely upon it, my dear sir, it is for the want of these observances, that our trade is disreputable; that even the men who sell to the trader, look upon him with loathing and contempt. I have embarked in this trade with the view of reforming its abuses. I have been laboring for years as a minister in reforming the abuses of slave-holding, and showing, and proving the sanctity of the relation of master and servant; but so many fellow-laborers are now in this part of the vineyard, that I have left it, and come in to more neglected places. This, sir, is the point of attack, and it should be our point of defense. Slavery is the corner-stone you know, sir, of our republican institutions. The relation of master and servant, is ordained of God, and sanctioned by his Church. The power of truth is wonderful. It has compelled many of the churches in the free-states, to acknowledge that our institutions are right. A minister, especially one who holds slaves, is not only received as a brother among them, but is counted worthy of double honor; of his full share, because he is a minister; and of superadded honor, because he is a slaveholder.

"Now, I have no wish to labor in this department, unless I can do so as a Christian minister. I want to reform the abuses of the slave-trade, and to make it as respectable as slave-holding is. They are all parts of the same system; each, a link of the same chain; from the African slave-trade to slave-holding, and the domestic slave-trade. If one link breaks; the chain, and all that depend upon it, fall to the ground. This, I repeat, sir, is the point of attack, and must be the place of our defense. The slave-buyer, and the slave-seller are equals in fact, and must be made so in public esteem."

"My dear sir," said Williams, "your arguments cannot be refuted except upon the ground, that the scheme is wholly impracticable. The white men who accompany slave coffles as drivers or owners, will never appreciate your motives, nor understand your philosophy; nor will the slaves themselves be profited by your labors. You do not seem to have thought much of Mr. Bullard's arguments. Have you given any attention to his view of the case? coarsely expressed, it is true, sir; but still, I submit, worthy of some attention."

"What! that negroes are not human beings?"

"No, but that the great masses of the American people, practically deny they are immortal! If the negro is immortal, why is he held as property, as the horse or the ox? If he is immortal, why is he bought and sold in the market? If he is immortal, why is not his immortal nature provided for? The truth is, my dear sir, immortality and slavery are wholly incompatible; you have no more right to chain an immortal man, than you have to climb into heaven, and put fetters on every angel of God. But I take the position that he is not immortal; and in this I am supported by every constitution and every law and every custom of the states or of society that treats him either as a slave or as an inferior being. All these constitutions, all such laws, all such customs of states or of society, are but Atheism, if slavery is wrong. They all rest on the principle that the negroes are below the human race, and therefore of right are held in bondage to their superiors. Examine the matter as you will, you will at last find that this is the turning point of the whole controversy, and it is useless and cowardly in us to attempt to disguise it. Let us meet it as men, and at the very point upon which the controversy does turn, or let us quit our defense.

"The Bible, I assure you," said Mr. St. John, "when critically examined, fully supports the system of slave-holding. Men who are wholly disinterested in supporting that system, in the quietness of their closets have, after careful investigation, reached this conclusion, and published the result of thoir inquiries for the benefit of the world. To suppose them insincere, would be to make them as ministers, leading thousands and tens of thousands of men and women down to hell, when they are watchmen on the walls of Sion, and are paid, some of them well paid too, for the very purpose of teaching them their duty, and pointing them to the narrow path that leads to heaven.

"Now, sir, you by your theory, do great injustice to these worthy persons. They are, I repeat, men of great learning, and men too, whose piety is attested by all the churches. They differ upon many points of theology and religious duty; but agree on this."

CHAPTER XXV.

AARON'S NARRATIVE.

"IT is impossible to describe the feelings of a man whose every hope is dead. I had longed for freedom, but it was for my child. I had hopes of happiness but all were for her. I had looked forward to a future, bright in proportion to my present darkness, and endured my sufferings, and still more, bore the full weight of my wrongs and hardships almost with cheerfulness, fully believing that when the day dawned at last, every shade of our night of sorrows would be chased away. But now I had nothing to hope! and the full weight of my sorrows settled down with its mountain load upon my pained and breaking heart.

"I had worked hard all my life; my limbs were stiff with toil ; my hair was gray ; my body almost worn out—and what was the result of all this care and labor? Here I was in a wild wilderness, hiding from the face of my fellow-man; without food; without clothes; without a house to shelter me; without a foot of land; without cattle or horses, or even a dog or cat; and what I felt still more keenly, without a coffin for my only child, or a cover to shield her body from the dust, or a spade even to dig with my own hands her little grave.

"I thought, and oh! how bitter was the thought, why it was that God made one man a slave, and another man to call himself his master! I almost repined, until better thoughts and better feelings came upon me, and then I remembered that this life will soon be over, and that another and a far longer one will come, when the slave and his master will meet on an equal footing before the God and Father of all."

CHAPTER XXVI.

AARON'S NARRATIVE.

"I COULD not bury the body of Lucy, for a day even, after I knew she was dead. I still took her in my arms, but her kind words, and her suffering, patient looks, and the faint voice calling, 'Father,' were all gone, and she too was gone.

"I was calm. I knew that suffer as I might, I ought not to grieve at a change which had freed her from the curse of slavery. The earth, wetted by my tears, received her lifeless form, and I knew that she had gone where no tyranny could crush—no cruelty oppress her. I marked the little grave; at night it was my pillow, in the daytime I could not leave it; I staid close by it, till this flood drove me away, to save my life.

"Yonder it lies, under the foot of that tall poplar tree, just on that little grassy knoll. I shall die soon, and oh master! as you have been so good to me, let me beg you now, to have my poor body buried by the side of Lucy's, that we may rise together in the last day."

I promised him that I would do so if in my power; and then he resumed his story.

"I had now no longer any wish for freedom or for life. All that I had loved and lived for on earth, was gone. The solitude of the wilderness oppressed me. I felt now, for the first time, its awful stillness. But for my Bible, my prayers, and what I believe is the presence of God, it would have killed me. The energy that had borne me up now forsook me, and the disease that my determination to escape had kept in check, now conquered its unresisting victim. In a few days I know I shall die; my cough is almost incessant, and my body is racked with pains. Master, in a few days more, I shall no longer be a fugitive slave but a free man. In a few days more it will be no crime to treat me with kindness, and no disgrace to greet me as a brother. In a few days more I shall be out of the control of the slave laws, that have so oppressed me, and under a far different system of government. I shall see Lucy, and be with her forever, and go in and come out with her without trembling, when I shall meet any of the inhabitants of the land to which I am going."

This coughing became almost incessant, and Edgar too felt assured that his life was rapidly drawing to its close. At his request he took him, leaning on his arm, to the grave where his Lucy lay. The water had now fallen so that they could walk there. When they reached it he stood over it for a moment in silence, and then lay down on the ground with his head resting on the head of her little grave. Edgar brought from his tent some blankets and pillows, and other necessary comforts, and after that they made that place their home. His whole time was occupied in reading to him passages from his Bible, such as he selected, for the whole of it was far more familiar to him than to Edgar.

CHAPTER XXVII.

HON. JOHN STRONG.

The honorable John Strong was elected to Congress many years ago. He was at all times a devoted friend of the people, and firmly believed that the representative has but to obey the will of his constituents. He also believed that a true party man, must at all times support the measures of his party. It so happened, while he was in Congress, that his party were in favor of a measure, to which a large majority of his constituents were opposed. Here was a conflict of principle. The powers at Washington and the powers at home could not agree; and Mr. Strong, after due deliberation, professed himself to his fellow members "true as steel, and firm as a rock," and voted. His constituents remonstrated; and it was plain to all, that his claims for re-election were gone.

But Mr. Strong got an appointment, a clerkship with a salary of fifteen hundred dollars a year, in an office in Washington. This consoled him, this more than comforted him. In due time, Mrs.

Strong was advised of this, and the honest-hearted woman thought the fortunes of the family were made and secured for life. Fifteen hundred dollars a year, to her imagination, seemed an almost inexhaustible mine of wealth. Fifteen hundred dollars for only one year! and work but six hours a day at that, and live in Washington! how fortunate was she that she had married a great man. ,

Mr. Strong, Mrs. Strong, and six little Strongs moved to Washington, and lived on in peace till another Pharaoh reigned, who knew not Joseph. Then things changed: Mr. Strong's services, and his vote were not so highly prized as they had been. His talents were now underrated. It was even thought that another could perform the duties of his place, as well as he. Mr. Strong lost his office; but got another, at seven hundred and fifty dollars a year. But his wife, was a "managing woman." Her first care when she came to Washington was, to get into "genteel society." Her next, to keep in that society. She soon found, to use her own phrase, that those who owned no negroes, "were looked down upon;" and Strong had no rest, till he consented to buy a negro. "Let it be a woman," said Mrs. Strong, for reasons she then assigned; and she was commissioned to buy one, with their scanty savings. But after several inquiries, she found that women were high, and therefore made up her mind to buy a girl. A poor, sickly girl at last was found, and bought at a low price. This girl was Patsy.

Years passed on, and Patsy grew up and was married, and the mother of three children; when one evening, after Strong and his wife had returned from a party, and were seated by the fire, Mrs. Strong said:

"Well, I have often advised you within the last year, to sell her; but you never will take my opinion on anything, till it is too late. I tell you the girl is sick, and will die on our hands, and be a dead loss to us, of fifteen hundred dollars. She has never been hearty since the birth of her last child, and now she is worse than ever. We've got to part with her, and the only question is, whether we shall get fifteen hundred dollars in cash—more money of your own, than you ever had at one time, in all your days—or whether we shall get nothing at all. Now, make up your mind to-night, for the man is to call to-morrow for his answer. Come now, John, don't be foolish, take my advice for once in your life. You know, when she wanted to live in the house on the alley with her husband and children, you opposed it till I reasoned you out of it; and then when they got into that house, we 've had no expense with the family. Her husband is a free negro, and gets good wages, and has nothing else to do with his money, but to take care of his wife and children."

"But," said Strong, "what will become of the children, if we sell her—of her babe; they are too young, to take care of themselves; and you have no time to see after them properly?"

"Well now, it does seem to me," said his wife, "that you have not one particle of sense; I mean of course, common sense. I know you have statesman talents enough to be President. Cannot the girls take care of the baby? and has not Jim always taken care of his family? Ain't he a Christian, and do you think he will let them suffer, because their mother is gone?"

"But, my dear," said Mr. Strong, "is not that an imposition on Jim?"

"How so?" said Mrs. Strong: "is it an imposition on you, that you have to take care of your children? Ain't he their father, and oughtn't he to take care of 'em? Won't it afford him pleasure to do so? What else has he to do with all the money he gets? He is a good carpenter, and I do believe, that at the end of the year he lays up more money than you do; or he would do so, if he did not spend it on his family."

"I don't want to sell the girl; she is a good girl and has been a faithful servant."

"But how, in this world, can we afford to lose fifteen hundred dollars? You 'll drive me distracted: it's no use to reason with you, and never was. We 'll all be in the poor-house in six months, and that too when the girls need part of the money to prepare for their sister's wedding. They must go to Martha's wedding, and they cannot do so unless great additions are made to their wardrobe. It will not be treating Mr. Leathers respectfully, if they either stay away altogether or go there among strangers in such a plight that they will not be fit to be seen. And as for Martha, she is so close that she won't let them have a single cent. You know that."

"Well, Eliza," said Mr. Strong, "it is useless to attempt to answer your arguments. I leave the whole responsibility of this matter with you. I think myself that Patsy's health will be improved if she is taken to a warmer climate. It may prolong her life."

Jim had often been told by Mr. Strong and Mrs. Strong and all the young Strongs that he was highly favored by being allowed to visit, and even to live with his wife and children; and from time to time he was reminded that Mr. Hunt and Mr. Wilson, and other gentlemen in the city, did not allow any free colored persons to visit their servants. Poor Jim felt grateful, very grateful for the blessings conferred upon him by the Strongs, and was willing and ready at all times to do such little services as lay in his power for so kind a family. He cut their wood and put in their coal; blacked Mr. Strong's boots, and as the young ladies grew up he carried parcels for them to different parts of the city, and in a thousand ways made himself useful to the family.

On Monday night after this conversation occurred, Jim was requested to go on an errand for Mr. Strong, down near the long bridge across the Potomac; and while he was gone the traders came and carried off his wife.

He returned and reported himself to Mr. Strong, and then making an humble bow went out by the back door to his house. As he approached he was surprised to find it all dark. He laid his hand upon the latch and listened for a moment, but all was still. He trembled as he went in and stood for an instant silent in the middle of the room. He called and a child's voice from under the bed, sobbing and low, said "Father, is that you?"

"Yes, Pauline, it 's me." His children rushed out and clung to him.

"Where is your mother, Harry?"

"Oh, father! men's come, and hit her hard, and put his hand over her mouth, and tied her, and took her away, and hurt little sister too. They comed just after you went away: Mr. Strong comed with 'em; and mother's gone."

Jim groaned—looked hastily in the cradle, and finding his youngest child there, sat down and took his little girl and boy upon his knees. He spoke not a word; no tears came to relieve his heart. There he sat in the dark and silent room, till both his little ones had sobbed themselves asleep upon his breast. He then put them in their bed, and sat down again; sat again in the dark, silent room, till the town clock struck twelve, and Jim aroused himself, and prepared to go to bed. He walked a step or two, and fell prostrate on the floor. A chill as of death, passed over his whole body. Cold sweat stood in great drops upon his forehead. His limbs were stiff and motionless; but his mind was more active than it had ever been before. His whole life had been one of sorrow and suffering; and all these sorrows, were now poured into his swollen heart, in one bitter, burning agony. What had he done more than others, that he should be thus singled out from among men, and made to suffer as man had never suffered before? All around him were men; some with high honors, others with wealth, and nearly all with abundant sources of comfort and happiness; even the poorest, were rich in the love of their wives and children; but he had no wife now, and his children were slaves. Their mother's fate awaited them, and one by one, they too would be sold. He was about to pray, and then he thought — God was no friend of his, and he would not pray to him. At last the fountain of his tears was opened, and his heart softened, and then he prayed—prayed in agony for his wife, for his children, for those who had sold her, for those who had bought her, and for those who made and sustained the laws under which she had been sold. A calm, as of oil upon troubled waters, soothed his heart; and he rested his throbbing head upon the bed, by the side of which he knelt. Was he asleep? or had nature given way, under the shock he had sustained? He was insensible for a time, and was then aroused by a soft hand passing over his forehead, and wiping the tears from his cheeks. He looked up; were those white wings that fanned him, the wings of an angel sent from God to strengthen him? were those words that fell like soft and delicious music upon his soul, the whisperings of the angel? and those hopes that soothed his heart, as they bade him be of good cheer, assuring him that his brother mechanics, and brother men would not suffer his little ones to remain much longer slaves, but would soon arouse, and speak, and write, and preach, and vote, and pray for GOD and FREEDOM; were they the delusions of a fevered brain, or—were they sober facts?

On that night, the flag on the dome of the Capitol waved in the wind, and displayed gracefully its stars and stripes as it spread with each passing breeze, and the angel that had borne that flag through the stormy battles of the revolution, stood by the side of it grasping its staff in his right hand, while in his left he held a golden censer filled with the tears, and groans, and prayers of poor Jim; which he was carrying to the Lamb of God.

Was it for this, that he had borne that flag amid the din, and dust, and shout, and uproar, and whirlwind of battle, at Bunker Hill, at Saratoga, at Yorktown and the Cowpens? Was it for this; when its folds were dripping with the warm blood of the heroes who fell beneath it, and it was overborne and trodden in dishonored dust by superior power, that he had raised it, and cheered with new hopes the failing hands of those who bore it; till at last, Victory placed her laurel crown upon it, and Peace folded it as a robe about her, and blessed it forever? The angel looked upon the censer filled with the agony and prayers of poor Jim; and then upon the flag, and burying his face in its sacred folds, wet it with his tears, and ascended to Heaven.

On the next Thursday night, all was life and gayety at Mr. Strong's. A new piano stood in the parlor; new Brussels' carpet covered the floor, and the three Miss Strongs, each in a new satin dress with lace collars and sleeves, received their guests. The party was, as all said, really a grand one. Members of Congress were there; a Secretary and two Judges; four attaches of the French and Prussian embassies, with close-fitting coats and elegant moustaches, were attentive to the hostess and her lovely daughters. Mr. Strong was happy. No one could have been more cordial or more kind. He went from room to room—complimented the young ladies on their fine dancing; their mothers on their youthful looks, and then in half a minute was seated at a card-table in a back room, talking of the good old times when he was in Congress, to General Bungo, the new member from Louisiana. Mrs. Strong was happy; the day had at last come, when their family was duly appreciated. The guests retired; the lamps were all put out save one; and Mrs. Strong said to her husband: "Did I not tell you to leave these things to me? and you did so; and now I hope you see that you have a wife?"

"Yes," said Strong, "Eliza, I am proud of you; you are indeed a helpmate and a treasure."

At eleven o'clock the next day, many persons who were at the party were seen slowly walking up the steps of the Capitol. They took their seats in their respective houses and talked of tariffs and banks, and the improvement of rivers and harbors; of the Constitution and its "compromises" and guarantees; of the greatness of our country and the advance of liberty throughout the world. But he who ventured to say that slave-holding is a sin, was looked upon by nearly all of them as a fanatic or a simpleton—one to be contemned or despised. Did they represent the *people* of the United States? Will they so represent them forever?

"I saw you at the party, last night," said Mr. West, a young clerk in the Treasury department to Mr. Irwin, also a clerk in the same department, as they met in their office early in the morning. "I hope you had a pleasant time."

"It was very pleasant indeed, while I was there; but when I went home the colored man who has the care of my room, told me that Mr. Strong, only last Monday night, sold his cook Patsy to Weston the trader, and ever since I heard that, I have a horrible taste of human blood on my teeth. I cannot wash it off. I cannot get rid of it. Every drop of coffee or wine that I drank and every particle of cake or food that I ate seems now to me to have been mixed with and steeped and soaked in that woman's blood. Bah! it makes me sick. I feel as if I had been at a feast of cannibals."

"You surprise me," said Mr. West; "you, a Kentuckian, to entertain such sentiments! Do you not know that if you utter them you will lose your office and your position in society? It is downright Abolitionism."

"Bah! the taste of that woman's blood is on every tooth in my head," said Mr. Irwin; can you tell me how to get rid of it? I would not live a week with such a horrible feeling over me, as I have this morning, for all the offices together that the government can give. I am sick."

"But it is your own fault that you are sick; you alone are to blame for it. Judges of the Supreme court were there, and they are not sick; members of Congress were there—they are not sick; even clergymen were there, and not one of them is sick. It must be your own fault that you have such queer tastes. You will be in favor of abolishing slavery in this District before long."

"I am in favor of it now," said Mr. Irwin. "It is of no benefit to any people to aid them in sin."

CHAPTER XXVIII.

AARON'S DEATH.

On the second day after they went to the grave, the sun rose beautifully bright; a few clouds were driven by the wind across the face of the sky; a breeze murmured through the leaves, and all was as balmy as a day in early spring. But Aaron was suffering intensely. He asked Mr. Reed to read one more passage in the Bible, and told him the place. Mr. Reed turned to it, and his eyes so filled with tears while he read, that he could hardly do so. It was: "The Lord hear thee in the day of trouble. The name of the God of Israel defend thee; send thee help from the sanctuary, and strengthen thee out of Zion."

Aaron then gave him his Bible. Mr. Reed thanked him for the present, and has ever since kept it as a sacred treasure. He looked over its pages and saw some writing on the blank leaves. Aaron told him he wrote it at his wife's request. She had been charged with murdering a child, of which she was innocent, and what he wrote was her statement of the matter. It covered all the blank leaves of the book, and was so badly written and so blotted that he could not read enough of it to understand it.

About noon of that day Aaron seemed to be much better; indeed Mr. Reed thought he would recover. He still had fever but his face was calm, and bore but few traces of pain. He talked of Lucy, and of the Bible, and of freedom, and of God and his hopes of heaven. He continually exhorted Mr. Reed to prepare for what he called life in earnest. He said, he forgave all who had wronged him; even those who had murdered his child. After awhile his agony returned. Then after a struggle he slept,—he slept,—

"And the sunshine of heaven burst bright on his waking,
And the song that he heard, was the seraphim's song."

The hunter went to his tent, and brought with him a spade, and some boards and clothing; with these he prepared the body of Aaron for the grave which he dug. He laid his body out, close by the side of Lucy's grave; and then, after taking some refreshment, prepared himself to pass the night as a watcher, by the corpse. He sat down on the trunk of a fallen tree with his back resting against a projecting limb, and there, wrapped up in his cloak by the side of a small fire, passed, what to him was one of the most serious and eventful nights of his life.

As the cold, stiff body of Aaron, dressed in white, was lying upon the ground, with his face toward the sunrise, the night dews gathered thickly over it, and a bright and beautiful star came out from heaven and looked down upon it, and trembled as it looked, and then passed on bearing the story of his wrongs to eternity. Another and another star came out, and each looked down on the corpse, as with the eye of an archangel, and trembled and went on its course, adding the story of Aaron's sorrows to its hoarded centuries of knowledge. Our hunter thought, these stars will all fade away into endless night, and be forgotten; but for all the ages and for eternity, Aaron will live on and on, and ever and ever on, full of happiness and love.

And how great! how wonderful was the change to Aaron! But yesterday, the basest white man in the land thought himself his superior, and could treat him with scorn; to-day, as he mingled with the hosts of heaven, angels and archangels bowed with reverence, as they met him and greeted him as a brother. But yesterday a fugitive slave! to-day a king and priest unto God!

Aaron is immortal, and the hunter therefore is immortal. He always thought so, but the thought was vague, and dim, and misty; now he grasped the truth, as a man grasps a great cable in his hand. Why then struggle for immortality on earth? What do Milton, and Shakspeare, and Goëthe care now that men are reading and praising their works? The good deeds which men may leave behind them, like the long, warm, lingering glow of a summer sunset, are all the works that even the best can look back upon with interest, after they have passed into the other life.

All men are immortal, and therefore all men are equal. And the petty inequalities of the passing hour, are but as when a great host of travelers is passing along an undulating road; one for the moment may be on ground higher than his fellows, but he passes over it and is gone; another, and another take his place, and they too pass on.

Man is immortal, and this great fact lifts the rich man above his wealth, and the king above his throne, and the slave above his fetters, and places all alike on the equal platform of MAN. Wealth or position, are but the garments of a day; whether they are on or off, the MAN remains.

Our hunter looked at the body of Aaron, and remembered how often that body had been sold: here yet lay the same flesh, and bones, and heart, and brain; who would buy it now?

He renewed his fire, looked around him at the

woods, and at the slowly moving water, and wrapping his cloak about him, took his seat again and was soon asleep.

He dreamed that he was in some island in the Pacific ocean, and saw a great crowd of savages with their faces painted in streaks of red and black, and quills in their hair, dancing around an enemy slain in war; and then they cut his body into small pieces and prepared it for food. He saw the priests of their religion stand over the loathsome repast and bless the banquet.

The scene changed—he was in a great city, and passing through a market-place crowded with people: he saw a woman with a tub covered with a white cloth, on a stall. What have you for sale, my good woman? She withdrew the cloth, and showed him human feet; he passed to the next. "What have you for sale?" a cloth was removed, and he saw a tub filled with human hands; the hands of little children, and of grown up men and women; he went to the next, and was shown human hearts, some almost warm with life; he went on to the next, and a man took the cover from a hogshead, and showed it full of ghastly human heads; he passed on to the next, the woman had no tub upon her stall, nothing but a napkin wrapped up and lying before her. "And what have you for sale?" he inquired. She unfolded the napkin, and showed him a jewel brighter than the morning-star, and spotted all over with blood. "What is that, good woman?" She drew his ear close to her and whispered, "It is a human soul, and these spots on it, are the blood of Christ." He passed on to the next stall, a tall man stood at it, and a beautiful young man by his side. "What do you sell here?" "This boy is for sale, I will take a thousand dollars for him. The others that you have just seen, sell only the dead; I sell the living."

"Do you sell his soul?" he inquired.

"Certainly I do. I sell you the whole living human being, as he now stands before you, from the crown of his head, to the soles of his feet. Sell his soul! of what use would his body be to any purchaser, without his soul? His body is but the covering of his soul: the thinking, talking, working intelligence, are all that give him greater value in our market than a horse. Sell the soul! what else is there for sale here?"

"I will neither buy nor sell men's souls "said Edgar, "Christ has purchased all of them with his own blood, and they belong to him."

"Ha! ha!" shrieked the whole crowd of sellers, at the mention of that name, "We sell the souls of the slaves, and buy the souls of the purchasers. Ha! ha!" And then in the shape of fiends they vanished from his sight.

He awoke; a screech-owl was seated on the limb over his head, shrieking Ha! ha!

He got down from his seat and renewed his fire, and walked about thinking all the while of his strange dream. "Is our state of civilization so low that some grave Senators whom the world delights to honor, are in truth but little in advance of the South-sea savage, with a fish-bone stuck through the cartilage of his nose, and eagles' feathers in his uncombed hair, and his face bedaubed with streaks of black and red paint? Is this the light in which posterity will view them? would some ministers too bless a cannibal feast? Where is the essential difference between the man who eats human flesh, and the one who buys and sells it? and who buys and sells the souls of his fellow-men, all spotted with the blood of their Redeemer?" He was young and inexperienced, and could see no difference. And he thought too, "Christianity abolished cannibalism in many islands of the South-sea, within a few years after the Gospel was preached to their inhabitants. Why has it not abolished the cannibalism of the United States? the selling of men, and women, and children in public markets, and in open day? "The reason may be," he said, "that savages were ignorant and poor, and the truth was preached fearlessly to them, while the slave dealers are rich and some of them intelligent, and awe the preachers into silence and submission."

With this dream and these thoughts the night wore away so rapidly, that he was surprised when the gray dawn of the morning broke upon him. He placed Aaron's body in the grave and withdrew to his tent.

He hurried his preparations for departure, set fire to the pile of brushwood, and the signal soon brought the men and boat to take him away. His success in hunting fully answered his highest hopes. The men took down his tent, and carried whatever was worth taking care of to the boat. When all was ready, he told them to wait for him a few minutes. He then made his last visit to the graves of Aaron and Lucy. The hot sunshine rested upon them, and the spider had woven her web over them. All was still as in the night—all was silent as the graves before him. He felt as if a friend had left him, but not forever—Oh no! not forever!

CHAPTER XXIX.

THE HUNTER.

EDGAR found Mr. Talbot still at the wood-yard, with the same cordial greeting, and frank hospitality, and eager inquiry for news. He told Edgar that he could get nearly as good a price for his venison and other game from some trading boat, as at New Orleans. He did not want to return to that place, because *he had deliberately made up his mind never to set up another type in any printing-office that sustained or apologized for the slavery of man.*

In a few hours a boat on its passage to New Orleans, stopped at the woodyard, and Edgar sold out his whole stock of game and hunting-gear to the clerk of the boat.

Soon afterward it began to rain; the hours hung heavily upon him until about nine o'clock at night, when he was cheered by seeing the lights, and hearing the sounds of a boat ascending the river. He held up a blazing torch, the bell of the boat rang out her answer to his signal, and in a few moments after taking leave of his host, he was on board. It was raining, and cold, and dark, when he got on the boat, and the change of scene was like passing into a fairy land. The boat was gorgeous as the palace of an eastern prince, blazing with lights, and decorated with vases of fresh flowers. Mirth and music, and a party of young people dancing, filled the cabin. Dazzled and half stunned, Edgar stood alone in the crowd looking upon the scene. Before he recovered from his surprise, a vision so full of grace and beauty swam before his sight, that his senses reeled as he gazed at the lovely object.

It was a girl in the full, ripe bloom of early womanhood, taller and larger than women generally are, with clear dark skin and exquisitely chiseled Grecian features, large lustrous black eyes that swam in liquid tenderness; her half-parted lips disclosed a set of teeth, even, and white as ivory. She stood at the entrance of the ladies' cabin, apart from the dancers, with her right foot extended and gently leaning as she looked at them. Her only ornament, a half-blown moss-rose carelessly placed in her hair, black as the raven's wing; her air of gentleness and purity, filled the atmosphere around her; sorrow and meek resignation spread over her oval face, and told too plainly that her heart was filled with grief.

While he was almost involuntarily gazing at her, a gentleman touched his elbow.

"Mr. Reed, I believe! I have not seen you on the boat before; when did you get on?"

"Oh, Mr. Ives! I am glad to meet you. I got on at the wood-yard, not ten minutes ago. I have been two weeks on a hunting excursion, and have seen the face of but one white person during that whole time, until I came on the boat. I am on my way to Pittsburgh."

"I am very glad of it, I shall have your company as far as we go; but we leave at Guyandotte, and will go across the state of Virginia to Richmond."

"Who is that beautiful young lady standing just in the shade of the door, at the entrance of the ladies' cabin?"

"That lady near the door, in a dove-colored silk dress with flounces, is Miss Mary Scott, sir."

"No," said Edgar, "she is not the lady; I mean the one near her, plainly dressed in black silk. She is wonderfully beautiful."

"Oh, that is Belle! Miss Scott's attendant."

"What is her name?" said Mr. Reed.

"Of course, Scott; as she is Mr. Scott's servant, she bears the name of her master."

"She a servant! Mr. Scott her master!" said

Mr. Reed: "Is there not a striking resemblance between her and Miss Mary Scott?"

"I have never seen any," said Mr. Ives drily, "and I have been acquainted with both of them since they were children. Miss Mary Scott has blue eyes and soft, brown hair; she is small. Belle has black eyes and black hair, and is large. Both have fine features, it is true, but they are very greatly unlike each other."

"It is no uncommon thing," said a gentleman who was standing by them, "for a master to have servants that greatly resemble his own children."

"It is not," said Mr. Ives, "but in this instance I have never observed any such likeness."

"I saw it but for an instant," said Edgar, "and now upon looking again, I can see nothing of it. It was an instant flash, and is gone."

"You seem to think Belle beautiful," said Mr. Ives. "She is so, but you have not seen a woman for two weeks till now, and of course they appear to better advantage than if you had not been so long deprived of their society."

The party danced on long after Edgar had retired to his stateroom and was asleep.

The next morning a group that formed a circle around a man in the cabin, were listening to his remarks; some with half suppressed pleasure;

others, with surprise at his boldness, and others, with anger.

Mr. Ives and Edgar went forward, to see and hear the cause of the excitement.

A middle-aged and intelligent looking man was standing in the midst of the crowd, the object of their attention.

"I tell you," said a gentleman to him: "it will not do to talk so here; you may *think* as you please, but it is, I assure you, really unsafe to express such thoughts."

The man raised himself to his utmost height, and fixing his eyes, glowing like coals of fire, upon the person who addressed him, slowly said in a clear, firm voice, "I am a free man. The right of free speech, is an inalienable and (speaking the words with strong emphasis,) an *unquestionable* right. I can no more surrender it, than I can annihilate my own soul. If my right of free speech conflicts with your slavery, one or the other of them must give way; and as I claim that my right is absolute, you have but one thing to do—take your slavery out of the way."

"Yes," said the first speaker, "but the slaves are our property, and such language as you are using, endangers our rights to what lawfully belongs to us. You have no more right to place our property or our safety at hazard, than we have to place yours. But go on, we 'll hear you out, and see what you have to say."

"I have but one thing to say," said the man, speaking calmly and slowly, "and it is this; Jesus Christ has said, 'whatsoever ye do to one of the least of these my disciples, ye do to me.' He has promised on the one hand, that he who gives to one of them a cup of water, shall not lose his reward; and on the other, he has threatened that whosoever shall offend one of them, it were better for him that a millstone were hanged about his neck and he were cast into the sea.

"He has established it as a principle of his government, that his disciples, and especially those of them who are poor, ignorant, needy, or in persecution or distress, shall stand as his representatives—as you treat *them* you treat HIM; and as it would be a sin, a blasphemy to make Jesus Christ a SLAVE, it is also a sin to make slaves of his poor disciples."

The gentleman then made his way through the crowd, and went to his stateroom.

Mr. Scott, who was present, walked quickly away. Others of the crowd sat down at a table, and commenced playing cards. Edgar was standing by the side of Mr. Ives while this litle scene was passing, and as he turned to say something to him, saw that his face was pale, and his brow shadowed with deep thought.

"What is the matter, sir?" said Edgar. "Are you unwell?"

"Oh no, sir, not at all! but that thought we have just heard, has startled me. It is, to me at least, a new view of the subject."

They parted; Mr. Ives went into the ladies' cabin—Edgar, to another part of the boat.

About the middle of the afternoon, Edgar saw Mr. Ives standing thoughtfully alone. He rallied him upon his gravity. Mr. Ives replied, "Indeed I am serious; I cannot, even if I wished to do so, get rid of the thought we heard this morning. It haunts me like an accompanying spirit. I have been examining it, and tracing it in its details and results. I have always thought that principle in the government of our Saviour, one of the clearest proofs of his supernatural authority and goodness, that the whole narrative of his life affords us. If I entertained a doubt of the truth of the Christian religion, this principle would remove that doubt."

"Why so?" said Mr. Reed.

"It was," said Mr. Ives, "comparatively of but little value to the disciples who lived with him. As they became identified with him, their sufferings increased. And so it continued, for a century and more after his death. He must then have looked far into the future. He knew that his person would be venerated and intensely loved. He intended to transfer this veneration to his disciples, as a protection and blessing. This piercing and accurate foreknowledge, proves him divine; and this protection for his disciples, proves him infinitely good. By this provision, he has girdled the whole earth with a blessing, that rests, at all times, upon the most needy and the most deserving."

"But what," said Mr. Reed, "is there new in this matter, that it should excite you? I have read it a hundred times, and you seem to be familiar with it."

"There is nothing novel in the principle; it is as old as Christianity, and has been held as a doctrine by all churches, from the beginning of the christian system to the present time. However much men may have differed upon the doctrines of Christianity, there never has been, so far as I have heard, any difference whatever upon this subject. It is its application to the negro race, that has startled me. I have lived with persons of that race all my life, and have read from infancy this Testament, and yet until this day, the thought has never occurred to me that this great principle is applicable to them."

Mr. Bridgeman, the gentleman who had made the remark, now came in view. "Let us," said Mr. Reed, "enter into conversation with him, perhaps he will startle you again, by some other new application of an old truth."

They went to him, and alluded to what he had said in the morning. "I have," he replied," no wish to annoy any one, by conversation on a subject which may be disagreeable. My right of free speech was questioned, and I determined to assert it at the very time and place, when it was disputed. I have said all that I wish to say on that subject."

"You have said a great deal," said Mr. Ives.

Mr. Bridgeman looked at him calmly and said: "Yes; I felt an impulse to say it, that I thought wrong to resist; and I would have said it, even if I had been thrown into the river the next moment. I hope it will be received in the same spirit in which it was made."

Mr. Bridgeman and Mr. Ives looked at each other steadily, after he had spoken, and Ives again said: "You have said a great deal sir. I do not as yet fully comprehend it; it cannot be done in a day; but simple as the thought appears, it may change and color my whole future life."

Mr. Bridgeman said: "Yes, it may do more

than that; it may color and control your eternal life."

The boat rapidly ascended the river. One day Mr. Reed passed by Mr. Ives, who was sitting at a table in the cabin, with a pen in his hand, and paper on which he had been writing lying before him.

"I see sir," said Mr. Reed to him, "that you give yourself but little rest, even when you are traveling."

"I did not mean to tax my brain with much thought," replied Mr. Ives; "but the remark made by the gentleman several days ago, has been so strongly impressed upon my mind, that I cannot avoid tracing out upon paper, the principle and its application to the colored race. It seems to me, that truth alone, has sufficient power to overthrow the whole system of American slavery."

"Slavery has existed in this country two hundred years, and it has not yet done so," repliod Mr. Reed.

"True, but the truths of Christianity have not been applied to slavery in the two hundred years, otherwise it could not have withstood their power," said Mr. Ives.

One afternoon, Mr. Reed saw Mr. Ives standing on the side of the boat next to the Ohio shore, and approached him. He did not observe until he got near him, that two ladies were with him, Miss Mary Scott and Belle.

"That is the State of Ohio," said Mary to Mr. Ives, and then turning to Belle she said, "you know, of course, that it is a free state."

"I know that Ohio is a free state, but did not know until now, that the land I am looking at, is the State of Ohio."

She gave one long, lingering look, at the land before her. Her eyes filled with tears, and to conceal them she went into the cabin.

CHAPTER XXX.

MR. AND MRS. LEATHERS.

Two months after the wedding of Bennett Leathers, Colonel Moore, a venerable gentleman long a citizen of Willoughby, about ten o'clock in the morning, cane in hand, was seen walking composedly up the avenue that led to the mansion of Mrs. Tullis, now Mrs. Leathers. His portly person was well dressed, and on his face was a calm benevolent smile. He was, as he deserved to be, at peace with himself and with all the world.

Mrs. Leathers had been his tenant since the death of Mr. Tullis. Three days before, another year's rent (eight hundred dollars) became due; but with that delicate respect which becomes a gentleman, Colonel Moore had deferred his call, to avoid even the appearance of haste.

The shutters in the front of the house were closed, but although the Colonel observed it, it did not attract his especial attention. It was early, quite early, and as Mr. Leathers was not yet in business, there was no necessity for rising sooner. His wife too was rich; time therefore was of less value to him than it is to some others less fortunate in life.

He rang the bell, and was surprised to find that the noise was so loud, from the very gentle pull he gave it.

He paused, and then turning round, buttoned his coat tighter around his neck, took off his hat and smoothed it with his glove.

No one came.

He rang again, gently as he could, but again the sound was much louder than he intended to make.

He stood now longer than before, and looked upon the leafless shrubbery in the lawn.

Still all was silent.

He rang again, harder than before, and then stood for a moment; then he went out upon the pavement before the door. The calm, benevolent look had left his face. His cane was tucked under his arm. Upon looking around, he saw the shutter of a window in the second story of the adjoining house partly opened, and a female's face looking out.

He raised his eyes and hat to the lady. "Your neighbors are late risers, madam?"

"I do not know that sir, I think they are all awake."

"I have rung the bell three times, madam, and no person has yet answered my call."

"A very good reason for that, sir, they have all moved away."

"Moved, madam! moved away!" said Colonel Moore, striking the end of his cane upon the pavement. "They gave me no notice of their intention to do so. When did they move, madam?"

"I really don't know sir. They were here a week ago to-morrow, I am sure; the next day the house was still, and I have not seen them since."

"What, madam! run away?"

"I can't say that, sir. I have told you all that I know."

"I'll follow them to the ends of the earth!" striking the end of his cane hard on the pavement.

"I think, sir, that is as good a place as any other, to search for them."

"Did you observe them making any preparations to go off, madam?"

"Yes, sir. They were sending their fine furniture out by the alley to a vessel at the wharf, for four or five days before they went away."

"What induced them to go, madam? Mrs. Leathers had a large fortune."

"I do not know, sir. I heard Mr. Leathers say, it was wrong for a gentleman to squander his wife's fortune, in payment of her debts: and they have been a good deal troubled with bills lately."

And now, good reader, we ask you to mark with what frankness we state this fault of Mr. Leathers. Biographers sometimes draw a vail over blemishes in the conduct of their heroes: but this we shall not do. The practice is a bad one. The reader cannot mark the growth of the inner life of the person whose character he may be carefully studying; he cannot note as he should, the upward or downward course, unless he is furnished, at least, with the leading facts, that are steps upon the ladder of ascent or descent. But as we have stated this fact, it is but fair to Mr. Leathers and his friends, that we state also the circumstances that accompanied it.

A month had hardly passed after his marriage, before Mr. Leathers was called to the door to receive a bill. Bills from the jeweler; bills from the milliner; bills from half-a-dozen dressmakers; bills from the grocer; bills from the confectioner; bills from the baker; bills from the dentist; bills from the doctor; bills from the lawyer; bills for pew rent; for water-rent; from everybody, and for everything.

Mr. Leathers, of course, knew nothing about them. They were referred to his wife, and that amiable lady declared that each one of them was wrong; some of them she said, were for articles that she had never ordered, others for articles she had ordered, but never received; some, she said, she had paid; others were too high—none too low.

It seemed as if every man in Willoughby was dishonestly trying to ruin Mrs. Leathers.

When the first bills came, Mr. Leathers paid them promptly, and said to his wife, "It's better—much better to do so, my dear, than to be annoyed with these kind of people." The lady was silent, but not satisfied. The payment of one bill, however, seemed to be as one blow upon a hornet's nest. The whole swarm was out buzzing about him and stinging him. He continued to pay, till one day Mrs. Leathers gently remarked, "It is much easier to waste money, my dear, than to earn it."

"A very profound observation, my dear, and it does great credit to your intellect," said Mr. Leathers. "Indeed it does. But what shall I do? they will warrant me if I don't pay."

"Let them warrant," said Mrs. Leathers. And the warrants came thick and fast.

Mr. Leathers defended the suits, and found to his surprise, that from some cause all the magistrates and courts were prejudiced against him. He thought, perhaps, that it was because he had married a merchant's widow. (He could not say negro merchant, the word stuck in his throat.) He had lost his position, and hence was persecuted. He abandoned further defenses in despair; and said to his wife: "I see, my dear Martha, that Willoughby is no place for us. Let us go where we can enjoy our own in peace. I cannot stand by and see a dear, confiding wife robbed; robbed before my face under the forms of law; robbed, my dear, with impunity! It does not become a gentleman to do so."

CHAPTER XXXI.

THE ESCAPE.

The boat had passed Cincinnati, and was rapidly approaching Guyandotte, where Mr. Scott and his party were to land. It stopped, for some purpose, on the Ohio shore. Edgar was reading in the cabin, when he observed an unusual excitement among the people on board; men were running to and fro, and women looked alarmed, as if some great calamity had happened. He was told that some slaves had escaped from the boat. Parties were set ashore to hunt the fugitives. After an absence of an hour, a shout was raised, and Edgar saw with horror two men dragging Belle to the boat. Another woman came sulkily along with her captors. Belle looked the very image of despair; her eyes were swollen; her face pale as ashes; her limbs all trembling, so as scarcely to support her. But before they reached the boat, another party came forward and asserted that the captors had no right to take the fugitives (even if they were such) from the state, unless an examination was first had before a commissioner, and his certificate obtained to authorize them to do so. After much altercation, this claim was acceded to. A commissioner lived in the village, his warrant was signed, and the case was set down for hearing

Mr. Williams, the commissioner, was apparently about thirty years of age, a member of the legal profession, whose talents, from his modesty, were not yet so far appreciated as to afford him a living practice. Hence it was that he was willing to accept an office which, though humble, yielded him once in a great while five or ten dollars, as the case might be.

The alleged fugitives were brought into the court, and the commissioner, seated on the bench, commanded an officer in a rather supplicating tone, and with a familiar look, to provide seats for the crowd that thronged the hall of justice.

A citizen requested, on behalf of the alleged fugitives, that the proceedings should be delayed for a short time, till they could find an attorney who would attend to the case. This delay was granted with a condescending smile and wave of the hand, which seemed designed to impress upon all, that the commissioner was at heart a most gracious and benevolent gentleman.

After a short time they returned accompanied by John Peters, Esq., an attorney of the village, who stated that he had been retained for Belle and the woman Katy, and would soon be ready for the trial.

Mr. Ives went into the court-house, to which they had taken the captives. It seemed as if the light of hope had fled from Belle forever. Her face was pale, and her eyes fixed as in death. At first she did not observe Mr. Ives, but looked with a vacant stare round the room; then, as if she was slowly recovering her consciousness, she looked steadily at him. He went up and spoke to her soothingly and kindly. In an instant the fountain of her tears was unsealed, and she wept, and groaned aloud. All were silent spectators of her grief; even the rude men who had arrested her, seemed awed, in the presence of her overwhelming sorrow. She said, "Oh Mr. Ives, do help me! I am here among strangers, except Mr. Scott and his friends, and they, you know, are trying to take me back into slavery. You are the only person on earth, to whom I can look with confidence for help."

Mr. Ives turned pale, and then in a low voice, so that none but Belle could hear him, said: "Do you not know, Belle, that if I take your part in this controversy, it will utterly ruin me."

"I know that you are engaged to Miss Mary, at least I have no doubt of it, but she cannot be angry with you for standing by me in an hour of affliction, and doing all that you honestly can do, to aid me. Oh, Mr. Ives! I feel in my heart of hearts, that I have the right to be free. I have always had an undefined, but strong impression that I was born free, and have in some way that I cannot account for, been wrongfully deprived of my liberty."

"All slaves have such impressions, I believe," replied Mr. Ives.

"That may be, but I believe, I am of right free. I had rather die, than go back into slavery. I had rather be blown into powder fine as snow, than be taken across that river," pointing to the Ohio.

"Belle, I am sorry for you, but if I do undertake your defense in this case, it will work in an instant the utter ruin of all my hopes of honor, wealth, and happiness in this life. I would ever thereafter, be an exile from the state of my birth, and the graves of my fathers. And I will have to begin life anew, among people whose customs, thoughts, and feelings are widely different from my own; you know too, that Mr. Scott never forgives."

"Oh! I know it all, Mr. Ives. I would not ask you, if more than my life did not depend upon your aid. You can save me. Oh, for Christ's sake, do so!"

Mr. Ives reeled at the word, as if he had been

struck a heavy blow. "I would not do it for any fee, nor for all the honors of earth, for I know that it will blast my hopes of happiness, at the very place where those hopes are garnered; but I will do it for the sake of Christ."

Mr. Ives took Mr. Peters aside, and informed him, that he would aid him in the defense of Belle. He also told Mr. Scott, that he would do so.

"What, sir! you who have been my legal adviser for years; you turn against me? I did not expect this from you."

"Nor did I expect it. I regret that it is my duty, to take her side of the case, and apparently to disoblige you; but I have determined to do so, sir," laying strong emphasis on the word determined.

"Very well, sir. Your determinations are of course, in your own power. I cannot but regret your course, as it will deprive myself and all the members of my family, from ever again enjoying the great pleasure we have so often had in your society."

"You, sir, and the members of your family, will of course be controlled by your own views of propriety," replied Mr. Ives, "and whatever may be your future conduct toward me, I shall always look back upon the hours I have passed under your roof, with gratitude and pleasure."

"Good evening, sir," said Mr. Scott; "of course you will not accompany us to Richmond."

"Certainly not, sir. Adieu."

Mr. Ives stated to the commissioner, that he could not be ready to argue the case until the next day: it was postponed the more readily, because Mr. Scott had not yet had time to employ a lawyer. Belle and her fellow fugitive were ordered to jail, and the boat went on her way. Mr. Scott remained to attend the trial, with a Mr. Watts, who had been for many years an overseer of Mr. Scott's, and who was needed as a witness.

At nine o'clock the next morning, the alleged fugitives were again brought into the court, now closely crowded by people from the village, and the surrounding country. All of the spectators seemed to take a lively interest in the case.

Poor Belle looked haggard and care-worn. Her depression of spirits had greatly increased. Her manner, however, was more composed than it had been the day before. Sad as she was, she had still found time to bestow a little attention upon her toilet, and when seated by the side of her sable companion in suffering, every eye was fixed in admiration upon her.

The commissioner, with great apparent dignity, asked the parties if they were ready, and upon being answered that they were, he directed Mr. Scott to call his witnesses.

Mr. Scott proved by his overseer, that he had had possession of the girl Belle since she was about six years old, and that he saw a bill of sale for her in Mr. Scott's possession about sixteen years before, and soon after the girl came to his plantation.

Witnesses were then called, who stated that the girl Belle was on the boat when it landed at the village; that she left it before night, and upon search being made, was found with the other women, hid in some bushes near the village. That when her captors approached her, she endeavored to run, and when overtaken, exclaimed, "Oh! I had rather die, than live a day longer as a slave. Kill me if you please, rather than carry me back into bondage."

The claimant here said he had no further evidence, and the defendant being called upon, Mr. Ives informed the court that in his judgment no evidence was needed for the defendant, but that if it was, they had none to produce.

Mr. Scott had employed an attorney, Mr. Weston. Mr. Weston read the sections of the law of 1850, upon which he relied, and stated that the evidence in the case, seemed to make it too plain for argument, and therefore he would submit the case to the judgment of the commissioner.

CHAPTER XXXII.

MARY SCOTT.

Our lady readers wish, of course, to know as soon as possible, the views of Mary Scott respecting the conduct of Mr. Ives, and we must anticipate a little the course of events, to inform them.

Mary Scott went on with some friends to Willoughby, leaving her father to attend to the lawsuit.

Mr. Ives, upon whom she had placed all her hopes of happiness in this life, had been forbidden to see her. She could but obey the command of her father. Her own heart, too, condemned the conduct of Mr. Ives. Did he not know the principles of her father? What freak of folly was it that led him, in a rash moment, to take the side of Belle? True, he was a lawyer, and could, of course, take either side of a cause, and urge whatever arguments might suggest themselves to his mind, with all the force he could on behalf of his client; but still there are limits, even to professional license; and it seemed to her that Mr. Ives had, in this instance at least, passed those limits. She had not heard his argument, but had been told by those who did hear it, that it was a tissue of rabid fanaticism—it was worse even than that—it went to the very verge of treason, and if true would dissolve this Union, and tend at least, to deluge our land with blood. Could he, so mild and quiet a gentleman, not used to excitement, of sober judgment and good sense, be recklessly guilty of all these wrongs in behalf of a servant, that the whim of that servant might be gratified, in her wish to leave the only friends she had on earth, and venture alone and uncared for among utter strangers? And then it seemed to her, that he might, at least, have consulted her views, upon a matter so momentous in its results to both of them. Why could not others have been employed in his stead? It would have been far better, she thought, if Mr. Ives had paid four or five lawyers from his own money to defend Belle, than that he should have done so himself. They could have defended her, and secured all her rights, and he would have avoided the difficulties that his rashness had brought upon his affianced and himself; would have avoided the displeasure of her father, and all the consequences that resulted from it.

In addition to all this, he had cut himself off from all hope of preferment in life; who now would vote for him to fill any office of honor? who now would retain him as an advocate? who now could trust a gentleman who had, apparently in a moment, renounced the principles in which he had been educated, and who cared so little for the opinions of his friends, as to set them at defiance.

But in the midst of all these upbraidings her heart still took the side of Henry Ives. She had known him from his childhood, and always knew him truthful and firm to his convictions of right. She knew that he scorned duplicity, and made it a maxim in his professional life, never to misrepresent either the facts or the law of any case to save even the life of his client. Could it be that he was sincere in his new views?

Could he be otherwise than sincere? What motive had he to do wrong in it? He labored without hope of reward, for one of the humblest of the human race; labored against prejudice and power; against the known opinions of his relations and friends, and all the opinions of his former life.

Was he really a fanatic? that thought was far more dreadful to her, than if she believed him to be insincere. If it was fanaticism, what had produced it? and what remedy lay within her power by means of which she could reclaim him from his folly?

She was now alone in Willoughby, with a

large estate that would, at her father's death, be hers, which she would be unable to manage. She knew that her fortune was not the attraction that had drawn him; other fortunes, greater than hers, had crossed his path, and would gladly have won his attention, but their beautiful possessors had received nothing but politeness from Henry Ives. With all her wealth she was unhappy, and would gladly have resigned it for the moments of quiet joy she had felt in the society of her lover.

Why, if he still loved her, had no letter been received from him? He might have written without compromising his self-respect. Indeed it seemed to her, that it was his duty to write.

One day while seated alone in her room, a card was brought to her, and on it "Henry Ives," and below in pencil "at the Pocahontas House—very ill, but recovering from a serious attack of brain fever." Her eyes filled as she read it again and again, and placed it carefully in her drawer; and then sat down, and again took it, and read it over and over, till every word and letter was written upon her memory: again she put it away, and again, and still again she took and read it.

What could she do? Go to his hotel and see him? propriety and self-respect forbade it; the command of her wronged father forbade it. She sat down, and thought and wept, and again read his card, "very ill." He cannot come to me. He is sick, and a stranger, and alone, and perhaps uncared for. What brought him to this city? When did he come? "Brain fever!" and again she mused and wept; and then as if half unconscious, she carefully made her toilet—hastily and carefully—and again read, "very ill," and was on her way alone to the hotel. She was soon at his side, as he lay pale upon a sofa, their hands grasped, and all—all in an instant was forgotten and forgiven. He was no longer a stranger and uncared for, for one watched over him, whose pure affection was full of health and life.

Mary learned from Mr. Ives, that after he had separated from her father, he visited a northern city, wandering restlessly and unhappily among crowds of persons, all of whom were strangers, and among scenes in which he took no interest, as there was no one to sympathize with him. Every day increased his unhappiness, and time rested heavily as a great burden upon him. He seemed to have cut himself off from the sympathies of his race. At home, all would denounce him as a traitor; and one, too, whose treason was of no common dye. He might have killed a fellow-man in a duel, and been forgiven, and even elected to posts of high honor, the highest in the United States; he might have planned and conducted an expedition to carry war into a neighboring country at peace with ours; he might have trodden under foot part of the most valuable provisions of the Constitution of the United States; he might have denied that the Bible is a revelation from God, and thus as far as he could do so, have overthrown the only true system of religion on earth, and destroyed the foundations of private and public virtue; he might have gone much farther, and denied even the very existence of God himself—and been forgiven. But for denying the dogma, that man may have property in his brother man—there is no forgiveness. The pulpit and the grog-shop; the banker and the gambler; the judge upon the bench and the thief on trial before him, would all unite with one voice and denounce him; each echoing and re-echoing the other, with varied degrees of intensity; but all—all with the same bitterness of feeling—the same detestation for him.

The friends, too, of his early childhood, the schoolboys (now men), with whom he had gathered wild fruits, and roamed on many a boyish excursion, who had been proud of him in after life, they too, with all the rest, would pity and condemn him. And beyond all this, the one whose image was ever blended with all his dreams of home and happiness in life—she who, when he thought of a white cottage, seated amid orange-groves and roses ever blooming, and shaded by great trees—she, whom he pictured standing at the door to welcome his return; oh! all is over now; nothing but a wild and dreary desert lay outstretched before him, upon whose hot sands a noonday sun was ever burning, and the few footprints upon it were filled with the blood of the pale wretches that wandered hopelessly over it.

And what had he done to merit all this. He had believed from his childhood, for he had always been taught it by his parents, and at school and at college, and from the press, and from the pulpit, and everywhere, and from every source of instruction—that it is the right of every American citizen to read, and to believe and to obey the whole Bible. He had read it, he believed it; he with faltering footsteps had tried to obey it; he had opened his mouth for the dumb, and pleaded the cause of those who had none to help. He had been a friend to the poor and needy in the hour of trial and of peril; he had, as for Christ, taken the part of one of his disciples, and endeavored to rescue the Constitution of his country from the glosses put upon it, to make good men hate and abhor it; he had endeavored, at least, to show that that Constitution is the ally and the friend, and not the foe of Christianity; that it is worthy of the patriots who framed, and worth all the toil, and suffering, and sacrifice and blood shed in the revolution, of which it is the first and best fruits.

He had tried, at least, to prove that man, however degraded, ignorant, or debased he may be, is still too noble, too great, too glorious a being to be classed with beasts. And for this—only this—he was cut off from all hopes of wealth or honor, from happiness, from home. "The sky above him was brass, and the earth beneath him iron." The very atmosphere he breathed seemed hot, and thick, and stifling. Are these thy rewards, Oh, Liberty! are these the garlands with which thy followers are crowned!

He thought still deeper. *He* had advanced no new doctrine; he had invented no truth, but had applied an old and familiar one to a new subject. He had not made the fire, but had only taken a coal from an altar, and applied it to materials prepared before him. The beauty of the blaze, the heat of the flame were from God. He saw then where the hatred really attached; not to him but to Christ; and now he *felt* that Christ, when in the world, must of necessity, have worn a crown of thorns. The light was hated, and the humble man who held the lamp; the truth was hated, and the lips that uttered it. But he knew that that light, and that truth were from Heaven; that they descended together from the throne of God.

He knew, too, that although its rays are but shooting through the darkness, like pencilings of early dawn, the hour will come when it will fill our atmosphere—wrap the whole globe, and rest upon it with unnumbered blessings. And he became calm and hopeful, and waited patiently, for surely as God lives and reigns, his law will conquer.

Unable to support his great grief alone, he started for Willoughby, but on his way was taken sick, so sick that he could with difficulty keep his seat in the cars till he reached the place. He was taken to the hotel—brain fever followed; but now he was better, happier—how could he be otherwise under such care as recently he had received. Mary, too, was glad that the presence of a friend was of so great service.

CHAPTER XXIII.

MR. IVES' SPEECH.

We shall give extracts only, from the speech of Mr. Ives.

"It is necessary that I call your attention to the Constitution of the United States, binding alike upon all of us; and which all of us are under the highest obligations to support."

He then read from the Constitution: "No person held to service or labor in one state, under the laws thereof, escaping into another, shall, in consequence of any law or regulation therein, be discharged from such service or labor; but shall be delivered up, on claim of the party to whom such service or labor may be due."

I admit that this clause was intended, by those who framed the Constitution, to apply to slaves. If it does not apply to slaves, for what purpose was it placed here? Why, in so solemn an instrument, should the Convention have descended to the detail of providing for the reclamation of apprentices, and perhaps a few other persons, escaping from those to whom their labor might be due?

This clause is to be interpreted by the same rules that are applied to all other parts of this instrument, and to treaties, and to laws. All of these rules may be summed up in a single sentence, and that is, that you are, with a fair and honest mind, from all the evidence you can obtain, both within and without the instrument, to ascertain the very mind of those who wrote, and who adopted it, so as to carry into effect the purpose for which it was written and adopted. You are, if the cause is of doubtful meaning, to look to the debates in the Convention upon it; to the reports of the committees; to the debates in the Conventions of the several states, and to the essays written for popular consideration, at the time it was submitted to the people for their suffrages. The uniform practice of the several departments of the government, from the time it was adopted till the present, is also a matter of great weight, that by no means should be overlooked.

But this clause is not the *whole* Constitution. That instrument, from abundant caution, was *amended* after it was adopted. The object of the amendments, was to guarantee the rights, and secure beyond doubt, the civil, political, and above all, the religious liberties of the people of the United States. These rights and liberties were too dear—had cost too much blood, and were so essential to the happiness of mankind, that the people determined by these amendments to secure them. They were jealous of power in the hands of fallible men. The history of our own country showed that power may be abused, to the extent even of invading liberty of conscience, and the right to worship God according to its dictates. They formed the Constitution, to secure, among other things, the blessings of civil and religious liberty to themselves and their posterity. They amended it, to make assurance doubly sure.

The first of these amendments provides, "Congress *shall make no law respecting an establishment of religion, or prohibiting the free exercise thereof*, or abridging the freedom of speech, or of the press, or the right of the people peaceably to assemble, and to petition the government for a redress of grievances."

This clause, too, must be so interpreted, as to carry into full effect the very minds of those who wrote, and who adopted it; and to secure to the uttermost extent, the several rights enumerated.

Congress then can make no law "prohibiting the free exercise of religion." No one ever doubted, that the free exercise of the Christian religion was intended to be protected and secured by this amendment. That religion was, in its different divisions, almost the only one professed by the people of the United States.

The whole people of the United States, at the time they adopted this amendment, intended to secure to each man in the Union, the right to believe in God, and to obey him; the right to read the whole Bible, and to obey every commandment in it; and from the day that it was adopted down to this hour, every citizen of the United States has claimed this right.

This cotemporaneous, and uniform, and universal construction of this amendment, cannot be wrong.

By the word "FREE," they meant the unlimited exercise of religious freedom.

What is the *free exercise* of the Christian religion?

Christ himself, has informed us: That it is to love God with all the heart, and mind, and soul, and strength; and thy neighbor as thyself. On these two commandments, hang all the law and the prophets.

The highest exercise of the Christian religion is to obey God.

Christ says, "Why call ye me Lord, Lord, and DO not the things that I say?"

The inquiry then is, do the acts of 1793, and 1850, forbid any man to do anything that the

Christian religion enjoins upon him? or, command him to do anything that Christianity forbids? For if they either forbid or command any act inconsistent with loving God with the whole heart, and our neighbor as ourselves, they are contrary to the true intent and meaning of the amendment, and are nullities. And if so, it is the duty of every man in the United States, and especially of those who have sworn to support the Constitution; to maintain it, by insisting, both by example and precept, that the laws which are opposed to it are void; were so from the instant they were framed.

I know that it is often said that the Constitution was never intended to be applied to slaves. It makes no difference in this argument, whether this is so or not. It was certainly intended to apply to, and protect the President of the United States, the judges of the Supreme court, members of both branches of Congress, to all the officers of the government, and to every citizen of the several states of the Union.

Its application to such officers and persons, has never been doubted.

Has Congress, by either of the acts in question, commanded YOU to do any act inconsistent with your duties as a Christian?

* * * * *

Slave-holding is sin.

It is the claim by one man, to hold another man as his property, in such manner, as that the master has the power to compel the slave to involuntary labor during his whole life, without return for his labor; and to make the will of the master, the rule by which the conduct of the slave shall be guided and controlled.

The Bible does not, as a treatise on natural theology, first prove that there is a God; and then, having proved that fact, go on to state what he has done. It assumes it as an unquestionable fact; its first line is, "In the beginning God made the heavens and the earth."

Nor does it assert that all men have rights. That, too, is assumed as unquestionable as the existence of God. It forbids man to worship idols, assuming that he has it in his power to worship them or not. It commands men to remember and keep holy the Sabbath-day, taking it for granted, that his own will controls his conduct. It commands men to bring up their children in the nurture and admonition of God; because it recognizes, as the only true position of parents, the one in which they have the control of their own offspring. And so from the beginning to the end of the book, its every page is addressed to men in the condition of freemen, and not in the condition of slaves. It is then just as true that all men are by nature entitled to freedom, as it is that there is a God.

* * * * *

God is the Creator of the world, and all that are in it. It was *his* world on the day that he made it, and must be his world forever.

He made day and night, and man has no power to change them.

He made summer and winter, cold and heat, seed-time and harvest, and man has no power to change them.

He made those things that are property for man, and made man, and established his relations to property, to his fellow-man, and to himself; and man has no power to change these relations.

He read: "And God said, Let us make man in our image, after our likeness; and let them have dominion over the fish of the sea, and over the fowls of the air, and over the cattle, and over all the earth, and over every creeping thing that creepeth upon the earth.

"So God created man in his own image—in the image of God created he him, male and female created he them."

Here the distinction between man and property is clearly marked, and accurately defined.

Man is made in the image or likeness of God

God has given to man dominion over the fish of the sea, over the fowls of the air, and over the cattle and over all the earth, and over every creeping thing, that creepeth upon the earth.

This was made to Adam, as the father and representative of the whole race.

From the creation of man to this hour, in all ages, and among all nations, man has been everywhere, the Lord of all things in this world. From the naked negro lying in the palm tree's shade, to the Esquimaux tumbling amid the ice-drifts of the polar sea, all are alike conscious, although untaught, that man is master of the beasts of the field, and of all the earth. The lion cowers beneath his gaze, and shrinks trembling from his presence; the eagle flies affrighted at his approach, and the whale dives to the bottom of the ocean, to seek in its caves a hiding-place from his superior power.

In civilized life, the lightning obeys his call; comes from its home in the thunder-cloud, crouches as a spaniel at his feet, and flies at his command, the meek and silent messenger of his will.

The things that God has given to man for property, are property in all places on the earth, and have been property in all ages, and will be property to the end of the world. *He* stamped with his own right hand, the impress of property upon them, deeper than the footprints of gigantic birds on old rocks, and that impress remains forever.

When the horse in battle loses his rider; when treasures of an unknown owner, are cast by shipwreck upon the shore, or when the owner, tired of his property, throws it away, the finder may seize the waif or the estray, and take it to his own use.

If therefore the black man is property, he must always be so. If the present owner shall abandon his claim, the next finder may seize him, and subject him to his ownership. The emancipated slave may indeed roam like the wild horse in the desert, but is subject to be re-captured and subdued, as is the wild horse, by the first man who can seize him.

States and nations may make laws to secure men in their rights to property; but they have neither created property, nor conferred upon man the right to hold it. Men held property before they made laws.

The distinction between man and property, is as wide, and as impassable, as is the distinction between men and beasts. God has made a great gulf between them, wider than the earth, and deeper than hell. Property can never be made man, and man can never be made property. As it is certain that man cannot be made a beast, it is equally certain that man never can have property in man.

Legislation has indeed *declared* that some men are property, but God has stamped all such legislation, through his revealed Word, as a great LIE. Legislation has sometimes declared that Christ is not the Saviour of the world. That also, he has stamped AS A LIE.

Men have *the power* to enslave their fellow-men. So, too, they have the power to cut off their limbs, to put out their eyes, to shut them up in dungeons, to rob and murder them. Sometimes this is done under law, and sometimes without law, and against law. The existence of the power therefore, does not even tend to prove the right so to exercise it. The power to kill a man, is no proof of the right to do so; and the power to enslave a man, is no proof whatever of the right to do so. From the very nature of man as a free moral agent, he has the power to sin; but to claim that he has the right to sin, is simply to annihilate the distinction between good and evil, right and wrong.

* * * * *

God gave to the black man eyes, he therefore has the right to see.

HE gave him ears, therefore he has the right to hear.

He gave him a tongue, therefore he has the right to speak. He gave him hands and feet, and therefore he has the right to use his limbs.

God also gave him intellect, will, reason, judgment, passions, affections, feelings, and therefore he has the right to *will*, to reason, to judge, and to control his own conduct by their guidance, as fully as he has the right to walk by the vision of his own eyes. The master has no right to put out the eyes of his slave, and therefore has no right to crush or to control his will.

When man claims property in his fellow-man, where is his warrant? He has all the right to the things of this earth that God has given him, and no more. Where, then, is the authority by which one man can have the right to hold another man as property? It is not in the Bible.

Thou shalt love thy neighbor as thyself. Why? Because thy neighbor's rights are equal to thy own.

Do unto others as you would that others should do unto you; because, as your rights are equal, the measure of your duties is also equal.

And it is only by bursting through these walls of fire, and trampling these laws under foot; and stopping his ears to the voice of the Lord God speaking in thunder, that any man can seize his fellow, and deprive him of the rights that these commandments have conferred upon him.

There *is* a distinction between legislation and tyranny. The province of legislation is to protect men in their rights. "Governments are instituted for the good of the governed." Tyranny strikes down the rights of man. The distinction is as wide as the difference between right and wrong; the whole moral world rolls between them.

It may be as difficult to know the precise point where legislative power ends, and tyranny begins, as it may be for the late traveler to know when daylight has ceased; but he knows it is night, when he is groping in thick darkness.

Slave-holding is tyranny, because it deprives a man of all his rights: if it is not so, the word has either no meaning, or has been misapplied in all ages and among all men, and there can be no such thing as tyranny on earth.

You cannot surrender a fugitive slave without recognizing the rightfulness of the claim of the master to the services of the slave. All the fugitive-slave-laws, assume as their basis, that the claim of the master to the person of the slave, is a rightful claim.

The whole system of slavery, and the fugitive slave-acts—which are intended to sustain and secure that system—proceed upon the theory that slave-holding is not a sin. The Bible teaches us that it is sin; and this first amendment, guarantees to us the right to treat it as sin.

A slave is an article of property; may be bought and sold; can own nothing of this world's lands or goods; may have his wife separated from him forever; may have his children one by one sold before his eyes, into returnless bondage; he cannot learn to read even the name of God; may not, except at the will of his master, go up to worship God in his sanctuary!

As a MAN, he is an immortal being; and it is our duty, and our right to treat him as a MAN. Others may disregard this duty, and deny this right; others may treat him, if they dare, as property; but with our Bible in our hands, we cannot do so. The light that burns as of polished gold, upon all its pages, teaches us too clearly for doubt, that he is a MAN.

When God commands a man to do a thing, he gives him the right to do it.

He commanded Daniel to pray. The power of the Persian empire forbade him; but he prayed: and God by a miracle sanctioned his conduct.

He commanded the three holy children not to worship idols; they were commanded by the Persian king to do so; and God by a miracle sustained them in refusing to obey the king.

Christ commanded the apostles to preach the Gospel; they were forbidden to do so by the Jews, whom they refused to obey; and God by miracles sanctioned their conduct.

The whole Christian world has applauded this conduct of Daniel, and of the three holy children, and of the apostles for more than eighteen centuries; so that we have the direct sanction of God, and the unanimous voice of all the civilized world for ages upon ages, sustaining the principle, that what God commands men to do, He gives them the right to do.

* * * * *

Here then lies the radical difference between the one theory and the other. God never created a soul for slavery—nor a body, the mere habitation of the soul—to wear its shackles. The immortal being, swells beyond the limits of the fetters that encompass him; bursts them, as straw, into fragments. He walks with the sunlight of God upon his brow, and hosts of unseen angels cluster around him.

It is *our right;* the right of all the citizens of the United States; born with us as men, and secured, and guaranteed, and established by the wisdom of our fathers in this first amendment to the Constitution, to tret the fugitive *as a man.*

We dare not relinquish this right. It is part of our own immortality. We can no more relinquish it, than we can destroy our own souls. It is sacred, it came down from God out of Heaven. To relinquish it for a moment, is treason to our country, and apostasy from God. No, by the battle-fields of our revolution, and the blood of our fathers shed upon them; by the blood of each holy martyr, from the dawn of creation to this hour; by our love for the Bible, and the great truths it teaches; by the graves of our mothers, who taught us to read and love it, and by the holy dust that slumbers within their coffins; by every tie that can bind man to man, and man to his God; we cannot, we must not, we dare not, we will not relinquish for a moment only, this great right.

If an act of Congress commanded *you* to worship an idol; such act would be, by the Constitution itself, but a nullity. If an act of Congress commanded you not to pray, as Daniel was commanded; the act would be but void.

If Congress commanded you, as the early Christians were commanded, to burn but a single grain of incense at the altar of Cæsar; *you* might with impunity, as they did, at the loss of their lives, spurn the command.

If Congress forbids any man to preach the gospel, as the apostles were forbidden; such act would be void.

All of these examples, and a thousand more,

were familiar to the men who prepared and who adopted this amendment.

If the act required a commissioner to aid a robber in his robbery, it would be clearly void, for robbery is sin.

If it required him to guard the spoil of the pirate, or the robber, or to aid the robber in guarding it, it would be clearly void.

If it required him to condemn innocent men, not even charged with crime, into imprisonment for ten years in the penitentiary, it would be clearly void; because the act of condemnation would be sin.

If it required him to tear a husband from his wife, or the wife from the husband, it would be clearly void, for such act is sinful. God has said, "Let not man put asunder, whom God hath joined."

If it required him to tear the child from the parent, it would be clearly void, for the relation is established by God as an incident to that of marriage.

If it required him to defraud the laborer of his wages, or to withhold the wages from the laborer, the act would be a sin: so, too, is it a sin to aid or assist another to do the same wrong.

If it required him to deny to any man the right to keep holy the Sabbath day, it would be void; and so too it is, if it requires him to aid another man to do so.

If it required him to oppress any man, it would be void; and so too if it requires him to aid another man in his oppression.

If it required him to degrade human nature as far as he could do so, to the condition and level of the brute, it would be void; or to aid any other man to do so.

If it required him to deny that God created man in his own image, a little lower than the angels, and crowned him with glory and honor, the act would be void.

If the act required him to deny the authority of Christ to make the law, "Thou shalt love thy neighbor as thyself," it would be void.

If it allowed him to admit the authority to make such law, but commanded him to disregard it, or to aid another man in disregarding and contemning it, it would be void.

If it required him to be a respecter of persons in judgment, it would be void, for such act is sin.

If it required him to take the side of the oppressor, against the right of the poor and needy, and the oppressed, the act would be void; for such conduct is sin.

If it required him to sustain by his conduct, the dogma that man can have property in his fellow-man, it would be void; for that doctrine is as dishonoring to God, and as injurious to man as any that ever has existed on earth; and Congress can no more compel a man to recognize the rightfulness of this doctrine in his official or private conduct, than they can compel him to recognize the doctrine of transubstantiation.

If it required him to commit upon an innocent man, not even charged with crime, an act of great cruelty; as to put out his eyes, or to aid another man to do so, it would be void; and so, too, would it be void, upon the same principle, if it required him to aid another to crush the will of man.

Christ says, "whatsoever ye do to one of the least of these my disciples, ye do unto me."

And again he says, "whosoever shall offend one of these little ones that believe in me; better were it for him that a millstone were hanged about his neck, and he cast into the sea."

If Christ was here as he is described since his ascension, seated upon the throne, King of kings, and Lord of lords, with angels and archangels, and all the redeemed of the earth, worshiping at his feet; would not the very thought of sending *him* into slavery, be blasphemy?

If Christ was here as he was in the hall of Pilate, crowned with thorns, and you knew him, would you send HIM into slavery?

He is here; he is here in the person of his disciple. Christ himself is here. He says to you, "Whatever you do to this my disciple, you do to me." If you send her into slavery, you send *me* into slavery; if you send her to the auction-block, you send me to the auction-block; if you send her to the lash, you send *me* to the lash. If her flesh and blood are sold, *my* flesh and *my* blood are sold, as Judas sold it. If an act of Congress that should command you to worship a golden image would be void, because contrary to this amendment, these acts are also void, because they command you to do a greater wrong, and to commit a fouler and deeper sin. *These acts do, in effect, command you to abjure and to renounce the Christian religion, by commanding you to trample in the very dust the body of Christ, in the person of his humble disciples.* They demand of you, if it be possible, a still greater sacrifice. Christ has said, "better would it be for you, that a millstone were hanged about your neck, and that you were cast into the sea, than that you offend *this* little one." These acts therefore, command you to sacrifice more than life—your soul.

If you surrender your own liberty of conscience, you betray this great right not only for yourself, but for all the people of the United States.

No man can serve two masters: either he will love the one, and hate the other; or cleave to the one, and forsake the other. No man can serve God and Mammon.

We must then choose between these claims.

If we take the side of the master; we recognize his claim to the services of the slave.

If we take the part of the slave, we deny that claim.

This amendment to the Constitution was made for the very purpose of securing to us our right to obey God rather than man. It was adopted for that object, and Congress can make no law that conflicts, in any degree, or to any extent, with its purpose and meaning.

Christianity and slavery are antagonistic principles.

Christianity enters into the heart of man as into a great temple, and lights a pure and holy flame upon its altars. Slavery comes into the same temple, and extends her bloody hand, and extinguishes the last ray of its light, and fills it with the silence, and the corruption of the grave.

Christianity, as she descended from Heaven, proclaimed, trumpet-tongued, to all the nations of the listening earth, the immortality of man.

Slavery herds him with the beasts of the field.

Slavery robs the slave of the wages for his labor

Christianity commands that he shall be paid for it by the light of the setting sun.

Slavery denies to him the marriage relation. Christianity blesses that relation, and guards it by her protecting wall of fire. Slavery robs the slave even of the children of his love. Christianity places them in his embracing arms, and blesses the embrace.

I can add but little upon this part of my argument, except to say, that *your* writ will command the executive officer of this court to deliver the alleged fugitive to her claimant. Even if you shall be willing to encounter the horrors that compliance with these alleged laws, will, as sure as the Bible is the true word of God himself, bring upon you; you ought not to command, you have no right to command, another, less educated than yourself, to do so. He, too, is protected by this amendment to the Constitution. He too has liberty of conscience. He too has an immortality of happiness or of woe before him. You ought not command him to surrender Christ into slavery, in the person of his disciple. Your oath binds you to support the *whole* Constitution, in all its parts, including this amendment, and you have no right to violate it by commands to your officer to do a deed of sin and shame.

Upon the theory that the third clause of the fourth article has not been repealed by the first amendment, and that that amendment is to be inviolably preserved, execute if you can, that third clause of the fourth article; but in doing so, be careful that you require no judge, no commissioner, no marshal, no citizen of the United States, no man, whether a citizen or not, to do anything whatever inconsistent with loving God with all his heart, and his neighbor as himself; for this is the exercise of the Christian Religion.

But the laws of 1793 and 1850, require us to take the part of the master, and to aid him to take the fugitive back into slavery.

Congress not only has no power to pass any law that interferes with any man's religious liberty, but to make the matter still more certain, all power whatever to pass any law, that directly or indirectly interferes with any man's religious liberty, is by plain words expressly taken away and withheld from Congress.

Nor can they then pass any law by which any judge, or commissioner, or other officer of the government of the United States, may be compelled to aid in any degree in returning to his master a fugitive slave? For the judge, or commissioner, or other officer of the United States is, in his office, the agent for the government, of the whole people; and the law that strikes down his rights, strikes down their rights.

There is no difference, in principle, between a law that forbids us to read the Bible, and a law that forbids us to obey it, or if there is, it is better that we shall not have the power to read it, than that we shall be compelled to disobey it.

Just so far as slavery is in conflict with the Bible, these acts of 1793 and 1850 command us to do what the Bible forbids.

It is the duty of the people of the United States to love God with all their hearts, and their neighbors as themselves; and every law that interferes with this (as do the acts '93 and '50) pierces the very vitals of the Christian religion as the spear of the Roman soldier pierced the heart of Christ on the cross.

The claim, of right, to recapture a fugitive slave, requires the agency of officers and men who are guaranteed in the enjoyment of the right to religious liberty.

The slave-holding states claimed the right to recapture fugitive slaves: that was conceded to them. They then wanted the Constitution amended so as that Congress shall make no law "respecting an establishment of Religion or prohibiting the free exercise thereof." All the states wanted it and it was adopted by the consent of the slave, and of the free states.

The people intended, by this amendment, to secure to themselves and their posterity forever, the free enjoyment of religious liberty. If there lurked, in the Constitution before it was amended, any power whatever to interfere with any man's religious freedom, either directly or indirectly, they intended, by this amendment, to deprive Congress of all power to do so. And they have done it.

There is, there can be no question that Congress never had power, since the Constitution has been amended, to pass any law that directly or indirectly, to any extent, impairs any man's religious liberty. The only question here is, do the laws that sanction slavery and require the people of the United States to redeliver a fugitive slave, require any man to commit a sin?

These acts of 1793, and 1850, do require acts to be done, which Christianity forbids, and prohibit acts, which it enjoins.

These acts are therefore void. If Congress can make another, not inconsistent with the first, and other amendments to that instrument, let them do so, but until they do, you have no power to act upon the subject.

There is, sir, nothing novel in the fact, that Christianity is constantly making fresh and new application of its truth and light to old abuses. At the time this amendment was adopted, scarcely a man in the United States, thought that the moderate drinking of spirituous liquors was inconsistent with Christianity; now thousands of the best and most enlightened Christians in our country, think that it is so.

The whole matter then, results in this. If slave-holding is a *sin*, and to aid, abet, and support it, is sinful in any degree, then Congress can pass no law by which any man in the slave states, or in the free states, can be compelled to participate in that sin.

If slave-holding is contrary to the genius and spirit of Christianity, then it is an interference with religious liberty, to *compel* any man directly or indirectly to participate in it.

The slave-holders made their contract, by which they acquired the right claimed for them, and afterward made another contract, by which they surrendered that right, if it could not be exerted without violating the right to the "free exercise of religion."

If my theory is wrong, then there is not an inch of our soil, which is sacred to freedom. Neither the graves of the heroes of the revolution, nor the battle-fields upon which they poured out their blood, nor the domestic hearth, nor the altars of God, nor the mountain-tops, nor the caves of the earth, are sacred to freedom. Into all of these the slave-hunter may enter, and drag from them his shrieking, and trembling victim, back again into hopeless bondage.

But if my theory is true, and I do most fully believe it is so; then the first moment the flying bondman touches the soil of the free states, he is free. His flesh, and blood, and bones, and soul, are all then, under God, his own. The *slave* is left behind him, and he stands up a MAN. He can now worship his God according to the teachings of his conscience. He can now learn to read, and with his Bible open before him, look at the wonders it teaches; as he looks at, and loves the stars of Heaven. He can now be a husband and a father, and bring up his children in the nurture and fear of the Lord. He can now labor, and have his labor sweetened by the hope of reward.

If this theory is true, Congress had no right, and never can have, until the first amendment of the Constitution shall be repealed, to pass any law, by which any man shall be required to aid in the surrender of a fugitive slave; nor can any state do so, whose Constitution has in it a guarantee of religious liberty.

The whole inquiry rests upon this only. Is it right, or is it wrong for one man, in any degree, to aid another to re-capture a fugitive slave?

The natural feelings of humanity in every man's bosom, exclaim in .thunder-tones, that it is wrong! And the law of Christ, as firmly fixed as any physical law that governs matter, that "whatever (either good or ill) you do to one of the least of his disciples, you do to Him; and that you had better be drowned in the sea, than to wrong the least of those disciples," leaves no doubt in the mind of any Christian, that it is ruin to his soul, to obey this law.

We can swear then, to support our Constitution; nor will the oath come reluctantly from us, for it will express the warmest feelings of our hearts. Ay, we *will* support it; we will cluster around our national flag, its emblem, rejoicing with our children, amidst the green fields, and waving harvests, in days of peace; and in luxurious cities, where commerce rolls her golden tides along; and upon every sea, and every shore to which the sails of that commerce may bear us. And we will support it, as our fathers supported that flag, amid the din, and noise, and strife of battle and of blood, on the deck of the ship, as she careens at each broadside that she receives or gives; and on fields, where the dying and the dead are lying thickly around us, and the living are struggling for victory or death.

We will support it, because it is worthy of support. We do love it, because it is worthy of our love. It secures to us, the right to worship and obey God. The power to make any law, at all inconsistent with the fullest and freest exercise of any religious duty, is expressly taken away from Congress. They can no more compel us to deliver God's image into slavery, or to aid in the least, any other man to do so, than they can compel us to annihilate our own souls.

CHAPTER XXXIV.

THE PRISON.

Poor Belle seemed at first to be in despair, but as her counsel proceeded in his argument—as his flushed face and earnest tones showed how deeply he felt what he was saying—her hopes seemed to revive; and when he sat down, a smile—the light of life—lit up her features; she wiped a tear—a tear of gratitude from her eyes—and in low tones, but with a fervor that showed how full her heart was, thanked Mr. Ives for his efforts on her behalf.

The commissioner stated that, in view of the new course of argument pursued by the counsel for tho dofondant, ho would take time to deliberate upon the questions raised; and inquired at what time it would be convenient for the parties to be present and hear his decision.

Mr. Scott said that he would be absent on business for several weeks, and would then return to his home near New Orleans. If the decision could be postponed until his return, it would accommodate him.

Belle readily assented to this, and the commissioner said that in ten weeks he would decide the matter; and that the parties might prepare themselves, and then produce any additional evidence they might have, and if further argument was wished for by either party, both would again be heard. He said: "I shall be obliged, however, (greatly as I dislike to do so,) to commit the defendants to prison until the time I have set for delivering my opinion."

No change passed over Belle's countenance when she heard the order to remand her to jail. The other woman, who was much older than she, was greatly frightened.

She said, "she did not want to run away, but that she was 'suaded off." Her master asked her who persuaded her to leave him.

She then said, "Oh! nobody, master; I only took a walk out, and intended to come back directly, but it was dark, so that I could not find the boat.

The commissioner then explained her rights, and even went so far as to intimate that it might be that she would not be delivered up at all, but would be suffered to go where she pleased at the end of the time. But she was so frightened by the word jail, that after a few moments of apparent indecision, she said she would go with her master if he would forgive her, and she would never attempt to run away again.

Mr. Scott walked across the room, and said that he was satisfied with the order made by the court.

The woman Katy was taken to a steamboat on the river, and into slavery for life. If her eyes had been put out by the slaveholder, all would have denounced the act as one of great cruelty; her will was crushed—and but few men saw any wrong or cruelty in doing that.

Mr. Reed accompanied Belle to the jail. When they reached it, the jailer, Mr. Jackson, carefully read the commitment twice very slowly, and then looked at the writing on the back of it. "All is right. Is this the person who is named in this writ?" The marshal said, "Yes."

Belle was then told to be seated for a few moments in the front room, which the jailer's family occupied as a dwelling.

In a short time the jailer came back and said, "I will now show you your cell." Belle, without even the appearance of reluctance, followed him along a wide hall, until they reached the cell farthest from the entrance. Into that she was told to enter. She did so. The only furniture was a bed and a chair. There was no window, but the door was made of thick iron bars; these crossed each other, and left small openings of about an inch and a half square. The jailer closed the door, and Belle was locked in alone.

The jailer now left, and Mr. Reed lingered a few minutes, standing outside the cell. He said:

"Belle, I am very sorry for you, locked up here in this gloomy cell, and where the few that see you are all strangers; you are indeed a stranger in a strange land."

"You may think my condition an unhappy one, sir, but indeed I feel as if a load was taken from my heart. I would much rather live here all my life and die here, among strangers, than return to slavery. This air, close and foul as it is, is fresh and healthy compared with that of slavery. I breathe more freely. I am full of hope."

"What did you intend to do when you left the boat?"

"I did not know where to go—anywhere, where I could be free. I intended to teach music, French, German and embroidery, if I could get pupils, and to live quietly and keep the condition of my life a secret."

"Did you intend to go to Canada?"

"No, unless I found it necessary to do so, and then I would have gone even to the polar regions rather than be recaptured. Canada, I think, is too cold for me. I could not be known as a slave by my complexion."

"Well, Belle, I am sorry for you, I will do all that I can to aid you, and to make you comfortable while you are here. I will, with your permission, visit you often, and bring you books and papers, and a lady to see you who was a schoolmate of my early life."

"Come, do come frequently, and let me, if you please, see the lady; companionship is always pleasant, and (looking round) it will be doubly so here."

Mr. Reed bade her good-by and left the jail.

Early the next morning, as he was going to his work, he again called with some newspapers.

He found Belle very sad. The excitement of the previous day had gone off, and she was pale and nervous.

"How have you passed the night, Belle?"

"Oh! I have scarcely slept at all. I have been thinking, thinking, thinking all night long. Almost all the events of my life have passed in review before me as far as I can remember; and indeed, although I see much in it which, if I could do over again, I hope I should do better, I cannot see why it is that I should be a slave and be here? My crime, in running off, is but the crime of a canary bird, that flies from the open door of its cage. I have never in my life injured any one in property, person, or reputation. I have lived quietly and peaceably, as far as I could, with all persons. I have lived in the midst of society but almost alone in the world.

While they were talking at the door of the cell, the grate that led into the hall was opened and a gentleman came in who was a clergyman, and the chaplain of the prison.

His salutation to Belle was courteous and kind. "I came," he said, "to see you, because I believe it to be my duty to visit all who may be imprisoned here. I deeply sympathize with you and believe slave-holding a great sin. I have heard too of the defense made for you by your counsel, and have almost as deep an interest as yourself, in the decision which may be made. Whatever I can do to soften the pains of imprisonment while you remain here, if you wish, will gladly be done; and I have many kind friends among the ladies of the village and the surrounding country who will, if you please, visit you.

Belle's eyes filled with tears. She extended as many of her fingers as she could, through the aperture of the door to the minister, who grasped them as if she had been an old friend. He then gave her some tracts, and prayed with her—promised to call again soon, and went away.

In a moment or two after he left, Belle said·

"Will you bring the lady to see me to-day?"

"Yes. We will come this afternoon."

"I shall look earnestly for you, and shall count the heavy hours as they pass, until you and the lady shall visit me."

"Good-by, Belle."

"Good-by. I thank you for your call, and your newspapers."

CHAPTER XXXV.

THE JAIL.

THE description of this jail, may be of service to the reader. It was a brick building two stories high, with its front to the east; built ten or twelve feet back from the street. Between it and the street, was a post-and-rail fence; and along the line of the fence, standing ten or twelve feet apart, a row of locust trees. The entrance was near the south end of the building. That door opened into the room occupied by the jailer and his family as a sitting-room. At the south-west corner of that room, there was a staircase that led to the second story, the whole of which was used as a dwelling by the jailer's family.

To the right of the front door, and near it as you entered the house, was a large door made of very heavy iron bars, that so crossed each other, as to leave apertures of diamond shape not more than an inch wide. This led into a hall, made on the one side, by the east wall of the jail, and on the other, by the walls of the row of cells. In this hall there was a large stove, that in winter warmed all the cells. The hall was lighted by three windows in the east wall of the jail, all of which were crossed with heavy iron bars. The door that led from the jailer's room into the hall, was fastened by a large lock; then by an iron bar of great weight, that passed from one corner at the upper part of the door, to the lower corner on the opposite side; one end of this bar had a hole in it, which passed into an iron staple that seemed to have been built in the wall itself; the other end was fastened over a staple by a lock. In addition to these, and for greater security, as this was the important door of the prison, it was fastened by a padlock and chain which passed over the bar, and around it, and through the apertures of the door. No one had ever escaped from the prison, by means of that door; some had cut their way out, after weeks of labor, through the walls, but the door was thought to be entirely safe.

Each cell had to it an iron door, with no other fastening than a large lock; these doors were made of bars, which crossed each other.

The three windows that lighted the building in the east wall, were each about two feet square.

The minister made a remark that surprised Edgar. "I have visited," he said, "persons in these cells for twenty years, and have conversed with hundreds of their inmates. The prisoners are generally young persons—nearly all of them are either the children or grandchildren of rich men. Education alone, by which I mean, learning to read and write, independent of moral training, does not deter men from crime. Many of the greatest criminals I have met with have been educated and even talented men."

The lady alluded to by Mr. Reed, in his conversation with Belle, was Mrs. Johnston; she had heard of the trial and of the interesting young girl who had been committed to prison. She wished to see her, and with Mr. Reed called upon Belle about four o'clock in the afternoon of the same day just mentioned. Mrs. Jackson's seat was opposite the door of the hall, where she could, while knitting or sewing, see through the apertures in the door all that took place in the hall.

Belle received Mrs. Johnston with dignity and cordiality. She said, "that with the exception of the jailer's wife, whose domestic cares seemed fully to occupy her time, yours is the first female face I have seen since I have been here. Oh! it is so kind in you to come to see me." The conversation at first was a little constrained on both sides, but in a few minutes both Belle and Mrs. Johnston were as well acquainted as if they had been friends for years.

They were both seated on chairs outside the door

of the cell. During this conversation Mr. Reed had a better opportunity to notice Belle carefully than he ever had before. When her taper fingers were passed around the bars of the grate so as to be seen with distinctness, he carefully looked at the roots of the nails. They were purely and pearly white, not a shade of dusky yellow, the last trace of African blood, could be seen.

Mrs. Johnston said, "This is a dull, sad place, are you not afraid, especially at night ?'

"Oh no! dull as it is, and sad as it is, it is better, and I feel happier here than I did when I was at home."

"Why, were you badly treated ?"

"If you mean by bad treatment, blows, or harsh words, hard tasks, or want of food, clothing, or of rest, or of mental culture, I was not badly treated. I was educated with his daughter; we learned music and ancient and modern languages together; we slept in the same room, and ate our meals generally at the same table; my duties woro but little more than hers; my cares perhaps lighter. But," said she, rising from her seat and standing erect, "if you mean by bad treatment, to be deprived of the social companionship of my equals; and above all, to be claimed and held as a slave; then I was badly treated. When I was a mere child I longed to be free, and as I grew up, that wish became a passion. All my hopes of earthly happiness, are concentrated in one wish, 'for freedom.' Without it, there is no position that I have ever imaged, in which I could be happy. With freedom, and the bare necessaries of life, such as I am sure I could earn by my own exertions, I should be happy anywhere.

"Once, when I was quite a child, I visited with our family a collection of wild beasts. When I saw the lions, and tigers, and bears, and leopards, all pacing their cages from side to side, I loved them intensely, for I thought that their hearts and mine beat alike, in one wild, restless, enduring wish for freedom.

"And even now, whenever a bird flies over me, I envy the little creature the freedom it enjoys. I have sometimes been in the society of the blind, of the dumb, of the lame, and often of the sick; and asked myself whether my condition, with the blessing of all my senses, was not better than theirs; but I am sure that freedom with blindness, with sickness, with any calamity to which our race is subject, except perhaps insanity, is better than perfect health in slavery. Oh! I can from my very heart of hearts say, with Patrick Henry 'Give me liberty, or give me death!'"

She sat down and leaned her head for a moment on her hand, and then looking up with a sweet smile, said: "Excuse, madam, if you blame my love for freedom; it is the first time I have ever dared to open my heart to a human being, upon a matter that has preyed as fire upon it, all my life. I feel better now. I have given utterance to thoughts that I never before have had freedom enough to breathe aloud; and although in jail, I have greater liberty than ever I enjoyed before. It makes me happy to talk upon the subject, but I fear I weary you?"

"Not at all, not at all," said Mrs. Johnston: "I could listen for hours, for your words sink into my heart. Oh! if I could only do something to aid you, how happy it would make me. Will not Mr. Scott sell his claim to you?"

"I am sure he will not. I have often heard him say, that he would not part with me upon any terms; and no one has ever even dared to make such a proposition to him."

"Do you think you will be free?" inquired Mrs. Johnston.

"I do not know. I have a presentiment that I shall. I heard the argument of Mr. Ives, and I am sure he is right; but whether the judge will so determine, of course, I cannot know. When Mr. Scott first talked of going to Virginia, my own heart told me, that by some means, I knew not how, my freedom would be the result of that visit. I still believe it as firmly, as I do the words of inspiration. It has always seemed as a spirit speaking within me, and assuring, and comforting me. It was that, that led me to leave the boat at the first opportunity. If I reason upon the subject, all becomes confused, and no way seems now to be open; but when I sit still in my cell, or lie awake at night, it whispers—sometimes I fancy almost audibly—and assures me, that I shall soon be free. And I love the silence and solitude of this jail, for that very reason. It seems as if I am not alone, but that another, a purer and a wiser one, is with me, comforting me with new hopes and assurances, that all at last will be well."

Mrs. Johnston wiped her eyes and said, "Belle, I am sure it will be so. I can no more tell how than you, but while you have been talking, a voice in my own heart has whispered; she *will* be free."

"Good-by, dear Belle, I will come with the minister and see you when he makes his morning visit to the jail. He is deeply interested in your welfare, and since he was here, he says that he can neither think nor talk of any other person than you; and the solitude that you so much love will, I am sure, be sadly disturbed by calls from all the ladies of the neighborhood."

"I thank them, indeed, for their sympathy. It is

wholly unexpected, and I fear, undeserved, but it is the first time in my life that I have ever been so treated. Oh! affection from others, is at all times, the warm life-blood of a woman's heart; and when that heart has been dry and withered from childhood, and exposed to the scorching heat of slavery, it is more precious than streams of living water in the desert to the traveler who is perishing with thirst."

Mrs. Johnston said, "I am sure, dear girl, you will be free. We have a nice school-house here, with a large grassy yard and a swing in it. We will have the school-house whitewashed inside and out and get you a school, and you must live here with us and teach the children. You will join our church, won't you, Belle? and be a member of our sewing circle, and we will all be so happy together."

"You forgot," said Belle, "that I am called a colored person."

"Oh I did forget that indeed, and now that it is forgotten I will try and never remember it any more. If you are colored, I am sure that you are whiter and better than a great many persons about here who are white. What church do you belong to?"

"I am not a member of any society of Christians. The churches where I have lived have presented no attractions to a person who is claimed as a slave. I have wished for several *years, for the companionship* of Christians in church fellowship, but have been so situated as not to have it in my power."

Mrs. Johnston replied, "Indeed you have suffered a great loss—the loss of the highest pleasure of life—but when you shall be discharged from this place and be free, then, if you please, we will receive you with open arms, for I am sure from your very countenance that you are a Christian—as good a one as the best of us."

"Good-by, Belle, I will see you in the morning. It is getting quite late now and I must go. I have taken leave of you twice already. Put your little fingers through the grate again and let me shake them once more. I wish I could kiss you, but these bars prevent me. It is not the first time though that prison bars have separated persons who love each other."

Belle extended her taper fingers through the bars; Mrs. Johnston seized them, held them for a minute, and wiping her eyes departed. As we passed through the door we could still see the little fingers shaking, as if to bid us farewell.

CHAPTER XXXVI.

MRS. JOHNSTON.

Mrs. Johnston boarded with the Rev. Mr. Stillman, the minister of a church in the village. As she and Mr. Reed walked to his house, she said,

"Cannot you do something more for that beautiful girl? It seems to me very strange that she should be in a jail! She is not accused of any crime, and she owes nothing to Mr. Scott. He is her debtor for the work she has done for him. I thought that jails, in Ohio, were made to keep wrong-doers in. Mr. Scott ought to be in it—not Belle. And while I think of it, how does it happen that our jail here is made a slave-pen? I have often read descriptions of slave-pens, but always supposed, till now, that they were places far away from us—at least, that they existed only in the slave states. But here is actually a slave-pen in our village—and I am part owner of it too—for only last year (she said it with a sigh) I was heavily taxed on my property to help build it. I have been told that James, the tavern-keeper, had the two women locked up in a room in his house, and kept them there for an hour or two, till the warrant could be made out. If any one of my tenants should permit any such thing, I would turn him out at the end of his term, and never let him have a house or farm of mine upon any condition. A grog-shop is bad enough, and they say that James does really sell liquor, but when in addition to that, the tavern is made a slave-pen, it is a nuisance, and the tavern-keeper who does so, should not be licensed again."

The beautiful young widow was quite animated while she made this speech—and stopping for a moment, and raising one finger of her little hand, she said:

"Oh! if I were a man, I would soon see by what authority, we people in Ohio have our property taxed, to build slave-pens for slaveholders! I would soon have all laws, that allow such outrages upon our rights, and such insults to our principles and feelings, repealed."

"But, madam," said Mr. Reed, "you forget that courtesy to our sister states requires us to —"

Mrs. Johnston interrupted him: "Courtesy, courtesy indeed, to keep a woman in jail! at the request of some brute of a man who claims to be her owner! So then, if I were in Kentucky, and you requested somebody to put me in jail, *courtesy*, as you call it, would require that I, and not you, should be imprisoned? If there is any courtesy to be exercised in the matter, it seems to me, that it would be better to seize and imprison Mr. Scott, and not the poor victim of his wrongs."

"But she is said to be a negress."

Mrs. Johnston: "She is not, you have only to look in her face, and you will see there is not one word of truth in the assertion. Even if she is, I cannot see what courtesy there can be in making our jails the prisons of a race, which, of all others, has been most deeply wronged."

The next day nearly all the men left the village early in the morning, to go about seven miles in the country to hear a political speech.

Mr. Wilbar, the blacksmith, could not leave, "because," he said, "it was his busiest day of the week." Two or three storekeepers, and two assistants remained; one tavern-keeper, a carpenter, and four young men, his apprentices and journeymen were, with Mr. Reed, all the men who did not go out to the meeting.

The village had all the quietness of Sunday: the wind was blowing freshly from the south-west, about three o'clock in the afternoon. Mr. Reed was the sole occupant of the printing-office. As he was distributing type at the case, he thought he heard a cry of fire! he paused and listened, and again in a shrill voice, as of a woman or a boy, he distinctly heard the alarm, Fire! fire! fire! Without waiting to put on his coat, or to roll down his sleeves, he sprang down the stairs, and ran as fast as he could, toward the black column of smoke now plainly visible. As soon as he turned a corner, he saw with horror, that it was the jail. The wind was blowing freshly, directly upon the fire, which spread so rapidly, that by the time he reached the place, the whole roof was in a blaze. Just as he got there, a little son of the jailer, about four years old, appeared at the north-eastern window of the building, crying for help. The stairs were already on fire; so much so, that it was impossible to ascend them. The only means for rescuing the child was, by placing a ladder against the wall, and taking him from the window. The flames were rolling and roaring in thick masses all along the roof, on both sides, and the wind was blowing the fire directly in the faces of those who tried to go up to the rescue. No ladder was at hand; not a moment was to be lost. The carpenters soon brought one, and two of them, one after the other, ascended it nearly to the window; but just as they reached it, a gust of wind blew down thick masses of flame and smoke, and they were driven back. The boy had now fallen upon the floor, and was suffocating. The intense agony of the mother, who stood below, struggling to release herself from those who prevented her from climbing the ladder—her shrieks—her agonizing prayers, her entreaties to the men to save, oh, save her son! the groans, and cries of the women of the village, all of whom were there, and in tears; some wringing their hands, others praying aloud, others running to and fro and calling for help, presented a scene full of awe and horror.

Three efforts were made to reach the window, and at each time the ascending persons were thrown back by the rushing, whirling, devouring fire. The smoke rolled down in masses, black, and thick, and hot; and amid it large flakes of fire were whirled by the wind in all directions. A shout was heard, "Stand back, men! the roof is reeling, and will fall;" and all the crowd, except those who held the half frantic mother, rushed to the opposite side of the street. In an instant a lad (a young carpenter) ascended the ladder with a hatchet in his hand; the wind for a moment had blown the flame away from the window; with one crash the sash was driven in; he disappeared for a second, amid the smoke, and then he was seen descending the ladder with the boy, who hung as if dead, in his arms, both with their clothing all on fire. A loud shout from the whole crowd, rang out. Mrs. Jackson rushed to the ladder, and before the young man had reached its foot, she clasped her child in her arms.

Just then Mr. Reed inquired: "Where are the prisoners?" and one loud shout went up from all the men and women there—"The prisoners—the prisoners are burning to death!" A man ran to Mrs. Jackson, and shaking her by the shoulder, asked, "Where are the keys?" Mrs. Jackson looked wildly at him, and then hugged her unconscious boy to her bosom. "The keys!—the keys, Mrs. Jackson—the keys of the jail, where are they?"

"Oh! thank God my child is not burnt up—he is scorched badly—but he will not die—Oh! no, he will not die, thank God!—thank God he is safe."

"The keys!—the keys!—where are the keys of the prison, Mrs. Jackson? the prisoners will burn up." She still looked in a bewildered manner at the speaker, and again pressed her boy to her bosom, and kissed his blackened and blistered forehead.

"Oh! he breathes—he breathes!—I feel his little heart beat. Henry—my Henry is not dead! the poor boy is badly hurt; but he will get well;" and she rocked herself to and fro, and gazed fondly on the face of her son.

"She has lost her reason for a time," said Mr. Wilbar; "we have no time to lose; come, men—come, come—who will follow me?" he shouted.

"We must save the prisoners!" Some men ran in to search for the keys, and returned, saying, "they could not find them." While they were gone, Mr. Wilbar and others threw down a panel of the fence, and tore from the ground one of the large posts. Into the holes, mortised for rails, they put three handspikes, and as many men as could hold them, rushed with the post into the jail. At the first blow they surged upon the iron door, a shriek was heard from the crowd outside—a cry that the rafters were falling—and a shower of fire, ashes, and dust, filled the house. They still, with heavy surges, thundered their battering-ram against the door, till a crash was heard—the house was more full of fire and smoke than before, and the men all dropped the post and ran out. Part of the west side of the roof, shaken by the assault upon the door, had fallen in, and the flames rose and swept with redoubled fury over the building. All the windows in the second story were now filled with flame. Mr. Wilbar paused but for a moment, and then shouted. "Back men—come back! one more blow and the door will be opened. The prisoners are not dead yet. We can save them, and they must be saved."

Half-a-dozen men again rushed with him into the building, and again the blows of the battering-ram thundered against the door; but the cries outside, were now louder than before; the roof cracks—it reels—it is just about to fall; come out—come out, you will be burned in an instant."

Again all rushed out; two of the party, overpowered by the heat, fell in the street and were carried to the sidewalk; others were on fire, and water was thrown over them. After a moment's pause—an instant of apparent indecision—Mr. Wilbar again called, "Come back—come back! we must save them—we can—we must!" and rushed again into the building.

Three only followed him now: again they seized the post, and again, with all their force, heaved another blow upon the iron grate. It shook—the whole house shook; there was a louder shout without—a whirl!—a rushing sound!—a shower of living coals! and with a crash that seemed loud as an earthquake, the whole roof fell in!

Mr. Reed did not know how he got out. He was stunned and unconscious for a moment, and was roused by hearing Mr. Wilbar calling out again louder than before, "Come on, men—come on! the greatest danger is now over; one more blow, and the door will be forced."

No one as yet moved: "Come, men, for the love of God come! if they were your brothers or your sisters, would you not help to the very last?"

Just then some of the men who had been in the country, rode up at full speed. In an instant the post was again manned, and with the first surge the door flew open. Mrs. Jackson had now recovered her presence of mind; she was again, by twenty voices at once, asked for the keys: she seemed abstracted for a moment, and then said:

"I have forgotten where I put them." She prayed, Oh God! my God! enable me to remember where I have placed the keys; then rising, she seized an old carpet that lay near her,— plunged it into a bucket of water, and wrapping it round her person, walked into the burning jail; got the keys, and placed them in Mr. Wilbar's hand, just as the door of the hall was burst open. The door of a cell in which two boys were, was unlocked in an instant, and then the cell of Belle. All was darkness, and smoke, and stifling, roasting heat within it.

Mr. Reed stumbled over her prostrate form, lying at the side of the door; he seized her in his arms: at that instant his head seemed to burst out to double its usual size; his eyeballs appeared as coals of living fire; his ears rang with a hissing, singing noise; his lungs seemed to be all in flame: he groped his way, feeling in the dark; something obstructed his passage; he knew not what it was; he pressed the still form of Belle closely, and reeled, and stumbled; a hand grasped him—he heard the voice of Wilbar—he was on his feet; he heard a loud shout, as he passed the door, and amid flame, and dust and smoke, he fell! Water was dashed on him, and for a moment he was conscious that he was sitting on the pavement, with a crowd of women and men around him. A boy taken from the jail, was stretched apparently dead upon the pavement; another was in a sitting posture, crying, "Oh, mother! oh, mother! Oh, Lord! oh, Lord! to be burned to death! Indeed I am innocent of this crime."

Groups of women were around them, fanning them, and pouring water on them. Mr. Reed again sank down, unconscious of all around him.

CHAPTER XXXVII.

EDGAR REED.

Soon afterward the only consciousness he had was a sense, a dull, dreamy, constant sense of pain. He seemed to be roasting at a slow fire; at intervals it would blaze up, and then he would roll as in a sea of flame. His brain, and the very marrow of his bones seemed to be masses of red-hot iron. By degrees it slowly subsided, and then he thought he was struggling through thorns that tore his flesh at each step, and incessantly stung him from head to foot.

One day he awakened as from a dream, and found himself in a neat and well-furnished apartment, lying upon a bed as white as snow, and a lady—a stranger to him—sitting by his bedside, with a young child in her lap, and some sewing in her hands. As he looked at her she seemed surprised, and then with a smile, said:

"You have had a refreshing sleep, and are now much better."

"Where am I?"

"You are at the house of Mr. Stillman, the

minister. When you were hurt, we had both you and Belle brought here, and I am very glad to find you so much better."

"How long have I been here?"

"This is now the morning of the third day since the fire—you have been insensible till now."

She left the room, and presently returned with Mrs. Johnston. This lady looked pale and care-worn.

She came to his bedside, and stooping over him, inquired if he was not much better. "You must not talk yet," said she, "but must be as quiet as possible, until you obtain permission from us to satisfy your curiosity. Mrs. Stillman is your nurse, and I am the nurse of poor Belle."

"How is Belle?"

"Oh! you must not say a word. Be still. I will sit down, and if I think you able to bear it, will tell you the whole story. (She sat down.) I was at the fire before you got there. I had no hope for Belle's escape, and believed that in half an hour she would be burnt to death. I never had such horrible feelings. I could not live, I think, through another such trial.

"When the great iron gate was broken open, and the two lads were brought out, I knew that you would not return without Belle. It seemed as if you were in there half an hour, but I have been assured it was not more than two minutes. Just as you left the cell with Belle in your arms, the sleepers of the second floor, and part of the floor itself, fell between you and the iron door. A part of it struck you on the head, and you fell. All outside were for an instant appalled, and gave both of you up as lost, when the brave and generous Mr. Wilbar wrapped himself in a wet blanket, although he was already badly burned, and scarcely able to walk, and went right into the blazing fire and brought both of you out. You walked out while he held your hand—but fell as soon as you got outside the door. Both you and Belle were carried over to the pavement, and water thrown upon you; you revived for a moment, and then swooned away. We then brought both of you here, and have nursed you ever since. The neighbors, especially the young men from the two printing-offices, have been very kind to you, and we have always had more persons offer to sit up with you than would have been enough to attend five sick men. The doctor says that none of your bones are broken, though you are badly bruised, and have been burnt, but not so as to disfigure you. Oh yes! you will be able to sit up this afternoon, and walk across the room to-morrow, if you only take care of yourself, and not be restless and talk."

"How is Belle?"

"I have just told you, that you must not talk—we will do all the talking. Two women, I think, can do enough of that. Belle is better; she fainted very soon, and the doctor—Dr. Williams, do you know him? he is a very skillful and attentive physician—says, that was of great benefit to her and prevented her from inhaling the hot air; which, he says, might have killed her. She was more hurt by the falling of the floor than you, but is not so badly burned as you are. The doctor says, that a great part of your hurts have been caused by over exertion in beating the door open. Mr. Wilbar and two other men have been confined to their beds, principally from the same cause, ever since; and nearly every one of the men, and several of the women who were at the fire, have been unable to attend to their business. It was an awful time, and we thank God that no lives were lost, while at one time, when the roof fell in, it really seemed as if all the prisoners, and six or seven men had perished.

"Belle is able to sit up in an arm-chair. As yet, the Doctor allows her to talk but little. But you know that you cannot keep a woman's tongue entirely still, and she will talk in spite of all that we can do to prevent her. She was just inquiring for you, when Mrs. Stillman came in and told us, you were awake, and sensible of what is passing around you. In a few days, both of you will, I hope, be well again. You are a brave man, and saved that poor girl's life; and the whole country is praising the bravery and generalship of Mr. Wilbar. No one expected it of him, or thought that he was more than an ordinary man; but the occasion brought out his energies, and has shown that he is a hero."

They recovered rapidly. Still, neither of them were able to leave their respective rooms. Great solicitude existed in the minds of all of Mr. Stillman's family, and of Mr. Reed, for the fate of poor Belle. What would be the decision of the commissioner? Could he appreciate the argument of Mr. Ives? Even if he did so, had he *nerve* enough, in opposition to wide-spread public opinion, to discharge his duty? or would he decide the case against her, and shield himself from perhaps the upbraidings of his own conscience, and the censure of the best of the community, by appealing to the authority of superior judges?

"If the case should be decided against Belle, what," said Mrs. Stillman, "do you think Mr. Scott will do with her? He is no doubt irritated, perhaps very angry at the attempt of Belle to escape. She says, that his prevailing vice is avarice; and it is reported in the village, but I really do not know upon what authority, that Mr. Scott said, as he was leaving the place, 'that he would have to sell her, to pay the exorbitant fees of his attorneys in the case.' Do you think, if she should still be sick, when the ten weeks are out, that he will force her away from us, and sell her? Mr. Stillman became her bail in two thousand dollars, for her appearance and re-delivery on the day when the decision shall be made. Would it not be better to forfeit the bail, although it would utterly ruin us as to this world, than even to run the risk of her returning to slavery?"

Mrs. Johnston said, "For my part, if I were in her place, I would run away again; and if I could not run off, I would creep off. She says, she would rather have been burned to death, than return, even to the slavery that has been her lot. If she should go, and Mr. Stillman loses anything by it, he has friends who, perhaps, will see that he shall not be ruined."

Two days after this conversation, the folding-doors that separated the parlors in which Belle and Mr. Reed respectively were, were thrown open—the blinds of the windows withdrawn, as Mr. Reed's weakened eyes could now endure the light—and Belle, seated in a large arm-chair on castors, was brought into his room. He had told

Mrs. Stillman and Mrs. Johnston detached parts of his adventure on the island, and they had repeated them to Belle. He was now to relate the scene of Aaron's death; and she was brought in, to hear it directly from himself.

When he told them that Aaron gave him his Bible, all three spoke out at once: "Let us see that Bible?" He replied, "It is in one of my trunks at the tavern."

"Your trunks are all here," said Mrs. Stillman, "Mrs. Johnston ordered them to be brought here on the day of the fire." Mrs. Johnston blushed slightly. He told them in which trunk it was. The book was soon produced and eagerly examined.

"What is this writing on the blank leaves of the book?" Said Mrs. Johnston, "it is even worse than that of Mr. Peters, my lawyer. Did you ever see such a scrawl? It must be poetry, too, for I see that every line begins with what is meant for a capital letter, and all the words run together." She examined it with care, leaf by leaf, and then said, "I can here and there make out a word, but not enough even to conjecture the meaning." Mrs. Stillman examined it with no better success. She could decipher some words that Mrs. Johnston could not.

"What did Aaron tell you this was?" she inquired. Mr. Reed told her Aaron said it was a statement of his wife, written down by himself just before her death, in relation to the murder of a child for which she had been sold. Mr. Reed was lying, at the time, on a sofa; Belle was near him in the chair, when the book was handed to her. *"I have been accustomed,"* she said, "to such writing; the slaves on the plantation frequently got me to write letters for them and to read theirs. Bring me, if you please a pencil and a sheet of paper and I will try to read it; I think I can easily do so."

They were handed to her and she began, "This here child that I am 'cused of killin' I never did at all. I nursed it several months, and how could I kill it, for I loved it? and my child was only six months older than this one. I put both children together—my child and this child—in one bed and went down stairs to supper; when I cum back it was gone and my child was asleep where I left it.

"I don't believe this here child is dead at all. I believe she is alive yet, and has been tuk somewhere. Missus cum to me in jail and begged me to tell her all that I knowed about it. I told her that I knowed nothing at all about it—nor more I did. I never did kill that child in my life, nor anybody else's child; and I have been unjustly dealt by in the selling me away off into this wild country, among sich people as is here."

"Bravo! Belle," said Mrs. Johnston, "you ought to go to Nineveh and help Layard, or to Egypt and decipher the hieroglyphics there."

"Go on," said Mrs. Stillman, "I feared, when you began, that it was a confession of murder, and I am now relieved."

Belle smiled and proceeded. "This here child I nursed a good while. (She has put that down twice said Mrs. Johnston, it must be true.) It had a mark as big as a cherry, and of a whitish red on its left arm, just at the elbow."

Belle's pale cheeks turned paler. "That is strange," she said; and rolling up the sleeve of her dress, showed a mark on her arm exactly like the one described. The ladies carefully examined it, and looked over Belle's shoulder as she found out the several letters, so that they could see them for themselves.

"Go on, Belle—go on," said the impatient little widow, Mrs. Johnston: "she had a mole on her upper lip, near the corner of her mouth, and about half an inch above it." Both the ladies exclaimed:

"Why so have you, Belle, just such a mole, and just where it is said to be!"

Poor Belle turned still paler, and her trembling hand was scarcely able to trace the letters; her eyes, too, were dimmed with tears. Mrs. Stillman was composed. Mrs. Johnston changed her seat several times, and finally stood up again and looked over Belle's shoulder.

"Go on," said she, "let us have it all as soon as possible." "She had three moles on the right side of her neck below her right ear, and they were so that they looked like a little flatiron." The pencil dropped from Belle's hand—she had fainted. Without attempting to revive her Mrs. Johnston ran to the side of her neck, and there was the triangle described. Was she the lost child of Mr. Scott?—the niece of the man who claimed to be her master?—the heiress of the large estate he had gone on to inherit? There was another passage in the book, but it was so obliterated that no one could decipher it.

Mrs. Johnston, without waiting even to tell what she was about to do, put on her bonnet and went directly to the house of the commissioner. She soon returned with her brow knit, and her bright blue eyes flashing with anger: without taking off her bonnet, she seated herself and said:

"Don't you think that, after my trouble in going to see that man, I have come back without any paper by which Belle can be released. He would not even read the book which I took with me, though I assured him that now, when we knew what the writing was about, it was easy to read it.

When I found that, with all that I could do, he would not read a word of it, or even look at it, I told him all that has just occurred, and how certainly her identity, as the lost child of Mr. Scott's brother, is established. He did not want to hear even that, but I *made* him listen; and when I got through and asked him if he had now any doubt about the matter, he would not answer my question. I asked him to let Belle go free at once, but he promptly refused. All that I could get him to promise was, that if Mr. Scott's lawyer consented to his reading this writing, and examining the marks on Belle, he would do so. A pretty judge, indeed, who won't look into the truth unless the person whose interest is opposed to his knowing it, will let him! If we women only had the making of laws for a day, we would soon sweep away all these follies. But you *wise* men have the power, and use it to suit yourselves.

This discovery seemed to have almost wrought a cure upon both Belle and Mr. Reed.

Within a day afterward, Mr. Reed was able to walk across the room, with the aid of a cane. The news soon spread through the village, and in the evening Mr. Herbert, the chaplain of the jail; Mr. Wilbar, the blacksmith, and many others were seated in Mr. Stillman's parlor. The marks were examined, and each, now that the context was known, could read the scrawl in the book. No one doubted but that Belle was the identical person described in the writing; and that writing had upon it such evidences of its antiquity, and even of its genuineness, that none were able to doubt the statements.

But what was next to be done, was the great question of the evening? A dispatch was sent by the telegraph, to a lawyer in Willoughby, stating that the lost child of Mr. Scott, was found, and employing him to act as her counsel. They then wrote a full statement of the whole affair, and sent it to him by mail. Mr. Reed suggested, "that some one should go immediately to New Orleans, and begin to search for evidence of Belle's identity at that place, and employ suitable agents there, to prosecute the search; and then go on to Willoughby, and commence similar inquiries there; and in the meantime, to write fully to the lawyer at Willoughby, and urge him to make inquiries into the matter, with all possible diligence."

Mrs. Stillman said, "There was not sufficient time, to go both to New Orleans and Willoughby, before the time set by the commissioner for his decision of the case, would expire."

Mr. Stillman said in reply, "Now, that God has begun this good work, He will carry it on to the end: this discovery is providential."

Mrs. Johnston said to Mr. Reed, "I am sure you can succeed in establishing her right. After the perils you have encountered to save her life, and your success in that, I am sure that you can if you will, do what is needed in her behalf; but you are too weak yet to travel, and must not think of it; some other person must go, till you get well enough to attend to it."

Mr. Reed thanked her, and told her, "that he had made up his mind, to start with the first descending boat to New Orleans; and would go at all hazards, even if the boat passed down that night. That his health was such, that he could not labor, and the journey, he was sure, would restore him.

Belle said nothing; but her look—one long, earnest look—told him more distinctly than any language could, how full her heart was of gratitude.

Mr. Reed's trunks were already packed; and early the next morning, the sound of a boat was heard round a bend in the river. He was carried to the landing on a settee, by Mr. Stillman and others, and was soon on board. In a few minutes, he was on his journey. By the time he arrived at New Orleans, he was almost well; Mr. Stillman had imparted to him a large share of his confidence in the result of his mission. He could not doubt, but that he would succeed.

CHAPTER XXXVIII.

EDGAR REED.

THE first person, and indeed, the only one he looked for, after he reached his former boarding-house, in New Orleans, was Captain Carter, who had changed his boarding place, and the landlady could not tell where he could be found. Mr. Reed knew a cafe, that he was in the habit of visiting. Early in the evening he went there, and seated himself in one of the boxes, with a broiled bird before him. In a few minutes two gentlemen came in. One of the gentlemen ordered refreshment. Mr. Reed did not know his voice. In a little while he could not but overhear the words:

"When I was a boy, I shot four deer one morning, near Little Egg Harbor, in Jersey, and I will tell you how it was." Of course it was his old friend, Captain Carter. As soon as he had inquired after Mr. Reed's health, and before he had time to reply, he said:

"How many deer did you kill on your hunting excursion? you staid longer than you expected; what luck had you?"

"Do you remember, captain, that you promised

to eat all the deer that I killed? Well now, prepare to keep your promise. I killed seven, and wounded several others.

"Where are your deer? let me see them. You know that I am a man of my word; I will eat the whole of them, only you must let me take my time to do it. I did not say how soon I would do it. And then looking archly, he said: "You don't expect me to eat the wounded ones, do you?"

"Oh! no," not until I bring them to you.

"Come, show me the deer; it does me good to look at a lot of good venison, even if I have had no hand in killing it."

Reed told him that he had sold them for twenty dollars, to the clerk of the steamboat Pocahontas, as she was descending the river.

"Did you indeed? then I have already kept my promise, in part, for I have been eating of that venison ever since it came into market."

They seated themselves in a box, where they could not be overheard, and Reed then related to him briefly the matters of which the reader is already apprised, respecting Belle. After he got through with his narrative, Captain Carter fairly leaped to his feet:

"What! the old wretch, to make a slave of a white girl—a young lady—his brother's only child! he ought to be hung without judge or jury

I have known, for ten years, that he is a knave. You know that I have dealt for many years in fine horses — I had a pair of as beautiful bays as ever were hitched in harness. They were small, with fetlocks as clean and as slim as your wrist, and legs like a deer. They had small and beautiful heads, and carried them as blooded horses should; thick black manes, and broad, full tails; they were well coupled—as sound as a dollar, and as gentle as dogs. I sold this pair of horses to Scott for a thousand dollars; when I did so, I told him they were well broken and sound. He paid me the money, and in less than a month, one of them, by the carelessness of his driver, got hurt. What did the old scamp do then, but write me a note, stating that the horse was unsound, and that I must have known it when I sold it. This wounded me—it touched me on a tender point—for as I deal in horses for profit, much depends upon my reputation for honor in my sales. I returned his money instantly, took back the horses, and in less than a month had the one that was hurt as well as ever, and sold the pair for fifteen hundred dollars. I thank him for his meanness. It was five hundred dollars in my pocket; but still I know the man. I never sold a better pair of horses in my life, except a pair of blue roans that I bought in Arkansas—they were —

"Captain Carter, let me interrupt you? please excuse me for doing so, my business is urgent?"

"Well," said he, "what can I do for you?"

"I want you to help me find the evidence of this young lady's identity and heirship. There is no time to be lost."

"Let me see," said Captain Carter: "How old is she?"

"Twenty-two."

"What name did Scott give her?"

"Arabella Robinson, was what she stated it to be at the trial."

"When did she come on the plantation?"

"When she was about six years of age; which must have been sixteen years ago."

"Who brought her there?"

"I do not know."

"Where was she brought from?"

"I do not know; except that when she was a child, not more than three years old, she was stolen at Willoughby."

"Who stole her?"

"I cannot tell."

"Is she handsome?"

"Yes, beautiful, tall and graceful; with black hair, black eyes, fine lips, nose and chin, and a beautiful set of teeth, white as pearls."

"Does she look like Scott?"

"Her hair, eyes and, skin, are certainly different from his, which, you know, are all light; but her features bear so striking a likeness to his that before I knew better, I supposed she was his daughter."

"The scent is quite cold," said Captain Carter, "but an old hunter never will pause on that account, when he sees so many tracks before him."

The next day they drove out to Mr. Scott's plantation. "We must be cautious," said Captain Carter, "but we must begin here; this is the starting point." He inquired for the overseer; they were told that he had gone to the city. They then walked out around the quarters, and saw an old woman—one of the slaves of the plantation. Captain Carter shook hands with her as an old acquaintance, and placed, as he did so, several pieces of silver in her hand.

"Lord bless you, massa! I do not know you, but you knows me. I forget all my ole friends."

"Never mind," said the captain, "here is a young friend, who wants to inquire for Miss Belle."

"Miss Belle is gone to ole Virginia—down to ole Willoughby, whar I come from when I was young; whar I's got four children living now, I s'pose."

"You know Miss Belle then, do you?"

"Why lor', massa! how can I help but know the child? I's known her ever since she came here."

"Who brought her?"

"Ay there, you're ahead of me. All that I know is, that one time when I went in the great house, I saw her thar—a pretty little thing she was too. But here comes Liza; she, may-be knows, for she was house-servant then. Eliza came up—Uncle Joe shook hands with her too, and dropped a piece also in her hand. Eliza looked as greatly surprised as Molly, the old woman, had.

"Liza," said she, "this gentleman wants to know who brought Miss Belle here, when she first came in dis here place; does you know?"

"I don't know," replied Eliza: "she was fetched here in the night; but this I does know, that a month before she came, massa sent down to the city for Williams, the soul-driver, to come out and see him; when he came, we was all so scared, 'cause we thought some of us was gwine to be sold. Then he came again, and staid all night. He came in a carriage this time. The next morning Miss Belle was here."

"Thank you, Liza," said Captain Carter: "good-by."

As soon as they were seated in a carriage, Captain Carter said: "This girl was brought here by Williams. Scott must have heard of her, and sent him for her. He was gone a month; perhaps not all the time on this errand. Her true name is Arabella Scott; when she came here, she bore the name of Robinson. Williams bought her from some person by the name of Robinson; that person did not live in these parts. Did she tell you who this Robinson was?"

"Yes, she told me that she lived, at her earliest recollection, with a Mrs. Robinson, a widow, on a small plantation in a pine hill country; but in what county or state, she could not tell. I told her where I had been hunting, and described the country; and she said, that she had an indistinct recollection of having seen just such a country."

"That will do," said the captain, "I'll go right there."

Mr. Reed now made arrangements with him, that he should pursue the search with the utmost diligence, and write to him the result, as often as he could; and if he met with any evidence of value, if possible to bring the witnesses with him to Auburn, whatever might be the expense of doing so; assuring him that if they were successful, the young lady would have ample means to repay all his expenditure, and to reward him for his labor. To these terms he cheerfully agreed. Mr. Reed was soon on his way to Willoughby.

CHAPTER XXXIX.

MARY SCOTT.

Mr. Ives recovered so far that he was able very soon to dine with Mary Scott. She was entertaining him with an incident that happened to her fortunes since she came to Willoughby. Among the slaves that her father obtained from her uncle's estate, was a beautiful boy, about sixteen years of age, named Lewis. She described him as yellow as gold, with flowing, glossy-black hair, and large lustrous eyes, full of activity and intelligence for a person in his condition. Within a few days after he became her property by the gift of her father, the boy ran away, and was trying to escape to the free States, or to Canada. No doubt, she said, he had been persuaded by some wicked person to do so; she did not see why he should have thought of such a thing, as he had always been well-treated, had plenty of food and clothes, and light labor. Nothing therefore but some mischief whispered in his ear by some vagabond, could have led him to take so rash, so sad a course. He was re-taken and in a few days she sold him to a gentleman who had taken him into the interior of the state.

"Sold him!" said Mr. Ives, "*you*, you, Mary! *you* sold him?"

"Yes, I have just told you I sold him; I got nine hundred dollars for him, and might have got twelve hundred if he had not diminished his value by his freak in running away."

"*You* sold him Mary? I can hardly believe my own senses! *You* sold him?"

Mary looked surprised by the intense feeling, and the energetic, though lowly spoken words of Mr. Ives, and saw that he was deadly pale. He trembled—his very lips were white. "*You*, Mary! you sold a boy, a fellow man, human flesh and blood."

The matter was too serious now to be concealed. The guests did not hear his words, but they saw that he was ill. He was assisted from the table, and taken in a carriage to his hotel. His fever returned with increased power, and all now feared he would die, but after several days of suspense, he slowly recovered.

Mary did not visit him. His language seemed filled with reproaches. She thought that he intended to wound her feelings; to reproach her. Sometimes too she thought that he was at least indelicately interfering with her acknowledged right to control her property. That at least he might postpone, until he became united with her in its ownership. The language seemed singularly strange for one so careful of the feelings of others as was Mr. Ives; so studious of propriety in all his attentions to her. Was it the lingering fever that disturbed his senses and now broke out again with increased force? After some days of unhappiness she came to this conclusion, and half pardoning, again visited him. He was again in his room upon the sofa, and alone and half uncared for; and again when she saw him, her heart, in spite of all her reasonings, forgave him.

"Henry, I have heard that you have been very ill indeed. I feared each day that I should hear of your death; but now you will recover. What have you been thinking of while you were sick and alone?"

"Of you, Mary, when I had power to command my thoughts, and of Lewis in all my hours of delirium."

"Of Lewis! and for hours at a time, Mr. Ives?"

"Yes, I have, wholly without effort on my part, been thinking of Lewis; the boy that you sold."

"Tell me what you thought? I will not; indeed, I will not be angry with you again. I have made up my mind that you are, at least, a little eccentric, and I will endure your vagaries for the sake of your good qualities. Tell me, Mr. philosopher, what you have been thinking about Lewis?"

"Mary, I will tell you a little now; perhaps, at another time, more may occur to me."

"I was burning with fever, and tossing restlessly upon my bed, and then became calm, and slept; a half-waking, restless, feverish sleep. I saw the white cottage in the orange grove, shaded by tall trees, and surrounded by hundreds of blooming flowers; I saw you at the door, wife—my wife—more lovely than ever, your eyes bright with welcome, as you extended your hand to greet me: and then in an instant the whole scene was changed. The cottage, and all its trees and shrubs, and flowers, and the green grass on the lawn were all gone, and in their place a great desert of flat, wet sand, and in the place where the cottage stood, Lewis, alone, in chains, kneeling on the sand, and with outstretched arms praying for freedom. And then the scene changed, and Lewis was not alone. Thousands, and tens of thousands—millions of men, of all colors, and all in chains, old men and young men, old women and young women, and children, and infants in their mothers' arms, stood around him, and chains fine as spider's web, but firmer than steel, extended from Lewis, and fastened upon the fetters of every one of all that host of slaves, and strengthened and riveted their chains. They all kneeled and prayed for freedom.

One came, who seemed to be a minister of mercy, for he had vowed to devote his whole being to God; he looked with a cold, careless gaze at the sufferers, and passed on.

"Another came, and knelt and prayed: 'Thy will be done on earth as it is in Heaven,' and passed on his way.

"Another came, and read from a book before him: 'And they stripped him, and put on him a scarlet robe; and when they had plaited a crown of thorns, they put it on his head, and a reed in his right hand: and they bowed the knee before him, and mocked him, saying, 'Hail King of the Jews!'' And he, too, bowed the knee to Christ, but passed on, looking as he did so, without pity or mercy.

"Another came, and shouted for freedom, and equality, and republicanism, and looked in his turn, and reviled, and hissed, and traducod, and defamed him; and he, too, went on his way.

"Others, and still others, came. Some blessed the fetters that bound him, and others prayed that the links might be broken, but made no effort to do so."

"Well," said Mary, "that was really a curious dream; it seems to me as if you were not all asleep when you dreamed it. Your will, perhaps, controlled the gambols of your imagination. But what at last was the end of it?"

"I dreamed still, that as Lewis knelt and prayed, a fire came down and encircled him, as with a halo of golden light; and on it was written, 'Thou shalt love thy neighbor as thyself.'

"And then another flame also, encircled him, and on that was written, 'Do unto others as you would that others should do unto you.' His chains fell, and he stood up, a MAN, girded and protected by these great lights from the Throne of God. And other men gathered in crowds around him, and endeavored again to enchain and to enslave him; but could not do so for these concentric circles of fire protected him; at length they burst through them, and while thunders muttered above their heads, and the sky was black with masses of moving cloulds, (through which I saw something like a great right arm outstretched,) and filled with thunder, they again enslaved him and led him off to the markets, where human flesh and blood are sold."

"Well," said Mary, "that is a curious dream; it seems to me there's something in it. All dreams are not alike; some are really remarkable, and you cannot help remembering them. But I have heard it said, that if you never tell your dreams, you will soon forget them, and never be troubled with them. I half wish you had not told this to me."

Mary went to her present home. The dream; did he invent it, to rebuke her as gently as he could, but yet as strongly? Was it indeed wrong to sell her truant slave? She leaned her head upon her hand, as she sat alone in the twilight in her chamber. She had sold the boy, but what of that? her father, and her grandfather, had bought and sold slaves. The minister of the church of which she was a member, bought some; and when occasion served, sold others; many of the best members of the church had done so; and why was it her duty to know more than these? or to set up for herself a higher standard of duty than that adopted and practiced by those whom she most venerated on earth? True, she thought that the habitual dealing in slaves, could not but be wrong. The men whom she had occasionally seen engaged in that trade, were persons with whom she could not associate; and she could not but condemn their conduct. But they followed the business for mere gain. She had not been controlled by such motives. If her boy had remained, she would have been kind to him; but he ran off, and all her friends advised her to sell him. He was a slave before she sold him, he was only a slave now; it was a mere transfer of ownership. The boy's mother was dead, she knew nothing of his father, except only, that she had heard he had been sold two years before, and taken to Tennessee. Mr. Ives did not condemn her for holding Lewis as a slave, but only for selling him! Where was the difference between holding and selling him? If the one was right, the other could not be wrong, unless indeed, she had sold him to an unkind master; but she had not done so; the purchaser was kind, a gentleman of high character and well-known benevolence.

But still in spite of all her reasonings, her heart was not at rest. "He was my property," she said; and an almost audible voice answered her, "Who made man your property?" She started, and thought of the concentric circles of light, and the words of fire: "Thou shalt love thy neighbor as thyself." "Love a negro as I love myself? make my own rights, and feelings, and wishes, the measure of my duties to a negro?" She sat still again, so still that her heart was almost silent; and rose, and said half aloud, "They are God's words. The common Father of the human race, lays the same duties, and confers the same rights alike upon all his children."

Early the next day, she sent a servant to inquire for Mr. Ives' health, and when she was told that it had improved, she again sent the servant with a message, that business required her immediate absence, for a few days, from Willoughby; bade him take good care of himself, and in an hour was in a stage-coach on her journey.

CHAPTER XL.

BELLE SCOTT.

The hopes which were entertained of Belle's speedy recovery proved to be delusive. Some permanent injury, that defied all remedies, seemed to have been inflicted upon her by the fire. She was not scarred nor were there any external marks of injury, but she was scarcely able to walk. Her spirits too became more sad each day, as the time drew near for the decision of her cause. She was sweet, and mild, her whole soul seemed to be bathed in an atmosphere of resignation, gratitude and love; but at times she would start and grow pale, as if just awakened from a fearful dream.

For a few days after the fire, the neighbors showed her much sympathy; some no doubt visited her merely from curiosity. But now things had resumed their usual course at the parsonage. The attraction of novelty had worn off. Mrs. Johnston was still the same devoted friend; Mrs. Stillman still kind and hopeful. Mr. Stillman looked sad, and sometimes sighed, but he also looked firm; as a man does, who knows he is right and is determined to persist in the course he has chosen. Why he was thus sad and thus firm will be more apparent from the following dialogue.

The parties are Mrs. Upson, the hostess of the evening; Mrs. Turton, Miss Williams, and Mrs. Jones, seated at the tea-table of Mrs. Upson, in the village of Auburn.

Mrs. Jones. "How is that girl who was hurt at the fire?"

Mrs. Upson. "Getting better; but she is unable, or pretends to be unable yet, to walk out of doors.

Mrs. Turton. "Well! what is this world coming to! Our preacher's wife went up to Mr. Stillman's last week, just to make a short call. Mrs. Stillman insisted on her staying to tea. She seated her, at the tea-table, right down by the side of that mulatto girl, Belle; and she declares that the odor was so strong that she could not eat a bit; and that poor Mrs. Stillman was so mortified that she could hardly look her in the face."

Miss Williams. "Why, how can that be? I have heard that she is a white girl and a great heiress. Indeed I have seen her, and cannot see a single trace of the negro or mulatto about her.

Mrs. Upson. "Oh! that was a nice story got up by the Abolitionists here, only to get the girl off;

but it did no good; it was hardly a nine days' wonder."

Mrs. Jones. "And that pert little Mrs. Johnston, who was so vain of her wealth and beauty, has met with a sad fall; people are talking about her all over the town and neighborhood; they say that she eats with that mulatto and treats her as if she was a sister. I guess some people presume too much on their wealth and influence."

Mrs. Jones. "Why, la me! The whole country are laughing about that young widow and her pet mulatto. As for poor Mr. Stillman, I do pity *him!* He and his wife are under the influence of Mrs. Johnston, because she contributes ten times more to their support than anybody else;—they are afraid to offend her; but on the other side old Mr. Rounds, who is one of the ruling elders of his church, called at our door yesterday and shook his head and said, that it did seem to him, their church never would have a settled pastor; they have had four ministers in five years; and now Mr. Stillman will have to leave, or the Church will be divided, as more than half his congregation entirely disapprove of his harboring that negro girl.

Miss Williams: "I wish I were only able to make good to Mr. Stillman, all the losses he will sustain by his hospitality to that poor girl. His conduct seems to me eminently praiseworthy. He has taken care of the sick and the hungry—and proved himself, by his good deeds, a minister whose example is a commentary upon his public teaching."

Mrs. Upson. "Well, my dear girl, no one blames him for his benevolence; we only censure him for his imprudence. He could have discharged all the duties you praise so highly, to the girl, without making her an inmate of his house, and a companion for his wife. He could have taken her to negro Tom's house, just by his church, and Tom's wife would have given her all the attention she needs—and Mr. Stillman could have called daily, if he pleased, and seen that she wanted nothing. If he had done so, he would not have insulted and outraged so large a portion of his church members as he has done, by trying to break down the God-made distinctions between the white and the negro races."

Mrs. Jones: "It's a great pity, too, that he did so just at this time. His church, which had been distracted, and almost divided upon the liquor question, had become in a manner united, and are now more divided than before. It is plain that he will have to leave."

Miss Williams: "I think if any church will not

let their minister take such persons into his family as he thinks best—the sooner he gets away, the better it will be for him. It may be worse for the church, but he will gain by the change."

Mrs. Upson: "Oh! you know, Jane, that a minister is a public person, and his example does more good or more harm than that of others. He ought, therefore, to be circumspect in proportion to his influence."

Mrs. Jones: "That word influence, that you have just used, reminds me, too, that another of the elders told me that Mr. Stillman, by his conduct in this affair, has utterly, and perhaps, forever impaired his influence, especially over those that are without. He said that Col. Nippers, our state senator, used frequently to go and hear him preach; but he declares he cannot do so conscientiously, now that he has turned Abolitionist, and that many others are in the same state of mind. The influence of a minister is his most precious jewel, and one that he cannot take too much care of."

Miss Williams: "I don't know how it is, but I have observed that those ministers, who are always taking care of their influence, as they call it, are good for nothing else. I have never seen, in either the New or Old Testaments that the apostles and prophets were men who took care of their influence—so far from it, they, every one of them, seem at all times utterly to have disregarded it, and discharged only the duty in hand, whether men would hear, or whether they would forbear—whether they were pleased or offended."

Mrs. Upson: "You are quite severe, Jane."

Miss Williams: "Indeed I am on this the greatest vice of our ministry. Taking care of their influence, is but a name, under which they cloak their cowardice and time-serving. The influence most cared for, is their conjectured influence over the rich or the great. Whenever I hear a minister talk of taking care of his influence, I think at once, that it is but the mean wincing of a time-server, shrinking from known duty, under the pretense, which he generally knows to be false, of being more useful by leaving known duties undischarged. All such men are injurious to the churches, and the sooner they are turned out of the ministry the better."

Mrs. Upson and Mrs. Jones together: "Why Jane, how you do talk."

Miss Williams: "If a few others would talk so too, and act also in the same spirit, our churches would not be as they are now, so cold and dead. The rule, fixed as the law of gravitation, 'that he who will save his life, shall lose it; and he who will lose his life for the Gospel, shall save it;'

applies as directly to the influence of ministers, as to their lives; and they all know it. As long as ministers are permitted, under the plea of preserving their influence, to stand aloof from unpopular christian duties; each in his turn may do so, and every duty be left undischarged. This vice, is the great maelstrom that draws down to death the usefulness of all who indulge in it. This practice, is the spendthrift's promise, to pay principal and large interest next year; while the debt is due now, and he can pay it if he will."

CHAPTER XLI.

MARY SCOTT.

Two men were in a parlor of a hotel. One of them was tall and handsome, his face showed marks of dissipation, but not of recent excess; it was an old wound of which you saw the deep, broad scar. The other was younger—both looked like gentlemen.

A servant came in and said to the elder gentleman: "Mr. Watts, a lady wishes to see you in the parlor; and wants you, if you please, to wait a few minutes, and she will come in."

"Who is she?"

"I do not know," said the servant: "she is young, and very pretty, sir. She came here only an hour ago."

"Some person," said Mr. Simmons, "who has servants for sale, I suppose, sir."

"Probably so," said Mr. Watts. "I know of nothing else, that could induce the lady to call on me. But to resume our conversation, I saw in a newspaper, an advertisement of a sale of slaves, which is to take place to-morrow in ——

county. Shall we go there to purchase? Fifty-two are to be sold for cash, to the highest bidder."

"I, too, have seen it," replied Mr. Simmons, "and knew the gentleman very well, when he was alive, whose property is now to be sold by his administrators. He was a distinguished preacher, whose name you have often seen in the newspapers. He wrote a great deal in support of slavery, and denounced the fanatics of the North with a degree of severity that made them wince and feel, to the core of their hearts, the sarcasms that dropped as vitriol from his pen."

"Well, well!" said Mr. Watts, "we ought by all means then, to attend the sale. We owe it to him as a debt of gratitude, to make his property sell as high as our competition can effect it, without injury to ourselves. I have often heard of the gentleman, but had not the honor of an acquaintance with him. Will you go? or shall I?"

"Oh! do you go by all means. I am here among those who have known me from my childhood, and could not bear to be seen as a trader purchasing slaves. You are almost a stranger here, and have been long accustomed to the business."

"I'll go, sir," said Mr. Watts, "but you really must get over the shyness that so afflicts you. You *are* a trader, and will have to share the losses as well as to enjoy the profits of the trade. You never fail to pocket your share of the profits. I *have* received profits from the trade and *losses* too. I have lost nearly all my friends, and my self-respect."

"You are in bad spirits this morning. Why should you lose your self-respect? Was not your father a slaveholder, and your grandfather? and were not all your ancestors slaveholders, as far back as you can trace your pedigree? *They* bought slaves and held them and sold them; and what are you doing now but buying and selling slaves?"

"Yes," replied Watts, "that is true, but they were planters—not traders."

"I cannot see the difference between the planter who buys and sells, and the trader who does the same, except that the one does not make it his regular business, and the other does."

"Difference or no difference, in principle," said Watts, "there is at least a great difference in the looks of a thing. Nobody whose opinion is worth a rush, thinks the worse of a planter for selling a slave, or thinks slave-trading a respectable business. I cannot for the life of me see, why the distinction should be made, but it *is* made, and whether it is rightly or wrongly made, is no difference to me. I feel, that I am in a lower position now than I was a year ago."

"That may be all true, sir; but even if it is so, you ought to conquer your prejudices. It is no worse to trade in slaves, than it is for a Northern judge to send one back again into slavery. No doubt, such judges feel themselves degraded and disgraced by such conduct; but they soon get used to it and learn to bear their misfortunes with due composure."

"That may be, sir; but nothing but the hope of making a fortune, and soon too, could make me continue in this business another day. I do hope, when I shall have made one or two hundred thousand dollars, to leave this business, and if possible, all my remembrances of it, and lead a quiet life on a plantation well stocked with slaves."

"That may be a bright hope, and I wish it may be realized; but, my dear sir, few persons who begin this trade ever leave it; they continue in it till they die. It has its fascinations, as all other trades by which money is speedily made; you buy and sell at a handsome profit till your reputation as an honorable trader is well known, and then you buy on credit, and have your notes to pay; and so it passes on from year to year until you become old, and rich, and die."

"Die a slave-trader!" said Mr. Watts with emphasis. "Die a trader, sir, I can never think of that."

"Well, that is strange; you said but half a minute ago, that you wish to retire and live on a well-stocked plantation. Is it any more dreadful to die a slave-trader than to die a slaveholder? Thousands and tens of thousands of men in this country have so died, and who thought their fate a sad one? Really, there may be a mighty difference, but my vision is too obtuse to see where it lies."

"Nor can I," said Mr. Watts, "but still I cannot endure the thought. I have had a fortune, and lost it, and must make another; and no other way than this, seems open before me."

"I, too, have lost a small fortune, but I do not feel as you do about the business. I have already made ten times as much as I had when I began life, and I intend to follow the business as long as I can make it profitable. I see no sense in a man's living on a sugar plantation, and making four or five thousand dollars a year, when he can make twice that sum in the trade, with the same capital. A man can live in Richmond or New Orleans and send out his agent, if he chooses, to buy and sell for him. His life will be as easy as that of the richest planter, if he pursues that course; and even if he attends in his own person to the details of his business, his life is not much more laborious than is that of gentlemen who give personal attention to the affairs of their own plantations. I have no qualms of conscience about the thing. The trade in slaves is but the trade in one of the great staple commodities of the United States. I have not the least objection to its being made as infamous as all the people in the world can make it. The fewer competitors the better for us. The more men you keep out of the business, the better it will be for those who remain in it. The infamy of the slave-trade, my dear sir, of which you complain so much, is really the greatest source of our profits. I have met in my time with hundreds of men who would gladly have engaged in it if they only dared to do so."

Here the conversation was interrupted by the entrance of a lady, who inquired for Mr. Watts.

"I am the person," said Mr. Watts, handing her a chair, "can I be of any service to you to-day, madam?"

"Yes," replied the lady. "I sold, some time ago, a mulatto boy to Colonel Rawlings, who told me he wanted him for a dining-room servant. I have since learned that he sold him to you. Is that so, sir?"

"I did buy a negro of Colonel Rawlings, and I

have no doubt, madam, it is the boy you sold him. He told me he had lately bought him."

"I wish to re-purchase the boy," said the lady; "what is your price?"

"Oh! my dear madam, I make it a rule never to sell any, while I am on my route, or gathering up a gang. I buy in the northern slave-holding states, and sell, generally, at New Orleans. It would greatly derange my business to sell before I get my gang into the regular market."

"But can you not sell *one*, sir? I wish, especially, to re-purchase this boy, and will give you any reasonable sum you may ask for him. I sold him inconsiderately, and greatly regret the act."

"Was he not your property?" inquired Mr. Watts, with a keen, piercing look.

"I got him from my father," replied the lady, "and regret that I have sold him. I have heard that you gave Colonel Rawlings nine hundred dollars for him, I will give you twelve hundred dollars, and you will thus make a handsome profit in a very short time."

"There is nothing in the world I would not do to oblige a lady, except to break in on my settled rules of business. That I can't do for any person."

"But, sir, I feel that I have done wrong in selling the boy, and wish to repair the injuries I have done him."

"Oh! as for that, madam, it is only a feeling common to all persons who sell slaves, especially after they are relieved from the pressure that induced them to sell. When the money is spent, then they are sorry, and repent."

"My money is not spent, sir, and my repentance proceeds from no such motive. Here, sir," said she, "laying on a center-table a roll of bank bills; here is money enough to repay you all that you have paid to Colonel Rawlings, and more, so as to leave you a reasonable profit for your nefarious business."

"Nefarious business, madam, in which *two* must always be engaged!" replied Watts with half a sneer. "Nefarious business! but, however, a lady has privileges."

"I feel the full force of your censure, and it is just. The buyer and the seller are, for a time at least, and in that transaction, equals. And because it is so, I want to re-purchase the boy."

"Well, madam, if that is your motive, we cannot engage in the same transaction. If it was wrong for you to sell to Colonel Rawlings, it must be wrong for me to sell to you. I cannot sell him to-day, madam."

"Will you to-morrow then?" eagerly inquired the lady; "if you will, I will wait here till to-morrow."

"No, madam, I have made up my mind, since I have been talking to you, to take him to my own plantation in Mississippi."

While this conversation was going on, a servant was busy in the room. The lady left the parlor, and in a few minutes heard a knock at her door; the servant entered.

"Don't cry, my dear leddy, don't cry so. I I heard myself all that the ould thrader said to ye, and all that ye said til him; don't ye cry so; me and Patrick is agoing away from here to-morrow, and Patrick, that's my ould man, that is, shall fix it for you; for all that ould Watts whouldn't take yer money when you was in the parlor, as soon as you come out, he sat down and counted it, and put it in his pocket-book. I saw him with my own eyes; so now he 's took your money, and he 'll be obliged to let you have the boy you want til buy. He can't help himself now, miss."

"Where is the boy?" said Mary, for it was she.

"Oh! he 's in this very house, madam, up-stairs in the garret, and the dhoor's locked; and Patrick takes up victuals to them, and 'tends to them."

"What! is this tavern a slave-pen?"

"Oh no, dear miss! it's not exactly a slave-pen. I have been chambermaid in hotels in the free states; they keep slaves locked up there, just as they do here, in the taverns up-stairs, to keep 'em from running away. I'll get Patrick to come up here wid me and see you; and sure you hardly would mind making us a little present, just for a keepsake, if Patrick helped the boy off, that you could get him again?"

The next day Mary was riding in a stage. She passed a man driving a lean horse in a small wagon. He was sitting on a great box, apparently of goods, and behind him in the wagon, sat Bridget. The man, when he saw her, gave two or three heavy raps upon the box, and the stage was soon out of sight.

Mary waited at Marietta, in Ohio, for her friends, Patrick and Bridget, to overtake her. The next day they crossed the river; the box was opened, and Lewis leaped out.

"Now will not the dear leddy, make Patrick a handsome present? only think of the risk that he ran, and all to oblige the swate leddy. He wouldn't have done it for any other person in this world, only for you."

"Thank you, madam, God bless ye! I'll remember ye forever! This is a twenty dollar gold piece, I believe?"

"Yes, it is twenty dollars."

"Is this for Patrick, or for me, madam?"

"For Patrick."

"Now, you dear leddy, I am sure you're not a-going to let Patrick have it all, when I've had just as much trouble as he?"

"Thank you, madam. That's a ten dollar gold piece, is it? God bless you! We 'll remember your leddyship forever."

CHAPTER XLII.

MR. IVES.

"WHY have you not called sooner?" said Mr. Ives, "I have not seen you for ten days. It is really cruel, to treat me as you have done. I have been sick; I am yet unable to leave the house; I have but few acquaintances here, and no friends except yourself; and the hours have passed heavily, with leaden weight, from your absence. Indeed I did not intend to offend you, by the remarks that I made about that boy. I was taken by surprise, and perhaps expressed myself in stronger terms than I should have used; but I am sure you will forgive me."

"Forgive you, indeed!" replied Mary, "forgive you! I thank you from my heart of hearts, for what you said, and for the terms in which you said it. I would not tell you where I was going, for fear that you would oppose me; and I had fully made up my mind to do what I have done, and so I thought it better to surprise you. I went, accompanied only by Julia, my servant, to the house of Colonel Rawlings, to whom I had sold Lewis, for the purpose of re-purchasing him; and there learned that his declaration, that he was buying him only for a domestic, was a mere *ruse;* that he had sold Lewis but a few days before, to a soul-driver, who had taken him to the western part of this state. I had made up my mind to purchase him, if it was possible to do so; and went on as rapidly as I could, until I found the trader. He refused to sell him to me, but I left on the table more money than he had given for him, and afterward got the boy safely off. He is now, I have reason to believe, in Canada. So that I have undone, as far as my efforts can effect it, the one great wrong of my life."

"You surprise me, Mary. You—you journeyed accompanied only by your maid, into the interior of the state, and then to the western part of it? *You* went to a slave-trader, and re-purchased the boy? *you* talked with such a man? I never have been so surprised in my life."

"There is nothing strange in what I have done. I thoughtlessly sold Lewis, and afterward saw that I had committed a great sin, and I determined, at every sacrifice of personal convenience, to undo the wrong. I felt, during every moment of my journey, a light heart. I knew that I was doing my duty, and that a good Providence was over, and protecting me."

"But could you not have done it as well by an agent?"

"No, not at all. No agent could have been filled with the same determined purpose to accomplish the result; and without such resolute purpose, the matter could not have been accomplished. I had personally sinned, and it was my duty, personally, to retrieve the wrong.

"I had, too, another motive. I know that you are worthy of me, and I could not but feel humbled when I thought that I had made myself unworthy of you. My very pride would have been a sufficient motive for my conduct; and that feeling, I am sure, had too much influence in controlling me."

"You are a noble girl, Mary, and I shall love you, if possible, more than I have ever done, for your generous, though singular conduct."

As Mr. Ives and Mary will not re-appear upon our pages, the reader may wish to know the sequel of their history.

That they were married soon after the conversation just related, my lady readers need not be told. But Mr. Ives could not return again to New Orleans, for all hope of a prosperous life there, was at an end. The slaves of Miss Mary Scott were all liberated. They were not turned out among strangers, to begin the world for themselves without the means of a comfortable subsistence.

They were brought to a free state, and there, upon well-stocked farms that Mary and her husband carefully aided them in selecting, were all settled. School-teachers, and the means of religious education were provided for them, and with many blessings from the old and young—blessings bestowed and received with eyes filled with tears—Mr. and Mrs. Ives left their friends, after promising to visit them often, and urging them to write, or cause letters to be written to them if anything should occur that might require their attention.

They then purchased for themselves a neat farm in Pennsylvania, and there, surrounded by kind neighbors and friends, they live in peace. Books, and flowers, and music, gladden their passing hours, and their home is filled with sweetness and love. Love to God and man fills their hearts, and the whole atmosphere around them.

CHAPTER XLIII.

SUSPENSE.

THE winter passed rapidly away, and the ten weeks of painful suspense were drawing to an end. Mr. Reed had written several letters to Mr. Stillman, the first one full of hope; indeed he stated that he had no doubt whatever, but that the identity of Belle as the lost child of Mr. Scott, could be easily and fully established. But his later letters chilled all these fervent hopes. He took a copy of the scrawl in the Bible with him, and had shown it to the lawyer employed for Belle at Willoughby; who told him that it did not state in any part, either the name of the child or of her parents, or the time or place where the matter occurred. All that was stated in the writing might be true, and still it might have no reference whatever to the lost child of Mr. Scott. In one of his letters of later date, he stated that his arrangements were such that he would be at Auburn in the evening before the day set by the commissioner for deciding the case, and that his friend at New Orleans would reach there about the same time. He stated also, that there was a link to be supplied in the proof, if the facts warranted it, and that was, to show that the woman Minte, who was sold to a man in the western part of Virginia in June, was the same woman afterward married to Aaron. He had no doubt whatever that she was the same, but as yet no proof could be found to establish that essential fact. How had Minte been transferred from Virginia to Alabama? by whom and when?

Poor Belle was sinking fast under the heavy weight of her accumulated sorrows. She tried at times to be cheerful, but the light of earthly hope had almost left her. Her fate hung upon the decision of a single man. Public opinion and the power of the government of the United States, and prejudice, were all on the side of her oppressors.

If she should be surrendered, what would be her fate? Mr. Scott could, if he chose, put her as a field hand on a sugar plantation, to labor under the eye of an overseer, and to have her flesh torn by the whip; he could also sell her, at a higher price, for baser purposes. Thousands of women no better than herself, had been so treated, and what reason had she to believe that her lot would be lighter than theirs?

Mr. Stillman deeply sympathized with Belle, and looked forward to the day when the decision would be made, with fear and trembling and sometimes with hope. He feared for the life and fate of the poor girl; he feared also for the Church and for his country. The decision that would send her back into slavery would strike down, as with an iron mace, the religious liberty of every man and woman and child in the United States, at the North, at the South; at the East, at the West.

It was clear to him that our fathers had made one contract by which they bound themselves and their posterity forever to aid the slaveholder in his sin of oppressing his fellow man, by returning to him his fugitive slave; and it was also as clear that about two years afterward they made another contract for themselves and their posterity, by which the religious liberty of each man in the United States is fully guaranteed and secured; and that they intended, by the last contract, to repeal all things in the former contract that were inconsistent with it.

But would the commissioner see this as clearly as he saw it? If he did so, had he courage enough to adhere to the truth and the right, and to maintain the highest right of each man in the United States at all hazards and at every sacrifice that man can could make or endure? If the commissioner should sustain his own religious freedom, he would do so for all the people of the United States. If he betrayed it, he betrayed it for all mankind.

Mr. Stillman well knew that if the people could but see what really was at stake in the contest, they would, in every city and town and hamlet in the whole land, stand waiting with eager earnestness to hear the result; they would ask each other with quivering lips, are the rights for which our fathers left their homes in the old world and fled to this, when it was all a wilderness, yet ours? or are they taken from us forever? and will the men whom we employ and pay to protect us in them, betray us? Are the rights, for which our fathers bled on a hundred battle fields, wrested from us? or are they safe forever? But it would require time to awaken the people. They will look upon him as an idle dreamer, who shouts in their ears—"Your religious freedom is stricken down and wrested from you!"

When Daniel was forbidden to pray, thousands of men had the same interest in the question at stake, that he had, but they could not either see or feel that any wrong was done to them. Thousands stood by when the Apostles were forbidden to preach, all of whom were as deeply interested in the right they were asserting as were the Apostles, and did not dream that any rights of theirs were involved in the contest. And in this country, part of the people have made laws by which their own rights, and those of all the people in the United States, to religious liberty, are stricken down, and nearly the whole land quietly acquiesces in the wrong. The reason is, that the people do not feel aggrieved by laws that are intended to oppress the black race of men. They have so long looked upon their oppression as a thing of course, that they regard it as right, or at least as inevitable.

On the evening before the decision was to be made, Mr. Stillman's family could not rest. As boats were heard, passing the village they hoped that some one of them would land and Edgar Reed would knock at Mr. Stillman's door. But the weary night wore away and he came not.

CHAPTER XLIV.

THE DECISION.

EARLY in the morning a pure blue sky, upon which the moon and stars seemed to have left still lingering, part of their light and glory, canopied the village of Auburn. All was calm and sweetly beautiful, as if the spirit of love and peace filled the air and hovered over the scene. From each house in the village, the slowly and gracefully ascending smoke rose in white wreaths until it mingled with the air, and the glorious sun, just rising, threw his long waves of crystal light, in luxurious beauty over the scene. The river was as a broad line of melted silver, moving slowly and majestically on, until hidden from view by a curve in its course.

Mr. Stillman prayed for Belle, and sobs from Mrs. Stillman and Mrs. Johnston drowned his voice, and they all rose in tears. The ladies embraced poor Belle, kissed her, and attired her for her appearance in court.

At the same time Mr. Scott, who had been in the village a day, was walking toward the court-house with the quick step, and hard, keen eye of a determined man. By his side was a man whom he had engaged to assist him; and along the street, going to the same place, the commissioner, with a roll of paper in his hand, was leisurely selecting his way, so as to avoid soiling his polished boots.

The ring of the anvil and the noise of the hammer stopped as he passed, and men put on their coats, and hastened to the court-house. It was soon filled; but those who were soonest there, were people of color from the village and the country, looking silently and earnestly at the gathering crowd. The commissioner took his seat. The officer announced that the court was in session, and commanded all persons to keep silence. By the side of the marshal were fifty strong men, whom he had commanded to aid him.

Mr. Scott and his lawyers, one of whom was a stranger, and the assistant he had employed, seated themselves at a long table in front of the commissioner.

One chair was yet vacant, and the people looked eagerly at the door for the person who was to occupy it.

At length it opened, and Belle, supported on one side by Mrs. Stillman, and on the other by

Mrs. Johnston, entered the room. Seats were provided for the group near the table.

Belle was radiantly beautiful. The paleness, as of death, which had so long settled upon her cheek, now, under the excitement of the hour, gave way to a hectic flush that spread over her face. Her eyes were bright as if her whole soul shone through them. Her long, jet-black hair hung in curls over her neck. No bride ever looked more lovely. But her attire was not that of a bride; she was dressed in deep mourning—an appropriate costume. Over her countenance despair brooded, as if he had clasped hands with death. She was calm in all her movements; but hers was the calmness of resignation to inevitable sorrow. Her eyes were fixed, her hands clasped, her breathing short and quick, as of a person who is suffocating. All eyes, for an instant, were fixed upon her, and then turned to the commissioner, who read his opinion.

CHAPTER XLV.

THE DECISION.

"The evidence," he said, "proved that Belle Robinson, the alleged fugitive, had been in the possession of Mr. Scott for many years; and during all that time, he had claimed her as his slave. Possession of personal property, especially when it is accompanied by a claim of ownership on the part of the possessor, is always, at least, *prima facie* evidence of the claimant's right to it. And as there is no evidence in this case, tending to disprove this possession, or this claim of ownership, the court had no difficulty in arriving at the conclusion, that the girl in question, was in fact, by the laws of Louisiana, the property of the claimant, John Scott.

"The next inquiry is: Is she a fugitive from service?

"On this question, the evidence left no doubt. The boat landed for a moment at the wharf of this town; it was nearly night; and the defendant, availing herself of the confusion occasioned by the landing, escaped, in company with another person, also a fugitive slave.

"This brings the case within the provisions of the act of Congress of 1850; and if that law is in accordance with the Constitution of the United States, the defendant must be surrendered.

"It might not be out of place to advert, for a moment only, to an alleged discovery, that the girl Belle is indeed a free person, and a niece of her claimant. But no evidence had been produced, which even tended to prove that the writing, which it is claimed identifies her, has any reference to her; nor does it appear by whom, or for what purpose, or when it was written! Such evidence could not be received against the girl; and by the same principle, it could not be received in her favor. It would indeed have afforded him great pleasure, to have found her free: the duty before him was unpleasant, but still it is not the less a duty.

"Is the act in question, in accordance with the Constitution of the United States?

"It is claimed that the acts of 1850, and 1793, are both contrary to the first amendment; which provides 'that Congress shall make no law respecting an establishment of religion, or prohibiting the free exercise thereof.' If, in fact, either of these acts of Congress do, in any degree, interfere with

30

the free exercise of religion—either of love to God or to man—do impair liberty of conscience; then the acts are void. Do they have any such effect? It is claimed, on the one side, that this girl is the property of the claimant, Mr. Scott, who perhaps, may have purchased her with his money; and that the laws of the state in which he lives, protect him in the enjoyment of this species of property, as they do of any other; and that therefore, his right to the restoration of it, rests upon the same basis, that it rests upon as to other kinds of property.

"On the other hand, it is claimed that the woman in question, is a human being; and to surrender her into slavery, is to partake of the guilt of the person, who holds or claims her as his slave.

"This may be true, if indeed there is guilt, in holding her as a slave.

"Slavery, in some form, has existed from time immemorial, and among all nations of the earth.

"It is true, that this does not prove it right. It casts, however, the burthen of proving that it is wrong, on the party who assails it.

"Have they done so here? The christian Scriptures have been referred to; and it must be admitted, that the arguments drawn from them, have been presented with ingenuity. On the proper exposition of the Scriptures, the sects into which the whole christian world has been divided, differ in many important points. But in the rightfulness of slave-holding, and its entire accordance with the Scriptures; there is among the Christians of the United States a singular unanimity of opinion. Catholics and Protestants agree, that slave-holding is not sin. Indeed almost all the christian sects agree, that it is no sin, to hold men and women in slavery. They admit known slaveholders to their pulpits, and receive the sacraments of the church from their hands. They admit them to christian fellowship; while most of them are so strict, that they sever from that fellowship, a person who dances, or even attends a dance. Thousands of men who have been set apart to the office of the ministry, and who have devoted their lives to the study and exposition of the Scriptures, are daily proclaiming, by the most certain of all tests -*their conduct*— that slave-holding is not sin. This they do with heavy vows upon them, to rebuke all sin. This they daily do; most of them firmly believing in the eternity of rewards and punishments. Nearly all of these men are therefore daily, and with one accord, teaching and proclaiming to the public, that slave-holding is no sin. Under these circumstances, it would at least be an act of rashness in the court, to dissent from their continued and united testimony.

"I therefore adjudge that Belle Robinson is a fugitive slave, and that she be restored to her owner, John Scott."

The judge now signed a paper, already drawn up, and handed it to the marshal.

The marshal conversed for a moment in a low voice with Mr. Scott. He then approached Belle, and laid his hand on her shoulder: "You must now go with your master." A loud shriek was heard from Mrs. Johnston. Mrs. Stillman became pale as a corpse; a thrill ran through all the spectators in the court-room. The judge folded up his papers, and was about to leave the bench, but before he did so, said, "he had heard that evidence was expected that day, to identify the girl as a free person. If it came before the marshal had finally executed his order, by taking the girl out of the state, he would hear the evidence." He then left the court-house.

The deep, cold, gray eyes of Mr. Scott, glared like those of a tiger. The prey was his. He seized Belle, and drawing out a pair of handcuffs, placed them upon her wrists. The poor girl raised her eyes and her manacled hands, appealing to Heaven, and found relief from her agony in a burst of frantic grief. "Why was I snatched from the fire to endure the deeper horrors of this hour? Why was I born into this world, to find in it nothing but unmingled sorrow and suffering?"

Mrs. Johnston joined in her cries; turning to the men around her, she asked them why they who so bravely rescued the poor girl from death, now stood calmly while a worse fate awaited her? She called on Wilbar, to make one more effort to save the poor girl for whom he had once periled his life.

Wilbar asked Mr. Scott what price he would take for her?

"No price shall buy her. I will make an example of her, sir. I have raised her tenderly as my own child. I 'll now send her into the cotton-field as a hand, or I 'll send her to Cuba, and sell her there. Your town is not able to produce the sum, sir—she is not for sale; I have always told inquirers that no price will buy her."

CHAPTER XLVI.

THE SURRENDER.

Mrs. Stillman embraced Belle once more and kissed her. The sad procession moved from the court-house down to the bank of the river. Mrs. Johnston quickly descended the bank in advance of the party; went to a ferry-boat chained at the wharf; locked the chain by which it was fastened, and put the key in her pocket. The marshal said to her:

"This is a public ferry; I want to cross the river."

"The ferry is mine—the boat is mine, and you shall not have it for the purpose of taking that poor girl out of Ohio. My boat was not made to carry her (pointing to Belle) where she may be scourged until the blood from her torn flesh falls upon the ground—to carry her where she may be sent as a laborer into the cotton-field, to toil all day in the sun, without even the promise of reward."

Poor, poor Belle! hope had fled; she was sad as those who meet death in despair. Her senses seemed benumbed, her lips were white, and her tall form, and face deadly pale, would have made a fit model for an artist, to paint the mingled emotions of despair and horror.

A great crowd was assembled upon the shore, to witness the departure of the girl (as they called her) and her master. Mrs. Johnston moved about in this assembly, and tried every effort, but in vain, to induce them to rescue Belle by force. Two young men said, "they were willing to do so, if enough could be found to aid in the enterprise." Others said, "it is a sin, and a shame for her master to take her away; but they must submit to the laws of the country, until those laws shall be repealed."

"Are you not convinced that the acts you speak of, are unconstitutional and void?" said Mrs. Johnston.

"Yes," they replied, "we have no doubt but that they are unconstitutional; but until some court shall declare them so, we are bound, as good citizens, to obey them."

"Then, if Congress should command you to worship an idol, you would worship it," said Mrs. Johnston, "for four or five years, till some judge said the law was void; and if the judge was himself an idolater, and decided it was not void, you would, of course, continue to worship the idol all your lives?"

"But this case seems to us, to be different," said the men.

"How is it different?" said Mrs. Johnston. "Idolatry was the sin of the Roman empire, as slavery is the sin of America. It is as gross a sin to enslave a human being, as it is to worship an idol; and the surrender of this poor girl into slavery, is just as bad as it would be to pray in an idol's temple. Will you as Americans, submit to such outrages openly practiced before your eyes? You are entitled, each man of you, to the protection of the Constitution of the United States; and are recreant to liberty, if you allow such outrages upon your greatest rights. Your rights, in this matter, are the rights of all men; what you maintain for yourselves, you maintain for the whole race of man; and if you betray them, you do so for the whole human race."

"That looks like Nullification," said a man in the crowd.

"I don't care what it looks like," replied Mrs. Johnston. "The acts of Congress on this subject are void, and he who maintains them, does not support the Constitution of his country, but tramples that Constitution under his feet. Daniel, when he was forbidden to pray, and the Apostles, when they were forbidden to preach, had no such constitutional rights as we have, and yet they obeyed God rather than man. You will be doubly recreant to your duty, if with a constitutional provision made by your fathers, for the very purpose of making all laws that interfere with religious duty, merely nullities and utterly void, you obey such laws and permit them to be carried into effect before your very eyes."

"That looks like the truth, said one of the men; but we fear the consequences. It may be better to let such wrongs pass for the present, believing, as we do, that this reign of terror will soon end."

"Yes," said Mrs. Johnston, "but in the meantime this poor girl will be murdered, and then what will be your share of the guilt of her 'taking off?'"

The marshal sent one of his men to a neighboring grogshop, and a large crew of half-drunken men came shouting at his heels, to prevent a rescue. They were loud in their professions of love for the laws of the country, and for the Constitution of the United States, and for the Union. Men were in the gang, whose only virtue was their patriotism; who respected no law that interfered with the indulgence of their impulses and appetites, but who now were found to love one of the laws of the country. The basest loved the act the best. The most worthless were the most ready to lend their aid to carry it into execution.

Mr. Scott passed from one point to another, amid the crowd, silent, with compressed lips and flashing eyes, apparently enraged at the unexpected delay. At last a boat was seen ascending the river. The littleparty around Belle, now gathered still closer to her. Mrs. Johnston, again and again folded her in her arms, and wept in an agony of passionate grief. Mrs. Stillman, in tears, embraced her, and begged God's blessing upon her. Mr. Stillman took both her manacled hands in his, and prayed aloud for God's blessing, and that he would yet deliver her; he prayed in agony, as though he would take by force, the boon he craved—as a mother prays who begs for the life of her only son. The boat landed for a moment, and the party moved toward it; but the voice of Captain McBride rang out: "You can't bring your slave on board this boat, sir. I've made my boat a floating slave-pen long enough, and will do so no more. Mr. Scott stopped, and cast at the captain a look full of rage and contempt.

At this time three persons were seen descending from the boat; one, a man about sixty years of age, with white hair, and shabbily dressed; another, a woman who took the arm of a gentleman by her side, as they walked up the bank of the river, and who appeared to be a few years his senior. When she first stepped ashore, she made a low courtsey to the first person she met, and said, she was mighty glad to see him, and continued from time to time to courtsey to the persons she passed, until the pair moved out of sight.

The gentleman walked on apparently without seeing any one.

Another person got off the boat, but he stood to watch the landing of a pair of fine bay horses which he had in charge. He was a tall man, a little lame, and with a benevolent and humorous expression upon his face.

After the horses were safely landed, he followed the three other persons up the bank; the horses, led by a hostler from the tavern, followed him.

Mr. Scott looked at the man who first went up, carelessly, then with a searching and curious gaze, and a shade of anxiety passed over his face. He looked too, at the other man, and became pale. As soon as they were out of sight, he offered a hundred dollars to any one who would put his party across the river in half an hour. But there was only one ferry at that place, and the next, either above or below, was several miles off; no other boat could be had. The firemen and deck hands on the steamboat, as soon as they heard the captain say, "that it should never again be made a floating slave-pen," set up a loud hurrah for Captain McBride—and in the midst of it the boat went on her course.

The whole party were about to move from the bank, and go back to the tavern or to their homes, when the sound of another boat was heard. They lingered, and it came slowly on. It was running upon one wheel only. The boat had broken her shaft, and like a crippled bird, at last came ashore. Before she did so, a person was seen upon her hurricane deck waving his hand and handkerchief; when he came near enough, he was known by all as the young printer, Edgar Reed. A loud shout arose from the greater part of the crowd, while his confident air and manner told them that relief was at hand. A venerable looking gentleman, carefully dressed in black, supported by a gold headed cane, came ashore, and close by followed Edgar Reed, who first eagerly inquired for Mr. Carter; if he had arrived? No one knew Mr. Carter, but he was told that a man with a pair of fine horses had just got off a boat and gone up to the tavern. He smiled and said, all is right. He then went up to Belle and bade her be of good cheer. He was shocked when he found her manacled and heard that the trial was over. He then found Mr. Scott, and told him he had on hand evidence that Belle was his niece, and that he knew it, and that if he attempted to take her out of the state he should be instantly arrested as a criminal. After a brief conversation, the manacles were taken from Belle's hands, and the party went to the tavern.

CHAPTER XLVII.

THE SURRENDER.

Mr. Scott walked quickly across the room several times, with his hands clasped behind him, and then turning said: "What are we here for? What do you want with me?"

"We have met here to see if we can compromise this matter."

"Well, what terms do you offer?"

"We wish you to recognize Belle as the only child and heiress of your brother."

Mr. Scott staggered back as if one had struck him, and said, "She my brother's child? preposterous. I will submit to no such imposition, sir. I have heard, since I came here, that some such story has been afloat, but by whom it has been started, or for what purpose other than to make a nine days' wonder, and excite sympathy for the fugitive, I do not know."

"Is this your answer to my proposition to compromise? I make it, sir, said a lawyer Mr. Reed had employed, "to save you from exposure, and, perhaps, more disastrous consequences."

"Exposure—consequences!" said Mr. Scott; "I neither heed the one nor the other."

The lawyer, Mr. Hinman, now said: "I see, Mr. Scott, that you are not fully informed of the position we occupy. I have here, in my hand, a bill in chancery drawn up in Willoughby, and brought with me, hoping that you will compromise the case, and save the expenses and other incidents of litigation. It is at your service to read."

Mr. Scott sat down and read the paper, which gave in detail, with dates and places, a concise history of his treatment to Belle, and asked that he should be compelled to pay over to her all moneys and property that he had received from his brother's estate.

He read it carefully, folded his spectacles, placed them in their case, and then said: "Well, here are assertions enough, but as I certainly shall deny every one of them that is material to the controversy, you, of course, expect to prove them;" and then, in rather a louder tone, "Where is your proof?"

Mr. Hinman quietly replied: "Our proof, sir, is in this village."

Mr. Scott: "Who have you here that knows anything about this girl?"

"We have Dr. Bryce, from Willoughby, who has already seen and examined her, and is willing to swear that he has no doubt of her being the child of your brother. Dr. Bryce, you know, was the family physician of your brother?"

Mr. Scott: "Where is he?"

"He is in this house, sir."

Mr. Scott paused, looked embarrassed, and then, without waiting for Mr. Hinman to complete his statement, said:

"I never cared a straw about keeping the girl as a slave. If she is willing to leave and go immediately to Scotland, where her grandfather came from, I will defray the expenses of her trip, and in addition to that, will give her an annuity so long as she will stay there. She has many relations in Scotland, who, no doubt, will receive her gladly, if she can find them and establish the relationship."

"That will not do, sir. We have invited this meeting for your benefit; not for hers. Nothing less than an unconditional acknowledgment of all her rights, and her full restitution to whatever property she is entitled, will answer our purpose."

"Restoration! property!" said Mr. Scott; "it is enough that I give her freedom and an annuity."

"Indeed, sir, you are greatly mistaken. But I must leave this place and return, early to-morrow morning, to Virginia. We are but wasting time in fruitless efforts to compromise. We have witnesses, sir, here in this house, whom I have seen and conversed with, whose testimony will, without doubt, fully identify my client as the only child and heir-at-law of your brother."

"What other witnesses have you than Dr. Bryce?"

Mr. Hinman stood quietly before Mr. Scott, looked him fully in the face, and said in a low, firm voice, we have here the Rev. Mr. St. John; and opening a door he invited Mr. St. John into the room.

The reverend gentleman and Mr. Scott looked at each other, and both were embarrassed. Mr. St. John extended his hand; Mr. Scott took it coldly and timidly.

"I have come here as a witness against you, sir: I regret it, and still more deeply regret the agency that my friend and parishioner has had in this unfortunate transaction. I recollect all his conversation as distinctly as if it occurred but yesterday, and I am now willing to testify to the whole of it, from the hour that he first saw this child to that when he saw her at your house, five years ago."

"Who is this friend and parishioner of whom you speak?"

"Col. Bennett Leathers, sir."

"Where is he?"

"He is dead, sir. He died four years ago, in Alabama, where he resided for the last twenty years of his life. I was with him in his last sickness, and heard from his own lips on his deathbed, only a few hours before he died, a full statement of his agency in this affair."

"Why have you not sooner disclosed it?"

"Because I got it from a dying man under the injunction of secrecy, until the proper time should arrive to disclose it: that time has now come."

Mr. Scott said with a sneer, "The statements of a dead man cannot affect me. They were probably the ravings of delirium; at all events, it is not evidence."

Mr. Hinman said, "That is true, sir, but we have living witnesses in this house, whose testimony cannot be so easily got rid of; if you please, I will introduce you to my friend Mr. Strong."

A poor, dilapidated, worn-out old man, whose hands shook as with an ague, gracefully bowed to Mr. Scott.

Mr. Scott returned his salutation by coldly saying, "What do you know of this matter, sir?"

"I know nothing whatever of the immediate transaction, sir. In the month of June, twenty years ago, I sold to a partner of Williams the negro trader, a girl named Patsy; I was then living with my family in Washington City. The bill of sale handed me by the trader, was a common printed blank form for such papers, and I inadvertently signed it, without first striking out the usual warranty, that the article sold is sound. Very soon afterward, Williams sued me on the contract for a return of the purchase money; a suit which ruined myself and my family. I defended the suit, and in the course of preparation for the trial, it became necessary for me to go into Virginia to cross-examine a witness whose deposition Williams took to prove the death of the girl. I did so. The witness was a farmer named Hilliard. Afterward I met the same man in the south-eastern part of Alabama; to which place he removed soon after he gave his deposition.

"He bought a woman named Minte, at the time the girl died that I sold to Williams, and he saw the girl both before and after her death. He told me, that he brought Minte with him to Alabama."

"Well, but what has all this to do with the matter in controversy here?" said Mr. Scott.

"It has this," said Mr. Hinman, "this woman, Minte, was the nurse of your brother's child."

"Another dead witness!" sneered Mr. Scott.

"The dead leave traces behind them!" said Mr. Hinman.

Mr. Scott said: "What traces has this negress left, that affect me?"

"This book, sir, and these marks."

Dr. Bryce was then called upon. The passage in the book which was so covered and obscured that Belle could not read it, had been submitted to some chemical process that removed the obscuring matter, and brought out distinctly all the letters. It was a statement that the middle and little fingers, on the left hand of the child, were grown together as far up as the second joint, and that Dr. Bryce had cut them apart.

Dr. Bryce produced an old day-book, in which he had made an entry of the fact, that he had performed the operation on Mr. Scott's child. Belle was brought in, her fingers closely examined, and the scars were there.

Mr. Scott reeled and sank back in his chair—looked around him as if for aid, and closed his eyes; then starting he piteously inquired, "Have I no rights here?"

"Certainly you have," said, Mr. Hinman, "and all your rights shall be respected. It is your *wrongs* that we are opposing: every wrong redressed is a right established."

Mr. Scott interrupting and turning to Mr. Hinman said, "I will give half her fortune and her freedom for the sake of peace. Will not that satisfy you?"

Mr. Hinman, coldly and rather contemptuously: "*No, sir.* It is growing late; I must leave to-morrow; time passes swiftly. Make your last offer or we shall abandon the conference, and you can anticipate the result."

Mr. Scott: "I have laid out thousands of dollars on Belle's education and maintenance. Can you not let me have that and interest? her fortune is large; I am her only uncle—she can well spare it; only repay me what I have expended on her without interest."

Mr. Hinman: "You expended that money (if indeed it has cost so much) without her request, and while you were doing so you were holding her iniquitously as a slave!"

Mr. Scott: "I will not contend; let me have ten thousand dollars and I will be content; she can spare it; she will not even feel the loss of so small a sum, and then we will part in peace, and she and I will be friends."

Mr. Hinman, impatiently: "Not a cent! not a cent, sir!"

Mr. Scott: "What then do I gain by the compromise?"

"You gain this, sir; you are saved from the public exposure of this transaction; the expenses of a lawsuit, and it may be, from legal proceedings of a criminal nature."

Mr. Scott turned pale, sat in silence a minute and then said: "I am innocent, but circumstances seem to be against me; draw up the necessary papers for my signature and I will take the advice of my attorney upon them."

Mr. Hinman: "Your attorney is now here," bowing to him, "I hope to have his aid in drawing up the papers, and will do so instantly." He then sat down and wrote, for Belle had requested it, a deed of emancipation for her, and another paper by which Mr. Scott, under his hand and seal, acknowledged Belle to be the only child and heir-at-law of his brother, promising to account to her or her attorney for whatever money or personal property he had received of the estate, and resigning his office of administrator of that estate. This was carefully read, signed, sealed and attested in due form by witnesses.

CHAPTER XLVIII.

DREAM.

WHEN Scott left Auburn, accompanied by his lawyer, he did so on board a steamboat bound for Wheeling. He was harassed in mind, and wearied with the excitement and labor of the day, dejected and melancholy. Late at night he aroused his friend, and said:

"I have had a horrid dream. I thought I was in a strange country; there was a house which I knew to be mine; I was to live in it alone. By the side of the house, and not far from it, was an outbuilding thatched with straw. I stood quite near it, and saw a pale-yellow flame ascending from the straw, and looked, but the straw was not consumed. I was about to call for help when I saw two men near me. They looked at the flame, and then steadily at each other, with meaning and deep melancholy in their faces, and without saying a word, went away. I awoke."

"Well," said Mr. Ellerton, "I see nothing remarkable in your dream, that you should be alarmed about it. You are nervous and excited; to-morrow you will be refreshed and better."

"I do see something in it that I never saw before. That house is my home; that flame that burned, and consumed not, must, therefore, last forever; those melancholy men have gone to that place before me, and know what it means."

He laid down, and after a brief sleep, again awakened his companion, and said:

"I have had another horrid dream. A great black dog was about to attack me. I felt utterly helpless; a man came and drove him away, and said, 'He will see you again at nine o'clock to-morrow.' What can that mean? I am not superstitious, but I never before have had such impressions from dreams. They seem to mean something."

"Oh, my dear sir," said Mr. Ellerton, "your whole nervous system has been shocked almost beyond endurance, to-day. The slamming of a door would startle you now, more than would the firing of a pistol at another time. Compose yourself, and after the night's rest you will be better, and laugh at what now strangely enough startles you."

The next day Mr. Scott arose pale and haggard. After breakfast he sat in the cabin alone, till he became weary, and then went out upon the upper deck of the boat, and looked at the beautiful scenery on the Ohio and Virginia shores. As he was about to descend, the boat made a lurch from some obstacle it met with—his foot slipped, the cry was raised: "A man overboard!" Two boys were sent out with a boat to pick him up; the steamboat paused for a moment, and the boys came back with a hat, in which was written, "John Scott." They were taken in, and the boat went on her way.

A lady and gentleman who were standing at a back window of the cabin looked out on the scene; saw the arm of the sinking man for a moment; saw the boys pick up his hat and return. The lady shed tears, and was sad; she did not know the name or the history of him who was lost; she knew only that a brother had gone to his long home, and that grief must fill the hearts of some household when they would learn his fate.

CHAPTER XLIX.

COL. LEATHERS.

Fifteen years have rapidly passed over the married life of Bennett Leathers. He has been made wiser, by his increasing years. His wild lands have greatly risen in value. He has sold them, and their proceeds, added to the fortune he obtained by his wife, have made him rich. He is now Colonel Leathers, and has often been a member of the Legislature; and has been talked of by his friends, as a suitable person for Governor of the state. Some indeed, have gone so far as to hint, that he should be President of the United States. But Colonel Leathers has always disclaimed any such wish; and has frequently said to his friends, that he is sighing for retirement, and the peace and comfort of domestic life.

The services that have given him distinction, are but the outgrowth of the principles of his early life. He has been a consistent statesman. A single profound thought, has given unity of purpose to all his political life.

"All negroes and mulattoes would be better off if they were slaves." This has been the maxim that his partisans have always carried upon his banner in every contested election; and under it, he has always triumphed. And when a grateful posterity shall strike coins to commemorate his virtues, this must be the motto which they will place upon them.

Acting steadily upon this principle, the world is indebted to him, for the profound policy exhibited in the statute books of some of our sister republican states; by which all free persons of color, are driven from the state, as a punishment for their impudence in being free; and under which, so many free persons of color, from the free states, have been imprisoned, and sold into slavery, for the gross crime of breathing the air, or treading the soil of those states.

His zeal against all Abolitionists, has increased with his years. He always looked upon the whole race with as much contempt, as so amiable a gentleman can entertain for any persons. But still, he has had some compassion for their errors. He knows how weak human nature is, and how deluded even honest men may be. He has not therefore, ever suffered his feelings so far to master his judgment, as to be willing to hang any of these poor creatures, who may by chance have fallen into his power. To whip them, or tar and feather them, has always seemed to him, to be just judgment in mercy. With Mrs. Leathers, the world has not gone on quite so well.

What trifling incidents affect the happiness of life! A spark, light as the feather from a swallow's wing, may fall on the ground, and perish as it falls. Another spark as light, may fall in the swallow's abandoned nest, and set fire to the contents, and then to the roof of the house to which it is built, and the house and a city may, in an hour, be but a mass of smoking ruins. Commercial disasters may follow from this misfortune, and their effects may be felt around the world.

One day, as Mrs. Leathers was quietly seated in her chamber in the second story of her house, a robin flew into the room. The scared bird fluttered from place to place, in its efforts to escape; and as it did so, it brushed from the mantlepiece a tumbler, which fell on the hearth. "Oh, my teeth!" said Mrs. Leathers; but do not imagine, reader, that any sudden pangs of toothache afflicted the lady. She had outlived all such infirmity. Her teeth lay upon the hearth, all broken into fragments. No dentist, not even the most persevering of the profession, ever visited the lonely part of the state in which she lived; and Mrs. Leathers was condemned to pass the residue of her life without teeth. At first, she encountered great difficulties from their loss; but time makes amends for many losses, or lessens their burden. She could eat no solid food; but in a few months, she grew so enormously fat on mashed potatoes, that she was unable to walk. She sat in a great arm-chair in her room, and read all the novels that the diligent Colonel Leathers could collect for her. Some of great merit, she read twice.

Her greatest loss, was the want of society; for the Colonel was so busily engaged, in spreading his political principles far and wide over his own state, and all the neighboring states; he had so many letters to write, and so many speeches to make, that his wife had long ago been taught, it would be a disaster to the country, for her to occupy any portion of his invaluable time.

One day, a thought occurred to her new and bright, like a gleam of stray sunshine in the bottom of a dark well. Jule should sit in her room, and she would give Jule verbal instruction in religion.

Jule was sent for; she could but obey the call. She was about fourteen years old, a dull, sleepy-looking mulatto. Mrs. Leathers commanded her to be washed and clothed, and told her that she was promoted to the office of waiting-maid to her mistress. Jule gave a loud grunt, when she heard this; but Mrs. Leathers kindly thought it arose from her horror of being washed.

For the first few days after Jule was installed in her new place, all things passed on pleasantly to both parties. Mrs. Leathers was glad to have some person always near her to talk to, and Jule was pleased with her change from the quarter to the great house, and of food and clothing. But old habits, how firmly will they adhere to us, and how hard are they to break! When Mrs. Leathers thought Jule was most attentive to her instructions, a closer inspection showed her to be fast asleep. She called, but Jule did not answer. She almost shouted, but Jule nodded her head, still lower and faster. She shrieked, but Jule was in deep slumber, and made no reply. She had to ring her bell for the cook to come up and awaken her; but by the time the cook would reach the kitchen in the back yard, Jule was again asleep.

Necessity is the mother of invention. Mrs. Leathers, after a week of deep thought, hit upon an expedient to keep Jule awake, which has not yet been patented, and is, therefore, at the service of any person who may choose to use it.

She called Harry, the carpenter, and made him measure the distance between her seat and the extremities of the room. He was then ordered to make a long pole, like a broomstick, and in one end to insert a nail, sharpened at the outer point, and in the other a small hook. This was done and placed in her hands.

She sat now in her great arm-chair, which she entirely filled, dressed in an old, greasy, worn-out black silk gown, with this pole in her hand, like a sceptered queen on her throne.

Whenever she called to Jule, if she received no answer, the point was quickly applied, and it served the purpose fully to awaken her.

If she commanded Jule to come to her, and she failed to obey, the hook brought her rapidly near enough for her mistress to box her ears: obedience was now fully established. Jule kept awake while her mistress taught her the whole catechism, from "Who made you?" to "the end of all things."

CHAPTER L.

THE DEED OF EMANCIPATION.

Mr. Reed took the deed of emancipation, as quickly as he could, to Belle, who had gone early in the evening to Mr. Stillman's, and by the light of a lamp, which was held by Mrs. Johnston, she read the document, pressed it to her bosom, kissed the seal upon it, and looked at it as a child looks at a much-loved toy, and exclaimed, "Oh! thank God! thank God, I am now free! no more a slave! no more a slave, and I never can be a slave again!"

Mrs. Johnston seemed to be as much delighted as Belle; she skipped about the room with the deed in her hands, and said, "I always told you she was free, I knew that some day it would turn out so."

Mr. Reed then told them that Mr. Scott had acknowledged Belle, as sole heiress of her father's estate, and that she was entitled to the immediate possession. Belle received this intelligence with composure—almost with indifference—but Mrs. Johnston and Mr. and Mrs. Stillman were delighted to hear it.

"How much is it?" said Mr. Stillman.

"I do not know exactly, but from all that I can learn, I suppose the cash and stocks are worth one hundred thousand dollars, and the lands, negroes and personal property as much more," said Mr. Reed.

"Belle," said Mrs. Stillman, "you have a large fortune."

"I am free! I am free!" exclaimed Belle.

"But there are slaves," said Mrs. Johnston; "Belle, you are a slaveholder."

"*I* a slaveholder, and that too at the very instant I find myself free! Oh no! no! no! I cannot be a slaveholder; I will not take these people as slaves; I will set them free to-night!"

The lawyer who accompanied Mr. Reed, was sent for; and a deed of emancipation was drawn for all of them, with power to appropriate a sum of money from the estate for their present wants, until a suitable provision could be made for them.

After a weary and eventful day, they all separated for rest.

The next day, Mr. Stillman invited Mr. and Mrs. St. John, and others, to dine with him.

All were seated at the table; all joyously participated in the conversation; the gloom, the sorrow that for a long time had hung as a thunder-cloud over the house of Mr. Stillman, had passed suddenly away and joy, as bright sunlight, rested in its place. All seemed calmly happy. The lines that had begun to furrow the pure face of Mrs. Stillman, now converged into dimples radiant with gladness; Mr. Stillman, though still thoughtful, was too happy to conceal his emotions. Poor Belle was unable to leave her room, but each moment of her hours was a diamond sparkle of bliss.

Captain Carter sat near the foot of the table, and quietly conversed with a gentleman by his side, on the merits and prices of horses. From time to time, as he heard the voice of the Rev. Mr. St. John, slowly descanting on some sublime truth of Christianity, he cast, with his oblique eye, a look at him, while his lip curled with ill-concealed contempt.

General topics at first, on which none could differ, were discussed. Miss Jane Williams, however, was restive—she sat opposite Mr. St. John, and said to him:

"How do you ministers of the south, get along with slavery?"

Mrs. Stillman colored to her eyes—all the others at the table looked as surprised as they would have done, if she had thrown a stone at Mr. St. John; but the Rev. gentleman was calm as he had been at any moment in his life, and replied:

"I have had but little trouble on that subject;

my greatest difficulties have been with the slave-trade. I have been greatly afflicted on account of the manner in which it is conducted."

Miss Jane Williams was quite excited, "Oh! Mr. St. John, do not ministers, in the slave-holding states, have great trouble on this matter of slavery?"

"Yes, miss, they are greatly perplexed about it, and the perplexity is daily increasing. They do not do their duty."

"Why, do they not faithfully discharge their duty on that, as well as on other matters?"

"They are too timid, miss—they fear man rather than God."

"Do they preach at all on slavery?"

"Yes, they sometimes do, but in so timid and time-serving a manner, that it is distressing to hear them. Their sermons make but little impression, and I fear, do but little good."

"Well, they pray that their hearers may be enlightened on the subject, I hope," said Miss Jane.

"They seldom mention it in their prayers, and when they do, it is in such a roundabout manner, that not half their hearers, I fear, understand for what they are praying. It is almost as bad as praying in an unknown tongue."

"What can be done to induce them to speak out boldly, as men and as Christians, on this great duty?"

"I do not know. The best manner, I think, is for each minister to take to himself some portion of that subject, and by his own precept and example (for precept, you know, is entirely worthless, unless it be sustained by correspondent practice,) to illustrate the duties of Christians. Acting on this principle, I took to myself the department of the slave-trade, and labored for years in that branch of duty. After that, I labored about two years in the branch of duty connected with catching those slaves that escape. But my efforts were not sustained, as I think they should have been, by my brethren in the ministry, nor by the Christian public. I was a pioneer in the enterprise, and shared the fate of all pioneers;—I was misunderstood, neglected, and even persecuted."

The liveliest sympathy was shown for Mr. St. John by all at the table, except Captain Carter, who sat in silence, casting, occasionally, a glance at him.

Mr. Stillman: "My dear sir, you have labored, no doubt, faithfully, and you know that we always lose the honors and rewards of this world, in the ratio of our fidelity to Christian duty."

"Yes," said Mr. St. John, "it is so; I have always found it so."

A pause, for a minute or more, took place.

Miss Williams said: "Is it not shocking, that

parents sell their own children, Mr. St. John? Cannot some reform be made in that horrid practice?"

Mr. St. John, greatly surprised: "You mistake me, miss! I have not been understood, I fear. *I* do *not* think it wrong or unchristian, for parents to sell their children."

The whole party, except Captain Carter and Mr. Reed, looked at him with surprise. He proceeded: "We all agree, that slave-holding, so far from being a sin, is in exact accordance with Christianity. St. Paul, you know, sent back Onesimus to his brother according to the flesh, to be held by him as a slave. There is not a word against slavery, in the New Testament; and the Old Testament expressly sanctions it, and commands it.

"Now, to reply to your question, miss, I think you err on this subject—your philosophy is wrong. It is right to hold slaves; that must be regarded as a fixed principle—as a doctrine not to be disputed or disturbed.

All experience shows, that it is useless to hold them, without the power of selling them; because that power is an essential means of holding them. The master could not keep them obedient, unless he can hold over their heads, the terror of being sold; and in addition to that, they would be of no profit to their owners, unless they could sell them. If a man sells children, he must sell somebody's children; and I submit it to your own good sense, miss, whether he had not better sell his own children, than those of some other person!"

Miss Williams excited: "But did I not understand you to say, that you took, as your department of labor for several years, the reformation of the slave-trade?"

"Yes, miss, I certainly said so."

"You condemn the slave-trade then, of course?"

"Not at all, not at all. I am really glad that you thus give me an opportunity to correct an erroneous impression, which, no doubt, my too general remarks have caused. I condemn the abuses and wickedness, that too frequently prevail where it is carried on. I found nearly all my brethren in the ministry, engaged in endeavoring to reform the abuses of *slave-holding*, by introducing family prayer, and reading the Bible, to slaveholders and their slaves; and finding one department, as I believed, entirely neglected, I endeavored to reform the abuses in the trade, by the same means. My brethren, for more perfect access to the hearts of slaveholders, became, in many instances, slaveholders; upon the same principle I, for more full and easy access to the hearts of slave-traders, became a slave-trader."

Looking round him he said: "I see that you all look surprised; but I hope to convince you by the most exact logic that I was in the discharge of a high christian duty. The abuses of slave-holding, and the slave-trade were, and will continue to be, the means of assailing slavery itself; and we all wisely judge that a reformation of those abuses will be the best means of sustaining the institution. None of you condemn the conduct of those ministers who labor day and night with tears, to reform the abuses of slave-holding and to bring the institution itself more completely under the control of christian principles. Apply the same reasoning to the slave-trade and the line of duty is as plain in the one case as it is in the other."

Miss Williams: "How did you labor in this department?"

"As I have just told you, I became myself a trader and went with the gangs. At first I endeavored to abolish the practice of chaining the slaves in coffles, and succeeded in inducing one trader to abandon it, but so many of the slaves ran off, that we had to return to the old method of securing them. I then endeavored to introduce family worship and reading the Scriptures morning and evening to the slaves and to the men who conducted the coffles; but the slaves were so sullen and sleepy, and the drivers so profane and frequently so drunk, that I soon found I could be of no service there. As a last effort, I tried my uttermost to induce them to remember the Sabbath day but the men said no such thing had ever before been heard of,—that the slave-trade knew no Sabbath, and the trader did not care a straw (they used another and worse word) for it—and so after many faithful efforts I had to give that up also. If my christian brethren had sustained me, perhaps I might have succeeded; but as I was alone, with the world against me, I fear my feeble labors will be lost."

Miss Williams: "You condemn, of course, the African slave-trade, do you not, sir?"

"Not at all, miss, not at all. We who support and believe slavery to be right; have unwisely lost a great point, by yielding to the assertion, that the foreign slave-trade is wrong. If you will examine the arguments urged against it, you will find that they are generally directed against its abuses, and do not touch the vital question itself. They condemn the practice of crowding so many slaves together in the holds of the vessels, without adequate food or water, so that many of them perish on the passage; the cut-throat and piratical-looking men who conducted such vessels; and above all, the great fact that

Spaniards and Catholics were frequently officers of the ships, and cruel in their treatment to their slaves; these are the great arguments against the African slave-trade.

"But that too, should have been reformed. If only as many were brought over as the ships could comfortably hold; if the slaves were well fed and supplied with water; if Protestant Christians were officers of the vessels; then it is plain that the trade would be respectable, and would probably have continued to this hour. It is the abuses of slavery, and the slave-trade, that should be the object of our solicitude. If the slave-trade is wrong, then it follows inevitably that slave-holding is wrong too; if you condemn the one, you must also condemn the other; and if you sustain the one, you must also sustain the other.

Mr. Jones said: "I think I heard you say that you endeavored to reform the practice of hunting fugitive slaves with dogs. I suppose sir, of course, that you tried to abolish it altogether."

"No sir, not at all--not at all. The practice is necessary and proper. I know it shocks your prejudices to hear me say so; but a little reflection will convince you that it is only prejudice, and not reason that is surprised.

"Hear me then, for a moment. It is right to

hold slaves—*that is settled*"—laying his hand upon the table. "Now that right cannot be enjoyed, if every slave is allowed to walk off at his pleasure. The right to hold, implies the right to re-capture. This being so, if one runs off, it is right to hunt him. But you object, perhaps to the means used. Dogs, however, are found from experience—the experience of hundreds of planters, and for a hundred years—to be the best means of hunting fugitive slaves. But for them, many who have escaped and hidden themselves in dense forests and swamps could never be retaken. It is, therefore, right to use dogs. I did so; at first I put wire-muzzles over their mouths; but this put the poor dogs completely in the power of the fugitives, they killed them as fast as the dogs came up with them. This was extreme cruelty to the dogs, and was too, a great waste of money, for each dog killed, was worth, at least, twenty dollars. It made the dogs useless; I therefore took off the muzzles.

"This branch of the business really needed christian reformation, and still needs it. Those who are engaged in it, are too frequently low, vulgar men; very profane, and they actually desecrate the Sabbath, by following it on that day. I therefore went into the business, hoping to reform it; but alas! my brethren in the ministry did not sympathize with me. I could not convince them that I was right. I suppose, that their minds were so full of prejudice against the class of men who are engaged in it, that their prejudices extend even to the work itself—a very common case."

Captain Carter said to Mr. St. John: "Did you ever have any bad luck, while you were out with your hounds? It appears to me, sir, that sometimes mistakes might be made that would be quite unpleasant."

"Such mistakes do not often occur; but in that business, as in all other human affairs," said Mr. St. John with a sigh, "accidents will happen. I can never forget, that four or five years ago, I was out with my hounds, in pursuit of runaway negroes. The neighborhood had been infested for several days with something greatly destructive to poultry and pigs; it was difficult to determine whether the havoc was made by a negro, or a bear. I satisfied myself, that the mischief was done by a runaway negro; and came the more readily to this conclusion, because Colonel Nimberley had lost a slave, a large athletic negro, a few days before. I determined, if possible, to capture the creature, because he seemed to be unusually bold in his depredations; and his example might cause great mischief to all other slaves in the neighborhood. Accordingly I set out, one Saturday morning at daybreak, with five good hounds. It was a dark, drizzly, disagreeable day. About ten o'clock the hounds struck a trail; it was along a path that led through a great forest. The ground was nearly level, and thickly overgrown with bushes; these bushes and the trees were dripping with the rain. To make matters still worse, my horse became lame. The trail, at first, was hard to follow; my hounds wandered into by-paths, and then returned to the regular track, that led directly west from the Mississippi river. I should have told you before, that it was in the northern part of Louisiana. My mind was as gloomy as the weather. While I was thus sad, I thought of the hard task I had undertaken—to remove popular prejudice from a vocation, that is an essential part of the system of slave-holding, by showing the people, that all the duties that grow out of slave-holding, may be performed in a christian manner, and by a christian minister. But one of my brethren in the ministry in the country, sustained me, and he did so in theory only. That was the Rev. Reason Tarbut, a most pious minister—humble and filled with the odor of sanctity.

In the midst of my gloomiest thoughts, it occurred to me with great force, that our system of slave-holding is sustained by a great many of the churches in the free states.

"He that is not against us is for us.

"Nearly all these churches condemn going to theaters and dancing as sins; and do not condemn slave-holding as such: does it not follow that they regard slave-holding as a lighter matter than dancing or visiting the theater? It is either clearly right or grossly wrong.

"Assuredly, if northern ministers and church members really believe that slave-holding is wrong, they would not hide their light under a bushel.

"While these thoughts were crowding through my mind, cheering, sustaining, and encouraging me in my labor, my heart was warmed; but I was weary, hungry and wet. Sometimes the hounds would leave the trail, and wander for miles into by-paths, and again would take a fresh start. We went on till nearly dark, and I heard with great joy, that peculiar cry the dogs always raise when the object they are pursuing is close before them. I whipped up my poor jaded horse, and soon came up with the dogs and their game.

"How was I horror-stricken to find that the Rev. Reason Tarbut, to escape them, had hastily climbed into a tree. The good man had an appointment to fill on the next Sabbath; he was making a long journey on foot, and had taken this as the nearest road to his place for preaching. We had been following him all day. I soon relieved him. He was, I assure you, greatly frightened, and he had reason to be so, for my dogs were hungry and fierce."

"I suppose," said Captain Carter, "the dogs had followed him by the odor of sanctity? They must have been poor hounds, not to know the difference between the odor of sanctity, and the trail of a negro."

"My lead hound, Juno, had a bad cold that day," said Mr. St. John.

"But, my dear sir, that was not the worst of the matter. Mr. Tarbut had been convinced by my arguments, that the slave-system, as it exists in this country, is a unit. He was, of course, before he met with me, well assured that to hold slaves is right; he soon saw very clearly that the foreign and domestic slave-trade, and the means usually resorted to for the capture of runaway slaves, are also as just and well-founded in right, as slave-holding is. He was one of my earliest converts in the south-western country, and my firmest supporter. Now he was so scared by the hounds, that I cannot but fear his intellect was somewhat touched, for from that day to this, he never would say one word to sustain my views about the right and duty to hunt runaway negroes with dogs. So far from doing so, very soon afterward he removed to Iowa, and recently by a letter which I received, I am most sure that he has turned an Abolitionist, for he states in that letter, that he still believes the system of slavery is a unit, and also in another part of it he writes, that he believes it is a sin to pursue fugitives with hounds, or without them. Poor man! his mind never was of the first order, and now, I fear, that he is slightly deranged."

Captain Carter, during this reply, turned his face from the speaker; I fancy he did so to conceal a smile, and the smile seemed to be contagious; Mr. St. John observed it and said: "I fear that these details do not interest or perhaps offend you, but be assured, ladies and gentlemen, that from the African slave-trade down to the re-capture of slaves with dogs, there is an unbroken chain—the whole is but one system, and the beginning and the end are parts of that system. If you sustain, as I trust you do, slaveholding, the precedents and the consequences must be sustained also. If it is right to hold them, it was right to bring them here; if it is right to hold them, it is right to re-capture them, when they escape, by the best means that experience suggests.

"Did you ever meet with any other bad luck,

in that business?" said Captain Carter, with quite a long and sober face.

"Yes, sir; early one morning not long ago, I lost two of my dogs. I was in pursuit of a large, ferocious-looking negro man, who had a child with him. They were eating their breakfast—at least the girl was—when we came upon them. The man killed two of my remaining dogs, and injured the others, by which I suffered severely."

Miss Jane: "Well, Mr. St. John, your arguments seem to be logical, if the system is right; but I differ with you on that point. I do think it is not only wrong, but one of the very greatest sins that ever cursed our earth."

Mrs. St. John: "Oh, honey, how you are mistaken! It 's one of the nicest things in this world, to have a nigger to wait on you; to tote you a gourd of water when you are dry; to keep the flies off with a brush, when you are asleep after dinner. Beside, honey, we could not do without 'em at all in our country, 'cause it 's so nice to have 'em; and it 's respectable too."

Miss Jane: "Do ministers, in your state, generally own them?"

Mrs. St. John: "Indeed they do, when they are able. I know a minister that owns three wenches; whenever he and his wife wish to take a trip to the springs, you know, or to Philadelphy or New York; they just sell some of the children, and get the needful at once. Slaves are always a cash article."

Miss Jane: "Why, I do hope, that you do not approve of selling children from their mothers, madam?"

Mrs. St. John: "Oh no! I do not approve of such sinful waste. Willful waste makes woeful want, miss, as the Bible says. It is a sin to sell children; better to keep 'em till they are fourteen or fifteen years old at least, and then sell them; they'll bring double price, ma'am. One of our neighbors wanted to take his girls to some great springs; and so do you think, he actually sold two boys of about six years old, for eight hundred dollars. It was the greatest piece of waste I ever did hear tell of. Oh no, miss! I does not approve of selling children."

CHAPTER LI.

MR. ST. JOHN.

THE company all went away except Mr. and Mrs. St. John, who were invited to pass the evening at Mr. Stillman's.

"My dear sir," said Mr. Stillman to Mr. St. John, "you are mistaken respecting churches in the free states. They do not, as you think, *intend* to indorse the system of slave-holding. Men do not reach the truth by intuition; it is only to be arrived at, by patient thought, *No man's opinion upon any question which he has not investigated, is worth a cent.* Error is the natural product of the mind, even of cultivated men; except only, in those departments to which their culture has been applied. We have examined the subject of dancing and going to theaters, and have reached correct conclusions upon them. We have *not* examined, as we should have done, the subject of slave-holding; and as the result of our negligence, our thoughts upon it are either crude or erroneous.

"As light advances, the Church will also

advance; and this sin, as well as others, against which her armies array themselves for battle, will fall before it. The Church, with all her errors, *is* the light and hope of the world; and will reform every abuse, and expel every sin, as surely as God is in her midst.

"The Church was as united on the subject of the slave-trade, and supported that, as firmly as she now supports its result, slave-holding. Church members with us now, have entirely different views on that matter, and regard the foreign slave-trade as piracy."

"That, my dear sir, is a great delusion," said Mr. St. John. "The foreign slave-trade cannot be piracy, whatever opinions may have been rashly carried into laws to declare it so, as long as the domestic slave-trade is a respectable business. They both rest on the same basis: and the domestic slave-trade is the necessary result of slave-holding. The latter could not exist a day without the former. No master can keep his slave in subjection unless he has the power to sell him, for that is the greatest of all his means to coerce obedience. The Church then is in a contradictory position. She condemns the foreign slave-trade, while she supports slave-holding and the domestic trade."

"I regret," said Mr. Stillman, "that it is too

much so, but men cannot and will not sleep forever while such great matters as this question involves are before them. The acts of Congress and of the state legislatures, that support slaveholding directly or indirectly, will soon be declared void by the courts or be repealed by the legislatures and Congress respectively.

"Christianity has gained her present position, not by the world's favor, but by winning her way inch by inch in a hand-to-hand fight with her enemies. The brows of her soldiers have been covered with dust, and their shoes filled with blood, and behind them, is a path overspread with the bleached bones of those who have fallen in her battles, wide almost as the world and extending back through the ages to the cross of Christ.

"The practice of Christians is no rule of faith—we must go to the Bible."

"Certainly, my dear sir," said Mr. St. John, "that is the very book I rely upon to sustain me."

"Do you think it a sin for a slave to steal?" said Mr. Stillman.

"You surprise me, sir! certainly I do. Whoever doubted that?"

"Let me ask you, Why is it sin for him to do so?"

"Because God has said, 'Thou shalt not steal.'"

"We will take that as the stand-point of our

argument," said Mr. Stillman. "It is a sin for a slave to disobey any of the commandments. These commandments are laws to the race of man, and should control the conduct of each man in the world."

"Certainly, my dear sir, I have preached that doctrine for twenty years, to masters and to slaves alike. I never heard a human being doubt it."

"The commandments then bind each man. Has it never occurred to you, my dear sir," said Mr. Stillman, "that they *protect* each man in the world; and that *protection to human rights is their great object?* 'Remember the Sabbath day to keep it holy!' The object of this law is, that each man in the world may be protected in his religious rights. God, by addressing laws to free agents, has hushed the whole world into silence on the Sabbath, that every man, it may be the beggar on the dunghill, may worship him in peace. And so with the law, 'Thou shalt not steal.' Every man on earth is commanded to respect all your rights of property. It follows inevitably, that if the slave is bound by these laws, he is protected by them."

"Yes, sir, that is certainly so," said Mr. St. John.

"Then," continued Mr. Stillman, "the slave has the *right* to love God; he has the right to keep holy the Sabbath day; to honor his father and his mother; to respect the earnings of others, and to have others respect his earnings; to respect the marital rights of others, and that others shall respect his marriage relations; he has the right not to covet his neighbor's house, nor wife, nor man-servant, nor maid-servant, nor ox, nor ass, nor anything that is his neighbor's, and that his neighbor shall not covet his wife, nor anything that is his.

"But further, the duty is imposed by God; no law of man can interfere with the duty. The *right* to discharge the duty is conferred on us by God, and no law of man can take away that right."

"Yes, sir," said Mr. St. John, "that is very true and very clear."

"These laws are addressed," said Mr. Stillman, "to persons who may obey or disobey them?"

"Yes, sir."

"To free agents?"

"Certainly to free agents; they could not have the character of laws, 'obligatory rules for conduct,' unless addressed to persons, who otherwise might not act as they command."

"God had the right to make them?"

"Why certainly, Mr. Stillman, you surprise me, by asserting what no one in his senses ever denied."

"Now," said Mr. Stillman, "can a slave, of his

own free will, obey all these laws? can he keep the Sabbath day? honor his father and his mother? obey—freely obey—all the other commandments, unless his master shall permit him to do so?

"Do you not see that the master stands above the slave, and between him and his God, and that slave-holding deprives the slave of his free agency? Do you not also see that these laws presuppose that the persons to whom they are addressed can obey them if they will? You have admitted that they are addressed to the whole human race; to each man in the world; and by God who created all men: and does it not follow inevitably, that God intended that men shall be free?"

"The view is quite novel to me," said Mr. St. John. "There is some plausibility in it. The idea too, that each man is a separate center, and that all the commandments surround him, (as the planets roll around the sun) and protect him from the aggressions of all other men, is, at least, worthy of attention. It exalts humanity, and shows that the thunders and lightnings of Sinai are exhibitions of the benevolence and care of God for all human beings."

"But still," said Mr. Stillman, "my question is not answered. Can a slave, of his own free will, obey all these commandments, if his master shall choose to forbid him?"

"Is not your inquiry, directed rather to cases of abuse of the power, than to its legitimate exercise?" asked Mr. St. John.

"No, sir. The very existence of the power is the wrong. To obey God is the purpose for which man is created; and the existence of a power to prevent man from obeying him, is the existence of a power to defeat the purpose of man's creation."

"I will think of this matter. It is late. I must bid you good-night," and Mr. and Mrs. St. John went to their lodgings.

CHAPTER LII.

MRS. ST. JOHN.

WHILE the gentlemen were in conversation, Mrs. St. John said to Mrs. Stillman: "Oh dear! how I would love to take a good smoke. I always does so after dinner."

"Come with me," said Mrs. Stillman, "into a back room."

The ladies withdrew. Mrs. St. John lighted her pipe. "I hope it will not hurt you, dear."

"It will not hurt," replied Mrs. Stillman, laying a slight emphasis on the word *hurt.*

"Now, I'll tell you all about it," said Mrs. St John.

"Captain Carter came to our house, last Wednesday, three weeks ago, and asked me, if my name was not Robinson, before I married Mr. St. John? and I told him, 'Yes, sir, and a very good man Mr. Robinson was, too,' said I to him.

"Then," said he to me, "'My name is Joseph Carter, madam; I live in New Orleans, and I have come to see you on very particular business.'"

"I was half scared when he said that; and says

I to him: 'My husband that is, Mr. St. John, will be at home in an hour or two; stay and take dinner with us, and he will be back by the time it is ready.'"

He said: "'Thank you, madam.' Then says he: 'Do you remember a girl named Belle, who lived with you several years ago?'"

"That scared me worse than ever, because I did know a good deal about her; and more than it was right for me to tell, 'specially while my husband was away. But I studied over it a minute, and said: 'the girl you mention, lived with me and Mr. Robinson, about three years. Mr. Robinson bought her cheap of a trader; and we kept her three years, or thereabouts, and sold her to Williams, the trader. Williams said he wanted to buy the little thing; and hinted that she was kin to great folks, and they wanted her; and so we sold her to him. I would not have agreed to sell her on any account, only for her good; for I liked the little thing.

"When Mr. Robinson brought her home, he said, the trader asked him where he lived; and he told him, he lived away off from all the big roads, and where nobody hardly ever, could find the place; and the trader told him, that was a good place for the child, for her mother was trying to steal her. When she came to our house, she was greasy all over; and one of our neighbors said, he heard of a woman that greased a Dutch child with bacon rinds, and made her sit in the sun till she looked like a mulatto, and then sold her for a big price to a trader. But we thought nothing of it, only I saw that the longer the little thing lived with us, the whiter she got; 'specially, when I made her wear her sunbonnet whenever she went out of doors."

Mrs. Stillman coughed. "I hope the smoke don't hurt you, ma'am," said Mrs. St. John.

"It will not *hurt* me, I think."

"After we sold the child, we never heard any more of her, till about four years ago, when Colonel Leathers, who lived a good ways off, sent for Mr. St. John; and the man that came, said he was sick and liken to die.

"I went with Mr. St. John, and when we got there, Oh dear! what a sight it was, to see Colonel Leathers tumbling and tossing in his bed; and to hear him say, there was no hope for him."

Mrs. Stillman. "His poor wife, how I pity her!"

"His wife was dead then. She was a monstrous religious woman. She taught all her young slaves, one after another, the whole catechism, and did her best to make 'em Christians. She died only a year before Colonel Leathers did, and there was a great dispute about her death.

"She had two doctors, and one of them said, she died of apoplexy, and the other said, she smothered to death in her own fat. The dispute got so high, that the doctors used to shoot at each other with pistols whenever they met; till the neighbors got tired of it and made them drink friends.

"Mr. St. John sat down by Colonel Leathers' bed and began to talk to him about politics, but the Colonel said that politics was only vanity and vexation of spirit.

"Colonel Leathers had been a great politician in that county. The gentlemen all said that his principles was the very corner-stone of our republican edifice. Some of them wanted him to be President, but the Colonel always declined; he told them that it was honor enough for him to lay down the principles of the party, and it did not make any difference what man they got to carry them into practice, and that 'they had better get a northern man with Colonel Leathers' principles and leave him to enjoy in peace the sweets of domestic life.'

"Them was the very words he said, but where the sweets was I don't know, for his wife, they do say, always found fault with everything in this world. She thought so much of the angels, honey, that she could not bear anything that was not as perfect as an angel.

"Well, my husband that is, Mr. St. John, said to him, 'I do hope you will recover, sir.'

"He sighed and said, his work in this world was all done; and then he took Mr. St. John's hand and cried, and said, 'You knew me, my dear sir, when I was a young man, and that sermon that I first heard from you has had a great effect on my whole life.'

"Mr. St. John told him 'he was glad to hear it; that every sermon should make a lasting impression on the minds of the hearers.'

"'But you convinced me, sir, that the slave-trade should not be a disreputable business.'

"'I have long been of that opinion,' my husband said to him.

"'I determined, under the influence of that discourse, to marry the dear saint, my departed wife.'

"'I always supposed so, sir,' said Mr. St. John. And then he said, honey, that 'when he made up his mind to court Mrs. Tullis that was, he wanted to get good clothes,' for he said, 'it was no use for a man to court a widow without he wore good clothes.' And so he sold an old negro he had, named Joe. He put a bottle of whisky, where old Joe found it and stole it, and got drunk; and before he was sober, the trader had the handcuffs on him.

"Then he said, 'he knew that the nurse's child would be so much better off if it was only a slave;' and he made a bargain with a trader to sell the child to him; that he went up to the nurse's room, and took away the wrong child and carried it on board the vessel, and before daylight the ship was off to sea. And when he found out his mistake, he was mighty sorry, but there was no help for it, without ruining himself.

"He cried like a child, when he said this, and seemed so sorry for his mistake, that I pitied him from my very heart.

"He was a little flighty, at times, and seemed to think that, somehow or another, Mr. St. John was a kind of to blame for it.

"At one time he tried to blame the whole of it on to Mr. St. John; but he said, 'You know, my dear Colonel, that I had no hand in the matter,' and then the Colonel said, 'No more you had—no more you had.'

"Just before he died, we were both called up at night, and he gave Mr. St. John a great bundle of letters that he got from Mr. Williams, the trader; and told him where the child was, but that he must keep it a secret till the proper time.

"He gave him, too, a great big roll of papers that he wanted him to look over and publish, after his death, being his political principles; but

Mr. St. John said, 'he was only a preacher, and had nothing at all to do with politics;' and Colonel Leathers got him to write a note to General Blowell, and request him to have all his best thoughts spread out in the newspapers, at some presidential election, 'specially in the free states, because, he said, 'that was the place where light was most wanted.'

"And then he talked about Belle, and said, 'if she only had one drop of negro blood in her veins, he could die in peace, but as it was, there was no hope.'

"My husband tried to console him, and told him that it was only a mistake made in the dark; but he said, 'there was no hope for a man who, even in the dark, mistook a rich woman's child for a poor one's.'

"My husband told him, he must not despair.

"But the Colonel said, 'the difference between a white child and a black child was enough to drive any man to despair.'

"And so he died, poor dear man, and we staid till the funeral.

"Messages were sent out for all his relations and friends, and they came. Four of his wife's sisters were there, and his father-in-law. They were all a poor, miserable, broken-down set of people. They had been mighty rich once, but bad luck came on their husbands, and the whole of them got broke up, and there they are, living yet, as poor as they can be; and two of them, honey, looks like they drank; they were both a little tipsy at the funeral.

"Mr. Leathers was a great man. He was a fightin' colonel, and the people buried him with all the horrors of war.

"When my husband came home, Captain Carter told him all about Belle, and they talked the matter all over, and we agreed to come up here and tell all we knew, whether it did any good or not.

"Captain Carter went for poor old Mr. Strong, and he agreed to come with us. He told us, as we were coming here, that the worst day's work he ever did in his life, was when he sold his girl Patsy, and said, 'there seems to be no end to the troubles it has caused me.' His wife is dead, and he is so poor now, that he has to live with one of his daughters, and she, poor woman, is a widow, and has mighty little to live on.

"I hope the smoke is not disagreeable, Mrs. Stillman?

Mrs. Stillman was silent.

"La me! honey, why didn't you tell me that before? Here I have been talking and smoking an hour, and you, poor dear, have been suffering from the smoke. But I'm done now."

CHAPTER LIII.

MR. ST. JOHN.

VERY early the next morning, Mr. and Mrs. St, John were at Mr. Stillman's.

"I see it clearly now. I was awake nearly all last night thinking the matter over, and my views are clear enough, at least, for my own purposes, my dear brother Stillman. I have been in error all my life on a vital question, honestly so; but now, to-day, I am rid of the greatest of all errors in morals and theology. God never made one man to be the slave of another. He intends that the whole race shall be equally bound and equally protected by his laws. All stand on a level before him, as He is the Father of all the race."

"Take seats on the porch here," said Mr. Stillman, "or walk into the house, if you please."

"Oh no, sir," said Mr. St. John, leaning against a pillar of the porch, and touching his forehead with the fingers of his left hand. "Let me stand for a moment, while I state my views, that you may see whether I am right or not.

"The whole race of man should obey all the

commandments that God has revealed by means of his holy Word. It is their duty to do so; and when God commands anything to be done, he gives the right to obey his command.

"The right and the duty are both alike from God. Human legislation cannot impair or destroy the one or the other.

"But as a man has the right to discharge every duty required of him in the Bible, he cannot be a slave; for the Bible prescribes all his duties, and as a correlative, secures all his rights.

"Our duties commence as soon as we know right from wrong, and end only with our lives, and extend to every action; and it follows that our right to discharge them exists every moment, and in every circumstance in which we may be placed."

"I see that you understand my position," said Mr. Stillman, "and am glad you do so. It is very simple. No slave can, of his own free will, obey the whole Bible. Slavery is therefore wrong, for God gave us the Bible, and commands every man to obey it."

"It follows, my dear brother Stillman, that Congress can pass no law, by which any man can be compelled to aid in the surrender of a fugitive slave.

"It is a sin, to hold one of God's children as a slave; and therefore it is a sin to pursue him, when he escapes, and to aid the pursuers.

"Let me give an illustration that occurred to me last night. Many negroes in the South, are slaveholders. Many of the slaves are so nearly white, that is impossible to know they have any African blood in their veins.

"Now, suppose the case of a fugitive slave mother, bearing her infant daughter in her arms. She gets into a free state and dies. The daughter is adopted by persons able to give her the highest culture. She grows up to womanhood, and is beautiful, educated, and refined; and while she is standing with the bridegroom at the altar, with orange flowers in her hair, her beauty heightened by an imperceptible trace of African blood in her veins; a negro, with all the most repulsive features of his race, exaggerated by a countenance on which is written brutality and depravity of the deepest die — old, ugly, gap-toothed, wrinkled—seizes the bride as his fugitive slave, and commands the bridegroom, under these laws, to aid him in bearing her to his den of sin."

"That is a horrid picture," said Mr. Stillman.

"It is indeed; but, my dear Mr. Stillman, no man knows better than you do, that the sin and shame of the act, are not affected by the color of the actor or of his victim.

"I have thought of another case, my dear brother Stillman.

"A mother escapes with her boy, who grows up to manhood, and is a faithful minister of the Gospel. He gathers around him a congregation, who have been brought by his agency, into the fold of Christ; and while he is administering to them the communion of his broken body and shed blood, the master enters the church, drags him from the altar of God, and commands the congregation to aid him, under this law, in taking the slave back into bondage."

"I see, my dear brother," said Mr Stillman, "that you are thoroughly converted.

"It is all very simple; slave-holding is a sin, and laws can no more make it right, than they can make the polygamy of the Mormons right.

"Law is a rule of action prescribed by the superior, and which the citizen or subject is bound to obey. Legislation has no more authority to compel men to sin, than it has power to dethrone God.

"The whole legislative power of the world, cannot make it the *duty* of any man to sin; and can make no rule for the control of his conduct, which will require him to commit any crime against man."

"I am glad, my dear brother," said Mr. Stillman, "that your opinions are changed.

"The fugitive slave laws cannot be executed

without destroying religious liberty. The same blow which strikes down the religious freedom of the northern judge, lights with equal force on the rights of the southern planter.

"We do not deprive the planter of any right, when we refuse to surrender his fugitive slave; on the contrary, we secure to him his highest and greatest, and what should be, his dearest right—his liberty of conscience.

"We preserve this Union by refusing, upon this principle, to make such surrender; and we do even more than that, we keep the Union as our fathers made it—a Union worth preserving.

"The religious principles of all nations lie nearest their hearts and deepest in their affections. All history shows that he who tampers with this sentiment of the people, uncaps a volcano. It is the last right that any people will, knowingly, submit to have wrested from them.

"If the people of the free states shall really be convinced that their right of religious liberty is impaired by these acts of Congress, no power on earth can prevent them from throwing off such fetters. Many will do it at the sacrifice of everything that hinders them in their efforts to be free.

"But now, my dear brother, as the acts are merely void, nothing need be sacrificed to secure the right. It is safe. Our fathers, under God, have made it so; and we have but to adhere to the Constitution *as it is*, to have the free exercise of religion."

"True, very true," said Mr. St. John.

"Well," said Mrs. St. John, "honey, what will you do now with old Aunt Polly? She is your slave. What 's mine is yours, you know."

"I will set her free. The purpose is now fully formed in my heart to do it, as soon as I can execute the necessary papers, and bring her to a free state."

"Oh, dear me! I do wonder what the old woman will say, when she hears it; won't she be scared though? I've seen her cryin', honey, and heard her say many a time, and when I axed her, 'What ails you, Polly?' she wiped her eyes with her apron, and said, 'Missis you's mighty good to me, but it 'pears hard for a person to be a slave; and her master to sell off all her children.'

"But I never sold one of 'em. They was all sold, afore I bought her."

"You concur very cheerfully in the views of your husband," said Mr. Stillman with a smile.

"Oh yes, honey! I always does. You know, the Queen of Sheba wrote to Solomon, that a woman ought always to let her husband do all the thinking, and other out-door business, while she cooks the victuals, and makes clothes."

"The Queen of Sheba, my dear?" said Mr. St. John, "where did you learn that?"

"Oh! I learnt it either in the book of Paul or Solomon, I don't care which, its good Gospel wherever you find it. It saves a heap of trouble to the women, and pleases the men folks."

CHAPTER LIV.

DEATH OF BELLE.

Belle, wasted to a skeleton, was rapidly sinking to her grave. Consumption was doing its steady work upon her; her countenance was bright with hope, and at times, was almost radiant with light and love, to all around and above her. She was on the very verge of heaven, and knew that angels were holding over her a golden crown, richer and brighter than earthly monarch ever wore, and that her poor aching head, was nearly ready to wear it forever.

Mr. Stillman had encountered the rebuke of part of the members of his church, but he was both kind and firm, and those who at first were most opposed to his course, were now sorry for their conduct; while others, and they comprised the great portion of the best members of his church, grasped his hand more warmly and loved him with deeper fervor, and were the most attentive listeners to his discourses. The cloud had passed away—the sunshine came again with redoubled brightness and warmth. His church soon acquired the name of the 'Abolition Church;' but all the members were still as cheerful and happy, as full of love and goodness as they were when no such reproaches were cast upon them. They admitted that, if by "abolition," is meant, "*the application of Christianity to the sin of slave-holding,*" the charge is true.

An attorney was one day sent for by Belle, while Mr. and Mrs. Stillman were absent on a visit to a sick person, who wrote, at her dictation, several sheets of paper, which she signed, and others also signed it, who had been invited in by the attorney; after all was rightly done, he took the paper, carefully sealed up, with him.

A week afterward the bell of the little church tolled, and people went to the house of Mr. Stillman, and a procession of friends followed the remains of poor Belle to her resting-place. The red earth, in which they let down the coffin, seemed a bed of roses, for she who slept there, slept in peace.

Two or three days after the burial, the attorney called on Mr. Stillman, and told him that Belle had made her will, and left it in his care: witnesses were taken, and it was duly proved; in the first passage in it she made full provision for those who were once her slaves, and directed that they should be taken to a free state.

Mr. and Mrs. Stillman were by no means forgotten. They were abundantly rewarded for all their care, as far as a generous bequest in money could do so. They received thousands of dollars—enough to supply all their wants.

Mr. Wilbar, and all who assisted at the fire, too, were generously remembered. Mrs. Johnston (now no longer Mrs. Johnston,) had a very handsome addition made to her already ample fortune.

Poor Belle faded, as fades a sweet and lovely flower, whose fragrance still fills the air with perfume, and gladdens the heart.

CHAPTER LV.

MRS. REED.

OUR narrative must now close. Mr. and Mrs. Reed, formerly Mrs. Johnston, are married and living near Cleveland, Ohio. They have a beautiful mansion and a farm, and are contented and happy. Mr. Reed has retired from his business as a printer, and is now a farmer; one of that kind who reads books on farming, and talks of the best kinds of wheat, and the improvement of agriculture and horticulture, and the arts and sciences in general. He is a warm friend of freedom, and his voice is often heard urging his neighbors to vote for God and for Liberty.

Mrs. Reed is the same dear, kind-hearted little woman that she ever was; with a smile always on her face. She is still more an Abolitionist than when we first saw her, and is strongly inclined to support the doctrine of woman's rights.

The courtship of Mr. and Mrs. Reed would have been recorded for the especial benefit of the young, but she saw the sheets after they had been written, and seized, and still detains them. She says it is one of her rights, that her love-affairs shall be kept secret, unless she herself shall choose to disclose them. She insists upon it so strongly, and supports her claim with so many plausible arguments, smiling all the time, and yet so earnestly, that it is really impossible to withstand her appeals. We regret it, but where a lady is so firm in her purpose, it is difficult indeed, to do what she forbids.

She says that Mr. John Scott was a wicked man, but she always adds, (standing erect, and extending her finger, her blue eyes flashing as she speaks,) "THAT EVERY SLAVE-OWNER HOLDS HIS BROTHER'S CHILD IN BONDAGE!"

THE END.

www.ingramcontent.com/pod-product-compliance
Lightning Source LLC
LaVergne TN
LVHW021148110826
845150LV00005B/1152

* 9 7 8 1 4 2 5 5 4 6 8 4 7 *